the Lady Stole My Heart

AIMEE NICOLE WALKER

The Lady Stole My Heart
(The Lady is Mine, #2)
Copyright © 2018 Aimee Nicole Walker

ISBN: 978-1-948273-09-1

aimeenicolewalker@blogspot.com

Cover photograph © Wander Aguiar—www.wanderaguiar.com
Cover art © Jay Aheer of Simply Defined Art—www.simplydefinedart.com

Editing provided by Miranda Vescio of V8 Editing and Proofreading—https://www.facebook.com/V8Editing/

Proofreading provided by Judy Zweifel of Judy's Proofreading—www.judysproofreading.com

Interior Design and Formatting provided by Stacey Ryan Blake of Champagne Book Design—www.champagnebookdesign.com

Copyright and Trademark Acknowledgments

The author acknowledges the copyrights and trademarked status and trademark owners of the trademarks and copyrights mentioned in this work of fiction.

Dedication

This is for all the cancer warriors and those who fought in the trenches beside us. We may be scarred, but we're still beautiful.

The Lady Stole My Heart

Prologue

Maegan

"**F**RECKLES, WAKE UP." EVEN MY SLEEP-ADDLED BRAIN recognized the urgency in Elijah's voice had nothing to do with his need for sex. This didn't stop me from busting his balls.

"Again, Elijah? Damn, can't a girl get some sleep?"

"How the hell are you sleeping through that?" A loud thud finally penetrated my brain. I sat up so fast I knocked my head against Elijah's. "Fuck! I think you broke my nose."

I threw back the covers, grabbed the flashlight out of my bedside table drawer, and marched across the bedroom. "This is getting out of hand."

"Where are you going?" Elijah's words were muffled by the hand he still held over his nose. "You're naked."

"What's your point?" I asked, whipping open the door. "Have you ever known me to back down from a confrontation?"

I heard rustling sheets and Elijah's heavy steps on the hardwood floor as he hurried to catch up to me. "My point is wherever you go naked, I go too, but does it have to be to the attic when our resident ghost is banging around up there?"

"Elijah, I'm sure you faced far scarier things when you worked undercover." I glanced over at him and saw a dark shadow cross his handsome features. It was gone so fast I started to think I imagined it.

"There's just something more unsettling about ghosts. Why is he suddenly angry? Everything seemed fine until you invited the paranormal investigator here tonight."

"Lyric is gay and not attracted to me," I told Elijah.

"I know. I saw how he couldn't look away from Memphis at the barbecue. *I'm* not threatened by Lyric, but your ghost is."

Elijah had a point. We did have a peaceful coexistence until Lyric arrived. It *did* feel like Anthony was suddenly upset. Jesus. I had zero experience dealing with ghosts and their moods. I had no proof the ghost in my house was Anthony Bliss, the founder of our town who disappeared in 1850, but I knew it in my heart.

"Stay down here and make sure he doesn't lock me in the attic," I told Elijah after I stomped down the hall to the attic door.

"I can't let you go up there by yourself," Elijah blustered.

"What exactly do you think will happen to me? He's not shown any violent tendencies. He's just upset about something. I'm just going to have a few words with him."

"You're going to go up there and yell at the ghost?"

"Who said I was going to yell? I simply plan on talking to him."

"Do it from down here then," Elijah countered.

"Then I will have to raise my voice to be heard over the noise he's making." I could tell Elijah wasn't willing to let this go. I either hollered at Anthony from the bottom of the steps, or we risked getting locked in because Anthony seemed to think it was funny. "Fine."

"Thank you, Freckles."

"Anthony," I said as firmly as I could without sounding like a shrew. "We're trying to sleep down here." The noise inside the attic stopped immediately. Elijah nodded encouragingly at me. "You have nothing to worry about, Anthony. We're not trying to hurt you or even get rid of you. We're only trying to find out what happened to you. We think you deserve it. You can ramble around here for as long as you want. Okay?" No response.

"I'm taking his silence as an agreement," Elijah whispered.

"Me too," I replied. "Let's go back to bed. We don't have to be up for a few hours still."

Elijah slipped his arm around me and pulled my naked body flush against his. I felt his dick respond to my nearness, and I relished how much this man wanted me. "Now that we're both wide awake…" Elijah let his suggestion trail off.

"I could use the assistance of a killer orgasm to help me fall back to sleep."

"I live to be of service to your every need," Elijah said. "I could plunder your…"

"Just fuck me, Elijah." I broke from his embrace and ran down the hall, knowing he would catch me then love me until I was too physically exhausted to stay awake.

Chapter One

Maegan

Three weeks later…

"WAKE UP, SLEEPY HEAD," I WHISPERED IN ELIJAH'S ear. He was sprawled naked across our bed on his stomach with nothing but a sheet covering him. Our central air-conditioning was working overtime to keep up with the oppressive mid-July heat. Even though our unit was new and efficient, hot, humid air rose to the second story and seemed to hover there. Both Elijah and I tended to kick off the duvet and only cover up with the sheet.

"I don't want to get out of this bed. My heart is happy, and my dick is satisfied in ways we never dreamed possible. What more could I possibly want?"

I climbed onto the bed and straddled his hips, feeling his firm ass between my thighs. I couldn't resist grinding my bare clit against the fine cotton sheets separating our flesh. "We?" I asked. "You do know that you and your dick don't have two separate personalities, right?"

"He does have a mind of his own at times," Elijah said, stretching his arms and tucking them under his pillow.

"How about now?" I asked, leaning forward, grinding in earnest. "Are you both thinking the same thing? Something about being satisfied and wanting to be left alone?" Elijah arched his back, pressing his ass tighter against my clit. I could've gotten off from the friction alone, but it wasn't what I wanted. I relaxed my thighs, and he rolled over beneath me. The sheet shifted so the head of his cock and its first three inches peeked out from beneath it. "Your cock looks neither sleepy nor satisfied."

"Every part of me wakes up craving you, Freckles. I'm always hungry for more," Elijah said, slowly sliding his hands up from my spread knees while staring up into my eyes. I saw the truth in his soulful, brown eyes, and it never failed to make my breath catch and my pulse race. I wanted him more with every breath I took. "I will never get enough of you." Words every woman longed to hear were made better by the sincerity with which they were spoken. Elijah made me feel cherished, adored, and wanted. "I will reach for you until my last breath." His hands didn't stop their upward glide until his thumbs reached my bare lips, and even though I saw his naked desire to be inside me, Elijah took his time running his thumbs up and down the silky skin until one of his thumbs got impatient and pressed firmly against my clit.

"Oh," I said because he knew the perfect pressure to use while circling the sensitive nub. He knew how to make me writhe, moan, and groan. Elijah had turned me into a sex-starved beast. Maybe I was that way all along, but it took the right man to bring my true sexual self to the surface. He stroked his other thumb along my core, teasing and taunting, while he continued to circle my clit. I wanted to close my eyes and let my head fall back, but I couldn't look away. He'd ensnared me in his dark, lusty gaze. "Elijah." His name was a whispered plea to both slow time and speed it up. I wanted the feelings to last forever at the same time I wanted the waves of pleasure to wash over me right then and there.

"I'll make you feel so good but not yet."

I raised my hands and pressed them against the silk and lace bodice of the short, teal nightgown I wore. My breasts felt so heavy and ripe, my hard nipples were extra sensitive as they pressed into my palms, sending a jolt of pleasure to my clit. A sexy growl rumbled through Elijah, and for the first time that morning, I felt like I had the upper hand. I loved driving him crazy and testing the tenuous leash he kept on his lust.

"Show me your tits." His already gravelly morning voice had become animalistic and primal. He was moments away from giving me what I wanted.

I slid one spaghetti strap down my left shoulder, revealing only one of my girls to his hungry gaze. I massaged the full, firm flesh and pinched my nipples, one hidden beneath silk and the other exposed to his lusty gaze. I knew he wouldn't be satisfied until both tits were bared. He sure as hell enjoyed teasing my pussy, so why couldn't I enjoy teasing him too. I glanced down and saw his cock was dripping precum onto his taut stomach, but he wasn't at the level of desperation I wanted from him. I pushed the other strap down my arm then licked my thumbs before teasing my turgid peaks.

Elijah slid just the tip of his thumb inside my pussy, and just that little bit of friction was enough to set me off. "Lean over me, Freckles. Give me those pretty tits."

Some women were highly offended by tits, cunt, and pussy talk, and I felt the same way before Elijah came along. He made me revel in my femininity and celebrate my womanhood. I didn't need secret gardens and gentle lovemaking. I wanted to fuck, grunt, groan, and come like the animals we truly were. He reached me at my basest level, and I was whole for the first time in my life. I was so much more than a woman who'd survived cancer, a woman who couldn't give him children of his own, a woman who was incomplete because her ovaries no longer worked. I wasn't broken, dammit. I was who he wanted—needed—in his life. I was the one Elijah cherished and loved with every fiber of his being. I wasn't ashamed of my needs; I fucking embraced them. Right then, I needed to ride his cock until I came.

Elijah didn't try to prevent me from inching the sheet down until he was fully exposed, nor did he pretend he wasn't ready to sink into my heat. He was a gentleman though and held his lady's free hand while she lined up his erection to her core with the other. One snap of my hips buried him to the hilt, just where I wanted him. The sounds tumbling out of me were similar to a kitten's purr but edgier. There was nothing cute about the way we made each other feel.

I leaned forward as I began to move, bringing my breasts closer to his face. At first, he seemed content to watch them bounce and sway over his head, but then his patience evaporated in a puff of smoke. He reached for my breasts, massaging them and flicking his thumbs over my nipples at the same time he lifted his hips and drove his cock deeper inside me. Teasing time was over and the chase to orgasm ensued. The friction of my clit against his pelvis and the broad head of his cock pounding my G-spot so deliciously had me crying out his name and coming in no time. I stilled my hips, letting my inner muscles milk his orgasm from him. Elijah arched his neck into his pillow and gritted his teeth as he tried to stave off his climax, but I wasn't about to allow it. I reached behind me and firmly squeezed his balls.

"Fuck!" he roared, rolling me to my back and rutting between my thighs until he spilled inside me. Elijah collapsed on top of me, and I wrapped my arms and legs around his damp back to hold him against me. "Now my dick is satisfied," he said, nuzzling his nose against my neck.

"How about your stomach?" I asked.

"A few minutes ago, I would've said it was doing fine."

"And now?"

Elijah lifted his head and smiled down at me adoringly. "I need carbs and protein to nourish my muscles and brain after you fucked

4

me senseless."

"Good because we're due at Milo and Andy's house for Sunday brunch in thirty minutes."

Elijah's smile grew even broader. "I started to think those two would never get together. The stubborn asses held out during the months of renovations at the stores and apartment remodel above your businesses no matter how much you or anyone else meddled."

"Until good ole Anthony locked them up in the attic the night Andy performed his home inspection for my mortgage company."

"Or maybe they accidentally pulled the door closed, and locked themselves up there. I don't want to think about why the door automatically locks when it's closed. It feels like a scary movie where the homeowners are trying to keep an evil entity locked up."

My heart squeezed painfully in my chest. It was probably ridiculous to feel so caught up in the history of my new home, especially the ghost residing with us, but I knew Anthony wasn't some evil spirit. I had never felt any animosity from him. My cat and dog, Rascal and Lulu, weren't afraid to live in the house, and pets were known to be sensitive to paranormal activity.

"Anthony isn't evil, Elijah. He's lonely and restless. I want to help him find peace."

"I know, Freckles. I wasn't trying to put your spectral buddy down. I just meant it's very odd to have that kind of lock on an interior door. It makes perfect sense to have exterior doors lock automatically when they shut, but not an attic door. Something very wrong happened in the attic."

A shiver of dread snaked down my spine. "Hopefully, Lyric will arrive soon and solve the mystery once and for all. I'd expected him to be here by now."

"Me too," Elijah said. "Maybe you'll hear something from him shortly." Then he slid from between my legs and kneeled between them, smirking when he saw the mess he left behind.

"You should just go ahead and pound your chest like an ape."

Elijah pounded his chest and did his best Kong impersonation, making me laugh. "We're down to twenty minutes now," I told him.

"Quit lying there looking all sexy and satisfied then. You make me want to forget about food and stay in bed all day."

I sat up, removed my nightgown, and tossed it aside, loving the way Elijah's appreciative glance felt like a caress on my bare skin. I slid off the bed knowing damn well he'd follow and join me in the shower.

I heard his phone vibrating against his bedside table and looked over my shoulder when I reached the bathroom door. Elijah scowled when he looked at the caller ID then declined the call.

"Not feeling chatty?" I teased when he got off the bed and walked toward me.

"Unknown number. I never answer those. Whoever it is will leave a message if they're legit and really want me to call them. Now, let's get in the shower so I can rub soapy hands all over your gorgeous body."

"I was just about to say the same thing to you." I glanced at the clock. "Fifteen minutes."

Elijah answered by swatting me on the ass.

"You're late," Milo said when we walked inside the little house he and Andy were living in until the remodeling was finished on the place Andy bought on Lover's Lane. The home and the name of the street were perfect for my brother and the only man he's ever loved.

"I'm two minutes late, Milo," I replied. "It's hardly worthy of the pissy scowl on your face."

"That's not why he's pouting," Andy said, entering the room. "He's mad because Memphis texted to say he wasn't coming."

"Why? Is he feeling bad?" Memphis never missed Sunday brunch or French toast Wednesdays."

"He was vague and just said he was sorry, but he wouldn't make it this morning. I sent a follow-up text, but he hasn't replied."

I pulled my phone out of my purse and sent a quick message to his phone. Maybe he hadn't heard Milo's text come through. *Hey, cutie. Is everything okay?*

I've had the same group of friends for most of my life and a brother who knew me better than I knew myself, so I never knew I was missing anyone until Memphis moved to town. Milo and I were drawn to him immediately, and he became such a vital part of our lives that we couldn't believe he hadn't been there all along. I knew he was conflicted about Lyric coming to town, even if he hadn't said anything. Memphis's crush on the paranormal investigator was well-known, but he never used his cousin's friendship with the man to wrangle an introduction. In fact, Memphis appeared to resist any attempts Emory made to introduce them, so you can imagine my surprise when Memphis offered his spare bedroom to Lyric for the duration of the investigation. I wasn't the only one who stared in wide-eyed wonder and held my breath while waiting for Lyric to answer. Surely, he'd say no even though he couldn't seem to take his eyes off Memphis, right? *Wrong.* He agreed to stay with Memphis then appeared to fall off the face of the earth over the next three weeks.

I watched as Memphis seemed to pull tighter and tighter inside himself every passing day without Lyric arriving in town. Sure, he said the right things and laughed in the appropriate places, but his smile never met his eyes. I was convinced his absence from brunch had to do with Lyric. Had the brooding, mysterious man changed his mind about staying with him? Did he change his mind about coming to Blissville altogether? I quickly checked my email app, but there were no new emails from Lyric.

I glanced up when I returned my phone to my purse and caught Milo watching me with a raised brow. "What?"

"Any news?" Milo knew what I was looking for, of course. I wasn't the only one who noticed Memphis's subtle withdrawal. I shook my head. "Well, let's eat while it's hot. Maybe we'll hear from him soon. I let Memphis know I would happily set aside a plate for him."

"Do I smell cinnamon rolls?" Elijah asked, sounding nearly as desperate as the time I taunted him by tying his wrists to our bedpost and denying him the pleasure he sought from my body. I mean, I eventually gave him what he wanted, but not until he was sweating, cursing, and demanding I fuck him. It was a game we hadn't played in a while, and I planned to reintroduce it later in the week when my newest pieces of intimate apparel were due to arrive. Elijah bought me a membership to Worship Me, a monthly subscription that delivered a gorgeous piece of lingerie and a bra and panty set each month. Elijah made sure his ass was home early on delivery day.

"Yes," Milo said cheerfully. "I made them from scratch."

"What time did you wake up?" I asked him. Nonna's recipe took hours to make since the dough had to proof twice.

"I learned a new trick, and I'm eager to see if it was effective," he replied. "I did the second rise in the refrigerator overnight."

"In the refrigerator? I've never heard of that technique."

"Me either, but someone shared their own recipe on Facebook earlier in the week. Of course, I was silently gloating because there was no way in hell it could be as good as Nonna's. I saw a side note next to the instructions for the second rise which stated it could be done in the refrigerator, but it would take longer, so they recommended letting them sit overnight."

"There's only one way to find out if these monsters are as good as your nonna's," Andy said. "I'll throw myself on the sword and go first, Peach."

"You've already fallen on the sword once this morning," Milo responded cheekily. "Let Elijah give these buns a try." Andy scowled and crossed his arms over his chest. "I'm talking about the cinnamon buns, Slugger. Take it easy."

"I'm game to take one for the team," Elijah said gleefully. He walked to the counter where the cinnamon rolls rested in their pan and lifted one out with the spatula. He took a big bite and there was no misreading the pleasure on my man's face.

"Oh goody. I gave Elijah a foodgasm." I narrowed my eyes at my twin because I wanted to be the one giving any kind of *gasm* to Elijah. "Step up your game, Sis."

"There's no competition, Freckles," Elijah whispered in my ear after he wolfed down the big roll in three bites. "These are delicious, but you're the only thing I can't live without."

I claimed a sticky, cinnamon-y kiss as my heart melted. Elijah had come so far to be able to speak those words to me. When we first met, he ran from the attraction he'd felt for me because he didn't want to risk his heart ever again. This beautiful man overcame his fear to build a life with me, and I would strive to make sure he'd never regret it.

"Likewise," I whispered before I kissed him once more. "Let's eat," I happily said when I turned around.

"If you think you can tear your hands and eyes off your man long enough," Milo said.

"I can manage for a few minutes," I replied. "Care to make a bet on which Miracle twin can behave the longest?"

"Maybe another day when Andy doesn't look so devastatingly handsome in his light blue polo shirt. I didn't think his eyes could look bluer, but I was wrong."

Had there been a bet, I would've won because Milo found ways to touch Andy all the time. I adored how happy my brother was, so I didn't even tease him about it.

After breakfast, I checked my phone to see if Memphis responded to my text.

"Still nothing?" Andy asked.

"Nope. I'm worried about him," I said. Milo agreed by nodding his head.

"Come on," Elijah said, scooting his chair back and standing up. "I'm sure everything is fine, but we'll go check on him."

"We can take him some rolls," Milo suggested.

"Let's not get crazy," Andy said.

When we arrived at Memphis's house, I assumed the old black truck in the driveway belonged to someone visiting one of the ladies known as the Matrons of Maple Lane. Imagine our surprise when we peered through the window in his kitchen door and saw the reason why Memphis canceled his brunch plans with us. Lyric Willows had finally shown up in town, and Memphis didn't look too pleased we had interrupted.

Chapter Two

Elijah

"WHAT ARE YOU SMILING ABOUT, PARTNER?" ADRIAN asked when he joined me at the coffee pot on Monday morning. "I mean, I could guess." His rueful expression said he thought Maegan was on my mind. While she wasn't foremost right then, she was never far off. The reason for this particular smile wouldn't exist without Maegan and her friendship with Memphis Sullivan.

I was the first to spot Lyric Willows through the kitchen door and tried my best to steer the meddling Miracles off the deck, letting Memphis get back to doing whatever it was that made him cancel his appearance at brunch. I knew how much he crushed on Lyric, so the last thing I wanted to do was ruin his morning even though I was eager for Lyric to either calm Anthony down or help speed him along to his peaceful afterlife.

Milo and Maegan didn't take the hint, and in fact, doubled down on their attempts to get Memphis to open the door. Lyric must have said something to Memphis because he turned his head to look at his overnight guest. That's when Maegan and Milo strained their necks to see who the hell he was talking to. Memphis let us in, and Lyric made an excuse to leave which felt awkward. Later we learned why. Memphis had left his dildo, accurately named Big Bob, suctioned to the shower wall because he wasn't expecting Lyric's arrival the previous evening. He'd forgotten all about it until he started cleaning the bathroom the following morning and saw Lyric had hung his washcloth over it after taking a shower. Memphis was horrified, but the rest of us laughed until we nearly pissed ourselves. So, yeah, greeting Bob O'Malley, our desk sergeant, the next morning made me smile as I recalled the conversation in Memphis's kitchen.

"Something like that," was how I responded to Adrian. "How was your weekend?"

"We had a great time," he replied. "My parents watched the kids for us so we could spend the night in Cincinnati. Sally Ann bought me Diamond Club tickets to Saturday's Reds game for my fortieth birthday."

I let out a whistle of appreciation. "Are those the premium seats behind home plate?"

"Yeah," Adrian replied wistfully. "The entire experience was amazing. We ate a fancy dinner in the lounge prepared by a chef I'd seen compete on *Chopped*, and then we had a private waiter throughout the game who brought us as much food and drink as we could handle."

"Did you have to pay for the food and drinks?"

"Nope, all of it was included with the tickets. You just tipped your server after the last call. Let me tell you, the snacks available to us were much better than what you can get in the regular seats. Sally Ann got these pretzel sticks and queso cheese I've never found in the stadium before. And the seats were incredible. I felt like I was part of the action." Adrian chuckled. "Do you know what my wife had the nerve to say?"

"I'm not sure I want to guess, partner."

"She said, and I quote, 'This is the closest I'll ever get to Joey Votto without getting arrested.' Then she started snapping pictures and sending them to Josh."

"My husband knows nothing about baseball except he likes the way Joey Votto looks in baseball pants," Captain Roman-Wyatt said from behind me. "He likes the contrast between the red jerseys and white pants." Adrian and I were so involved in our conversation we hadn't heard him sneak up. He sure was stealthy for a big guy.

We both turned at once to face our captain. Luckily, the good-natured smile on his face said he wasn't too upset about Josh and Sally Ann swapping texts about how hot they found the baseball player.

"Elijah, can you come to my office once you get settled in?" he asked me. I noticed the jovial smile from seconds before was replaced with a strained one.

"Be right there, Captain." I could see Adrian looking between us out of the corner of his eye and sensed his curiosity. I had a pretty good idea about what the captain wanted to discuss with me. Afterward, it would be time to come clean to Adrian too. After all, as my partner, he had a right to know about anything that was a threat to him. Axel Washington was dangerous to anyone who came in contact with me. "We'll chat later," I said to Adrian before I followed Gabe to his office.

"I suspect you know why I wanted to see you," he said as soon as we were seated on either side of his large desk. Gabe Roman-Wyatt wore responsibility and dedication well. He appeared broader and taller behind his captain's desk.

"Is it regarding a previous case I worked on?"

"Does my husband make the best country fried chicken you've ever had?"

I only had eaten it once when Gabe invited me to dinner after I first moved to Blissville, but it was enough to answer with a resounding, "Yes."

"Tell me what's going on," Gabe said firmly. "More importantly, I'd like to know why I'm just now hearing about it, Detective."

Uh oh. The captain's formality let me know just how upset he was I hadn't informed him about the info I got from my former CO. "The last scum bag I busted is walking the streets free and clear of all charges because several of the witnesses disappeared, along with evidence from the locker. Honestly, it wasn't likely Axel would get convicted anyway. A sleazebag like him probably has corrupt judges on his payroll, and if not, his henchmen wouldn't hesitate to intimidate jurors."

"You've known this for how long?"

"A few weeks."

"Why didn't you say something, Elijah?"

I blew out a frustrated breath. "What could any of us do about it? Captain Barker said he's under surveillance and he'd let me know if he got word my cover was blown. Cap, I was deep undercover during the investigation. Axel won't easily find out my identity and track me down here."

"You don't believe what you just said, Elijah, so why are you expecting me to? If Axel has judges in his pocket, then he has cops hanging out beside them. How else does evidence turn up missing?" He had me there. "Captain Barker must've been worried if he called me behind your back. Do you know why he's worried?"

"I don't have a specific reason to believe he's worried about my safety. I would've heard from him if it was the case. He probably called you because he knew I wouldn't say anything unless I believed there was just cause to push the panic button."

"Yeah, that's pretty much what he said. He also might've thrown out an 'Elijah is a stubborn son of a bitch, but his instincts are unparalleled by any officer who's worked for me.' Captain Barker just wanted to make sure someone was taking the threat seriously."

"Of course, I'm taking this seriously, Cap. Do you think I want to see Maegan hurt? I wouldn't jeopardize Adrian and his family, or yours either for that matter. At this moment, there's just nothing to do. Captain Barker told me Axel appears to have gone straight."

Gabe snorted. "His clean living will last as long as his surveillance does. They'll need to turn one of his guys against him to get new evidence or hope someone from a rival biker gang takes him out for us. Otherwise, it's a matter of time before he looks to exact his revenge. I love the people of this town, Elijah. I cannot protect them if I'm unaware a threat exists. I will not allow Axel Washington to catch me off guard, so I need you to be more forthcoming with information." The captain knew how to make me feel like a selfish dick.

"Absolutely, sir. I apologize for not coming to you right away, and you have my word you'll be the first to know about any intel I receive."

"I appreciate it, Elijah. Has anything unusual happened lately that's concerned you? I hear you say you want to keep me in the loop, but your body language says you're keeping something from me."

"I'm not keeping anything from you. I haven't seen anyone strange loitering around, but I have more than usual unknown caller activity on my cell phone. That alone isn't enough to sound an alarm. There's nothing for us to investigate because they're not leaving behind threatening voicemail messages and the calls are untraceable."

"You're not answering the calls?"

"If it is Axel Washington or his gang of deviants, I don't want to make it easy for them to confirm my identity and where I'm living. Only people with your kind of clearance can access my employment files to see where I transferred to, and I haven't changed my driver's license or vehicle registration yet."

"That's wise," Gabe admitted. "Okay, it sounds like I'm up to speed now. I want to be the first to know if anything changes. Do not make me call your former captain for information."

"Yes, sir," I replied.

"You're dismissed."

Adrian didn't bother trying to disguise how eager he was to know what the hell was going on. "Not here," I said when I reached our desks.

"That's fine because a call came in when you were in Gabe's

office. It seems Mrs. Blankenbauer's chickens were stolen from her back yard last night."

"And it requires two detectives responding because?" I asked with a raised brow.

"She's not the only one missing chickens."

"How many people have chickens in Blissville?"

Adrian grinned and slapped me on the shoulder as we headed out. "It's the new trend. People are raising their own chickens for fresh eggs and selling what they don't use."

"Huh," I said, opening the passenger door of Adrian's car. "I grew up on a farm, and we didn't even have our own chickens. My mom said it was too much hassle compared to the cost per dozen at the store."

"There's no comparison between store-bought eggs and fresh ones," Adrian said. "I was hesitant when Sally Ann announced she wanted a coop with a few hens for fresh eggs. I prayed there would be an ordinance prohibiting ownership in town, but I didn't get so lucky."

"How'd I not know this about you? You never mentioned it."

Adrian started his car and put it in drive. "Well, it just never seemed to come up in conversation. 'What did you think about the Bengals draft picks?' 'Do you think this is Votto's last year to wear a Reds jersey?' 'Oh hey! Come on over to meet Elvis, Patsy, Aretha, and Gaga and take home some fresh eggs.'"

I howled with laughter. "Elvis, Patsy, Aretha, and Gaga? Are you pulling my leg?"

"Those are the names Sally Ann picked out. She raised them as little chicks, and I'm telling you she loves them just like any other pet. Our kids love them too, and our neighbors love the eggs Sally Ann gives them."

"I'm assuming Elvis is a rooster. I bet the neighbors don't like him."

Adrian snorted. "We were surprised to discover the chicks we bought included a rooster. The fat bastard is too lazy to get up early. He doesn't start cock-a-doodling until the sun goes down."

"You can't be serious."

"I'm serious as a heart attack, partner. He sleeps for twenty hours a day then struts about, eats, and shits before he starts making a racket at sundown. I'm telling you those hens eat it up too. They carry on and make a huge racket when he struts around in his separate pen. I don't speak chicken, but I'm pretty sure they're fighting over him."

"Stop it," I said, wiping tears from my eyes. "'Speak chicken.'"

"My life has become a crazy zoo, and it would get even wilder if I let Sally Ann have the goats she wants."

"Goats?"

"Oh yeah. Goat milk is huge. They put the stuff in everything these days. Marabel uses goat's milk in many of the products she sells. I guess Marabel is having issues with her milk supplier, so Sally Ann had the bright idea *we*," Adrian gave me a knowing smirk, "meaning *I* would raise goats and supply Marabel with the milk she needs for her store in exchange for goods."

"Blissville is turning into *Little House on the Prairie*. Soon everyone will be trying to pay for things with their chickens."

"It happened to Kyle last week at his animal hospital."

"Get out of here, Adrian," I said.

"Man, I'm not joking. It's the same little lady who's reported them stolen."

"Are you sure she didn't barter them for goods or services and forget about it?" I asked.

"I might believe it if three other people hadn't reported their chickens missing in the last week."

"Well, it has been a little dull around here lately."

"I'm grateful it's stolen chickens and not another dead body," Adrian said.

"Well, we hope the chickens haven't been harmed, but we don't know that yet."

"Bite your tongue. I don't want to tell little old ladies their chickens were snatched and killed."

"Do we have coyotes in the surrounding areas?" I asked. "Are there signs of a struggle? Excess feathers on the ground or blood?"

"Not that I'm aware of, but then again, I just heard about this from Officer Simanski."

"Joey's taken the previous reports?"

"Yeah, and he decided to bring it to my attention after Mrs. Blankenbauer's call came in this morning."

"Adrian, how is it possible we haven't heard about this before now? Last week, I heard about Betsy Watson getting caught sneaking away from Trevor Honeywell's house at seven in the morning when I was waiting in line at Books and Brew for coffee and pastries at ten after seven."

"Maegan makes you wait in line?" Adrian asked.

"You're missing the point."

"What *is* the point?"

"The point is it became public knowledge ten minutes after Betsy slinked away."

"I see what you mean. I don't know why Joey didn't realize we had a serial chicken snatcher on our hands," Adrian said, pulling in front of a yellow Cape Cod house with light blue shutters. "We need to act fast, partner. My wife and kids will lose their minds if someone snatches Elvis, Aretha, Patsy, and Gaga."

"We'll get to the bottom of this," I assured him.

"Then you're going to tell me all about the conversation you had with Gabe."

"Yes, I will."

Mrs. Blankenbauer was waiting for us at the front door when we walked onto her porch. She swung the screen door open wide to let us in. "It's about time you got here. I called twenty minutes ago."

"I'm sorry, Mrs. B," Adrian said quietly. "I had to wait for my partner to conclude his meeting before I brought him up to speed."

"Your name is Ethan, isn't it?" she asked me.

"Elijah Markham, ma'am. I'm sorry I caused us to be late. Do you mind if we take a look at your coop?" I didn't tell her I was looking for signs an animal had tunneled under the fence to snatch her chickens.

"You get right to it. I like that in a man. Are you married, Elijah?"

"Um…"

"I'm not asking for me," she said, waving her hand in front of her blushing face. "I have a beautiful granddaughter who's single."

"That's so thoughtful of you, Mrs. Blankenbauer. I'm not married, but I'm in a relationship."

"Is it serious?" she asked.

"Very."

"Mrs. B, Maegan Miracle is Elijah's girlfriend."

"Ahh, Little Maegan Miracle," she said with a smile. "It's about time she found herself a nice man. You better treat her good."

"I promise I will."

Mrs. B led us through the house to the back door in her utility room. "I didn't even hear a peep out of Jezebel, Betty, and Gloria last night or this morning. I think they must've muzzled the girls when they nabbed them."

"We'll check out the coop for any clues, Mrs. B."

"My daughter thinks I've lost my mind. I joke one time about trading my chickens for Fifi's vet bill, and she thinks I actually gave my babies away and forgot about it. I'm not as sharp as I used to be, but I know damn well I didn't give my girls away."

"I believe you, Mrs. B," Adrian said. "You stay inside where it's nice and cool while Elijah and I take a look around. We'll be back in after we finish taking pictures and looking for evidence."

"Okay. I'll see you boys in a bit. Don't worry about knocking when you're done. Just come on inside."

There were no signs the chickens had been in distress. I looked around the back yard and realized how secluded Mrs. B's lot was.

It was the last one on a dead-end street. Her chicken coop was surrounded by a fence and had a locking gate. Well, at least it did lock before someone cut through the padlock with a pair of bolt cutters. Her entire property was surrounded by a chain-link fence and backed up to a wooded area.

We took pictures of the empty coop, the cut lock, and the surrounding area. We also looked through the yard for any evidence our perp would've left behind. We didn't find so much as a discarded cigarette butt. When we returned to the house, Mrs. B was sitting at her kitchen table making a sign on a poster board with a black Sharpie. It said: GUARD YOUR CHICKENS!!!

We promised to keep her updated then knocked on her neighbors' doors. Not too many people were home, but those who were hadn't heard or seen anything out of the ordinary. If we were going to catch our perp, he or she needed to fuck up and leave behind some evidence.

"Okay, spill the details about the conversation with Gabe," Adrian said once we were back inside his car.

"There's not much to tell, partner."

Adrian listened without interrupting on our way back to the station. "This kind of bullshit happens all the time. The likelihood of Axel Washington finding you is small, but in the event he does, we'll have your back."

"Thanks, Adrian. I'll head on inside the station while you call Sally Ann and let her know she needs to guard the chickens."

"Quit busting my balls over my chickens."

"I thought they were Sally Ann's chickens."

"They are. I just slipped up."

I felt so much better after talking to Gabe and Adrian about Axel Washington, and I realized it was foolish to keep quiet about the situation. It didn't mean I was ready to tell Maegan she was living with a marked man. The time would come, but it didn't need to be the week the paranormal investigation started at our house.

When we got inside, Adrian and I divided the list of people whose chickens were stolen for follow-up phone interviews. I finished first, so I had a few minutes to do a bit of research and text it to Adrian while he was finishing up. He glanced at his phone mid-sentence then looked at me with suspicious eyes. Too curious to wait, Adrian clicked on the message icon and saw the link to a farm with milking goats for sale. He flipped me off and kept talking.

There was no fucking way I'd let him live this one down. Everywhere he turned, he would see goats. I laughed in wicked delight, earning a double flip.

Chapter Three

Maegan

"**G**OOD AFTERNOON, CUPCAKES," VANESSA SAID, breezing through the kitchen door in the rear of Books and Brew. Elijah ridiculously stood in line with our loyal patrons, but no one else with a close personal relationship with Milo or me did. There were only a few people I had a closer relationship with than Vanessa, and they were either blood relations or slept naked beside me every night. They didn't eat or drink for free, but they slapped their money on the back counter and left without being seen by the hordes of people.

Milo and I looked up from refilling the cookie trays for the front display cases. The Blissville residents had been especially ravenous and caffeine-crazy, even for a Monday. I suspected their hunger and thirst was for information about Lyric's sudden appearance in town rather than the items on the menu.

"Hey, Van," we both said at once.

"I stopped by Curious Things to chat and Bonnie said I would find you here. What's up? Did someone call in sick?" I normally helped Milo with Books and Brew for a few hours until my store opened at ten o'clock, so it was unusual to find me in the bakery after

22

lunch. We employed three part-time employees to help with Books and Brew, and Bonnie worked part-time at Curious Things. Our businesses were growing at a startling rate, and if we wanted more personal time off, we'd need to hire additional staff.

"The busybodies are in full force today since Lyric returned to Blissville yesterday."

"Saturday night," Milo corrected. It was hard to keep the smile off my face when recalling what we learned about Memphis and Lyric's first night together.

"Yes, he technically arrived at Memphis's house late Saturday night," I told Vanessa. "I had a chance to talk to him yesterday when we stopped by Memphis's house after brunch and later at my parents' barbecue."

"Memphis missed brunch? Interesting." She didn't know the half of it, and she wouldn't learn it from Milo or me either.

"What I find more interesting is the relaxed expression on your face," Milo said, changing the subject. "If I didn't know better, Mae, I'd say our sweet Vanessa recently got laid." Vanessa's expression didn't give her away, but the telltale blush creeping up her neck did. "Aha! You did get laid. It must've been a really good time too."

"Why don't you shout it a little louder, Milo," Vanessa hissed. "I don't think my mother heard you four blocks away. I absolutely want her to know I had a glorious weekend of hot, sweaty, no-strings-attached sex with a virtual stranger."

"Your mom is no prude," I said. Of course, the virtual stranger part might alarm her.

"That isn't why I don't want her finding out," Van said dryly. "She'd either take out an ad in the Blissville Daily News to celebrate the big event or get her hopes up I was finally settling down like the Miracle twins."

"And you don't think your weekend is a precursor to happily ever after?" Milo asked her.

One of our part-time baristas, Joe Thierney, poked his head

around the door leading to the shop. "I'm sorry to interrupt, but are the cookies ready? I'm getting looks out here."

"I'm so sorry, Joe." I walked the tray of cookies over to him and bit my lip to keep from smiling at the way he couldn't take his eyes off Vanessa. He was adorable but only twenty-five. Vanessa had a rule about only dating older men.

"If he were ten years older and didn't reside in the same town, I'd give him something to truly pine after," Van wistfully said when we were alone again.

"Okay, you were saying something about hot, sweaty, wall-banging sex with a stranger..." Milo prompted.

Vanessa's eyes glassed over, and a shiver rippled through her tall, lithe frame. It must've been one hell of a weekend. "Yes, but that's where it ended. I knew when I kissed him goodbye at the door of his condo I wouldn't see him again."

"You spent the weekend at his condo? Not some random hotel?"

"I know what you're thinking, Mae, and just because he took me to his home doesn't mean he'll invite me back. He was very honest and open when we met on Friday night. He said he wasn't looking for anything serious, and I assured him I wasn't either."

"Where did you meet?"

"We met in the hotel bar after my seminar ended." Vanessa wasn't just a skilled tattoo artist and a successful business owner. She was a true artist who liked to share her knowledge with others. She stayed on top of the newest trends and taught what she knew. I had gone with her on many occasions to her seminars to act as her canvas.

"Did you have a nice turnout for your seminar?"

"Full house," she said proudly. "The attendees were interactive and asked a lot of questions, so it made the day go by really fast. Afterward, some of us headed to the hotel bar to have a few drinks."

"And that's where you met *him*?" Milo asked.

Van nodded. "He bought us all a round of drinks. I assumed he was interested in Amber, who was blonde, busty, and younger than me." The thing I loved and hated most about Vanessa was she had no idea how beautiful she truly was. "Anyway, he joined us and made it clear right from the start I was the one who'd caught his eye."

"You mean, the tall, svelte brunette whose body is perfectly proportioned?" Milo asked sarcastically. "I can't believe it." I adored my brother so fucking much. He always knew the right things to say without hurting anyone's feelings. "Besides, her big boobs will start to sag before long while your breasts will stay higher, tighter, and firmer."

"My mystery man was very fond of my breasts," Van said ruefully. "Enough about me."

"Oh no," Milo said. "I'm not through with you yet."

"That's what *he* said on Saturday morning," Van said. I could tell she wasn't acting flippant either.

"What started out as one night turned into two?" I asked.

"Two *glorious* nights and one long Sunday afternoon. I didn't drag myself home until after six o'clock last night."

"I'm surprised you're able to stand," Milo remarked. Okay, there were other times I wanted to smack him. "Maybe he wasn't as good in bed as you think he was."

"Oh, yes, he was," Van said then sighed. "Bed, couch, elevator, shower, kitchen island, and up against the glass wall of windows overlooking the river while the fireworks exploded over Great American Ballpark."

"Wow," Milo said. "How the hell are you walking?"

"Women self-lubricate, darling," Vanessa said, crossing the room to pat his cheek.

"He liked more about you than your self-lubricating vag if he kept you around all weekend long," Milo replied nonplussed. "There must've been eating…*food*…and talking in between bouts of sex."

"Yes," Vanessa said softly. "I had an amazing weekend, but nothing changed. He kissed me long and tenderly like he hated for me to leave, but in the end, he walked me to the door, held it open for me, and told me it was lovely meeting me." I hated the sadness I detected in her voice, but I knew her well enough to know she wouldn't want either of us to make a fuss.

"You haven't heard the last of him, Van." I could see in her eyes how much she wanted to believe Milo's bold prediction. "I just know it."

"Thanks, Milo." She kissed his cheek then pulled me into a hug. Vanessa held on tight like she needed the support from me that I almost withheld based on her usual preferences.

"I know amazing things await you, Van," I whispered. I would accept nothing else.

Vanessa chuckled then pulled back. "I had no intention of talking about my wild weekend. I came here to talk about the *Paranormal Whisperer* arriving in town but got waylaid by the orgasm whisperer instead," she said, nodding toward Milo.

"Yeah, my O-meter gets tripped a lot," Milo said, tipping his head toward me. Like Vanessa, I wasn't ashamed of my desire to fuck and fuck often, so I ignored him.

"There's not much to tell at this point, Van. Lyric's here by himself on his own time and dime because the Bliss House mystery appeals to him as much as it does me, and he's not certain the network will air the show. He's doing research this afternoon at the library and talking to Homer at the historical society."

"When will he get started?"

"Tonight," I replied. "Lyric and Memphis are bringing over dinner from the diner then they'll start the investigation."

"They? I thought you said he was working solo."

"I volunteered Memphis to help him," Milo boasted. "It was just a gentle push, and now, I'll leave the rest up to them."

"Uh huh," Vanessa said with a knowing smirk. "You mean Memphis told you to butt out."

"He might've insinuated he didn't want me to meddle any longer."

Vanessa tilted her head back and laughed heartily. "Insinuated, huh?"

"You can go on your merry way now that *you* know what's up with *us* and *we*," he gestured between himself and me, "know *you* went down a bunch this weekend."

"Guilty as charged, but I wasn't the only one," Vanessa said with a wink. "Text me later and let me know how the investigation went. Maybe Anthony will sense their stubborn hearts and lock them up in the attic," Vanessa said, getting the last dig since that's exactly what happened to Milo and Andy.

Vanessa kissed us both on the cheek and left with a cutesy finger wave and swaying hips, and I headed back to Curious Things when it appeared the afternoon rush had settled down at the coffee shop and bookstore. Bonnie was still floating on cloud nine when I walked through the door between our businesses. She was a huge fan of Lyric's show and couldn't believe he was in town to investigate.

"I hope I didn't act like a nutty superfan when Lyric was here earlier."

"You didn't, Bonnie. You were full of helpful information, and you made him feel welcome. I appreciate it."

"It's my pleasure. Do you need me to stick around a little longer?"

I looked down at my watch and saw it was almost three o'clock which was her normal time to leave. "Heavens no. I'll be just fine. I know your Monday afternoons are busy with taking Jessie and Tyler to gymnastics and dance lessons. I wouldn't dream of interrupting your time with them." One of the things I loved most about Bonnie was her devotion to her grandchildren. I knew my mom would be the same way when Milo and I made her a grandmother. "I'll hire another part-time employee if things get too hectic for me to keep up with in the afternoons or when my days off create too much work for you."

"Sounds like a great plan," Bonnie said. "If your business keeps growing, you'll be hiring more help in no time. Well, I'll head out since you don't need me to stay. I'll see you tomorrow morning."

"Have a great night, Bonnie. I'll text you if anything amazing happens tonight."

"You're the best, Maegan."

After she left, the store was steady but nothing I couldn't handle. I locked up at five o'clock like normal and headed home since Lyric, Memphis, Milo, and Andy were expected to arrive at six. Lulu and Rascal rushed to the door to welcome me home. Lulu would be excited our guests would be bringing their dogs with them, but Rascal would most likely hide under my bed until they left. Andy and Memphis adopted Chihuahua siblings, Bull and Gigi, and Lyric brought his Great Dane to town with him.

As I expected, Lulu sent up an excited bark when she saw her friends and the newcomer while Rascal ran so fast he was a blur of black fur flying up the stairs to safety. Elijah arrived home shortly after, sniffing the air appreciatively.

"Honey, I'm home," he said, sounding like a husband on the old black-and-white sitcom reruns my nonna loved to watch. "I smell meatloaf, mashed potatoes, and green beans."

"You smell the green beans?" Lyric asked in disbelief.

"I do when they come from Edson and Emma's. They add bacon to theirs." Elijah rubbed his hands together gleefully. "Let's do story time while we eat."

"What was the book event you held for Valentine's Day?" Memphis asked me.

"Blind date with a book."

"Let's do that with the takeout containers. I pass them out blindly, and we eat whatever we get."

"Give me the meatloaf and no one gets hurt," Elijah playfully growled. At least I thought he was kidding. "Wait, don't even bother opening them." He took a deep whiff of the air and picked up a container off the table. "This one." Elijah opened the container and his loud whoop signaled he'd chosen wisely. "The rest of you guys can do the blind date with a dinner thing."

"Sounds good to me," I said. "What about you guys?" Andy, Milo, and Lyric nodded in agreement.

We all dug in after Memphis passed out the containers. "Lyric has news he wants to share with you while we eat, and then we'll begin our investigation."

"I'm so excited to hear all about it," I said eagerly.

"We've frequently talked about Anthony but discovering a second tycoon was living in the middle of nowhere really stuck out to me. What were the odds? What was the history between the two men, if there was one."

I had never thought it was odd that a steel magnate, Wallace Bennington III, had made Blissville his home not long after Anthony Bliss established our town. We knew Blissville was a progressive town back in the day, but I could understand how it seemed strange to an outsider. "They definitely had history," I agreed. "They were friends in New York City before either of them moved to Blissville. Anthony moved here with his family, and Wallace followed afterward."

"I think the men were more than friends, Maegan. I think it's possible Anthony did indeed run away in 1850."

"Are you basing this on something you found or gut instinct?" I asked.

"A little of both. I looked through two years of newspaper clippings which included many photos of the two men. I think it would be easy for people to miss the fondness in their expressions if they weren't looking for it."

"Huh," Andy said, sitting back in his chair.

"I compared photos of Anthony with Melanie to those of Anthony with Wallace, and there was a noticeable difference." Lyric tilted his head to the side. "Also, Wallace Bennington III fell off the face of the earth not too long before Anthony disappeared."

"He moved west, right?" Milo asked. "So many people had

wanted an opportunity to find their fortunes during the California Gold Rush, but the rich just got richer, and the poor got poorer."

"That's true," Lyric agreed. "The thing is, I spent hours online searching for information about Wallace Bennington III, and there was not one mention of him living in California. A man like him wouldn't move west without buying a hotel or something."

"True," I said softly. "He announced his departure and the townsfolk accepted it at face value. What about his family? Weren't they looking for him?"

"He was an only child and a confirmed bachelor. Once his parents passed away, there was no one to look for him. I did some digging, and he sold the newspaper for a song, most likely just to unload it. He sold his steel and iron works company for a shit ton of money though. It was enough to start over with a new identity and the man he loved."

"Wow," Memphis said softly. "That sounds romantic."

Milo winked at him from across the table. "Then Anthony faked his death and followed Wallace west a year later?"

"It was more like eight months, but yes. That's what I believe. Anthony relied on people believing he perished as part of the curse," Memphis said. "I think the men changed their appearances as best they could and started over." It was so cute how he'd become so caught up in the investigation. I knew a big part of it had to do with the man conducting the investigation, but that wasn't all of it. I knew him well enough to know he was a sucker for a happy ending.

"Back then, it could've been as simple as shaving their faces and changing their style of clothes," Lyric pointed out.

"If Anthony left here of his own free will, then who is haunting this house?" Elijah asked.

"That's what we're going to find out," Lyric replied.

He and Memphis headed upstairs to the attic to begin their EVP session while the rest of us went outside to enjoy the nice evening. It looked like we were finally going to get a break in the heatwave we were experiencing. Andy and Elijah talked about their upcoming softball game with Milo weighing in about the likelihood they'd have an undefeated season. I mostly listened to them talking because my mind was stuck on the information that Lyric told me at dinner. Were Anthony and Wallace lovers? Had they planned an elaborate escape to live out their lives together on the West Coast?

"I better go make sure they're not locked in the attic," Milo said, rising from his chair dramatically.

"Don't cause any more trouble," I cautioned.

"I'm only heading in to see if I hear them banging on the door. I promise I do not have ulterior motives." Andy and I snorted, earning a narrow-eyed glance from Milo that would make any cheesy television villain proud.

He was back in a few minutes with Memphis and Lyric following close behind him. "The gang's all here," Milo said dramatically. "What happened up there?"

Lyric opened his mouth to answer, but Memphis spoke up first. He talked so fast that I had a hard time following. It sounded like, "Elevated EMF readings…shadows moving…boxes knocked over…EVP session."

"I'm going to upload the session into my computer to see if our ghostly friend had anything to say. I'd like to come back and set up some video equipment in the attic tomorrow morning. Maybe try another session tomorrow evening? Is that okay with you guys?" Lyric asked us.

We agreed, and he assured us he'd be over early enough not to interfere with our work schedules. I offered them dessert, but I could tell by their swollen lips and dazed gazes they were eager to get back to Memphis's house to do more than play back the EVP session. Milo and Andy left immediately after them, giving me my first moment of quiet with Elijah since we left for work that morning.

"Alone at last," I said when he pulled me into his arms. The scent of tobacco wafted through the air.

"Bug off, Anthony," Elijah said. "I need some alone time with my woman."

"You still think it's Anthony's ghost after what Lyric found out?" I asked.

"I'm a cop who believes in hard evidence and not speculation, Freckles. Until I have proof that tells me otherwise, I believe it's Anthony's presence." A wide smile spread across his face. "I also believe Anthony got an eyeful up in the attic."

"You noticed their swollen lips and dazed expressions, huh?"

"Freckles, Inspector Gadget wouldn't need Penny's help to figure that one out."

I hugged his neck tighter and giggled against his chest. "Could I possibly love you more?"

"I'll let you give it your best shot. You're not coming with us, Anthony. You've seen enough action tonight."

"Guess what arrived a few days early in the mail?" I asked, waggling my brows.

"What's inside?" he asked, eyes blazing with lust.

"I didn't have time to open it."

Elijah stepped out of my embrace and headed to the table by the door where I place the mail each night. He picked the box up and just stared at it for a few seconds. Then he lifted it by his ear and shook it. "Sheer baby doll negligee with matching lacy thong and a pretty lace bra and panty set," he said as he returned to my side.

"What colors?" I asked, playing along with his monthly fun.

Like normal, he hoisted me over his shoulder and carried me off to our room where he would wait naked, hard, and horny for me to model my newest acquisitions.

Chapter Four

Elijah

WHEN I MOVED TO BLISSVILLE EARLIER IN THE YEAR, I had worried the transition from undercover work to small-town detective would be difficult. Of course, I had no idea I'd meet Maegan and fall in love so hard and fast it stole my breath. Adapting to my new life was amazingly easy and waking up at seven in the morning never felt so damn good. Of course, some days Maegan was up and out the door to open Books and Brew before my alarm went off, but it wasn't one of those mornings. Milo opened on Tuesdays, so I stayed in bed with my girl as long as I could, knowing she'd nudge me awake if I fell back to sleep with her tucked up against me. Once Maegan's eyes opened, her brain fired to life, and she never went back to sleep.

"Shit! Elijah, wake up! We fell back to sleep. Lyric and Memphis might be here any minute."

I jackknifed into a sitting position in time to see her sprint into our bathroom. So much for Freckles never falling back to sleep, but who could blame her after the night we had. I wanted to boast and brag that my bedroom skills kept her up all hours of the night, but it was the damn ghost. I mean, I rocked her world well and good, but

I was considerate enough to let my lady get plenty of rest. Anthony didn't give a fuck. He slammed doors, shifted boxes in the attic, and chain smoked his pipe in our room when we didn't pay him any attention. Finally, at about three o'clock, Maegan sat up in bed and calmly said, "Anthony, I won't be responsible for my actions if you don't shut the hell up right this minute. Lyric doesn't want to hurt you. He only wants to find out if you and Wallace made it to San Francisco, so why don't you be a good ghost and cooperate with him." Anthony's response was to slam our bedroom door shut, but he stayed quiet for the rest of the morning.

"I wonder if they heard anything interesting in their EVP session," I asked when I entered the bathroom. Maegan was already in the shower, and we'd leave Memphis and Lyric waiting on our porch for quite some time if I so much as looked at her wet, naked body.

"Jesus, even the way you scratch your balls in the morning is sexy," Maegan said.

Wait? I was scratching my nuts in front of her? I looked down. Yep, I was brushing my teeth with my right hand while my left hand was definitely between my legs scratching my sac. "Huh, it's a little soon for me to be doing that in front of you. I should act like I have a shred of couth until I can convince you to marry me." That remark woke me the fuck up. After Brandy's betrayal, I never thought marriage was something I'd ever risk again. It turned out I was wrong. I wanted every part of me, itchy morning nuts and all, to belong to only Maegan for the rest of my life and even beyond.

Maegan snorted. "Just name the time and place, buddy." Did we just sort of get engaged? "Besides nut-scratching, what other goodies await Mrs. Elijah Markham?" I noticed she didn't say Maegan Markham, yet, maybe she worried I was about to freak out and disappear like I did the first weekend after we fucked like animals. I did run from her, and she damn well knew it. "Please don't tell me you'll take your morning shit while I'm in the shower."

I nearly choked on my toothbrush. "Freckles, I don't even take a piss while you're in the shower now, yet you think I'm going to shit with you a few feet away?"

"Elijah, you were in the military for a long time, and I'm pretty sure your privacy was limited."

"True, but I've been a civilian long enough to know ladies would consider that a total dick move. I can assure you I will use one of the other bathrooms to take my morning shit if you're taking too long to do unnecessary things with your hair and makeup."

"Okay," Maegan said agreeably.

"What things will you let slide, Freckles?" I asked when I heard the water shut off and the door open. *Focus on shaving. Focus on shaving.* Men woke up with a semi hard-on, and we fired that bastard up to full speed with very little prompting. "Can I expect a seventies bush within a month after our marriage?"

Maegan laughed so hard I worried she might rupture something. "You won't have to worry about that, babe. I will permanently have smooth, hairless skin for the rest of my life."

"Like a side effect from the chemo when you were seventeen?" I asked, looking over at her. She was more beautiful than any woman had a right to be wearing nothing but a towel wrapped around her body and another wrapped around her wet hair. The summer months had added new adorable freckles across her nose and cheeks. I wanted to kiss each and every one of them.

"No," she said softly, making me worry I'd said the wrong thing. I hated that Maegan would never be able to carry my children in her womb, but not for selfish reasons. I didn't need biological children to be a father, and I hated that she might doubt her worth because of her inability to give them to me. "I had laser hair removal treatments, so I'll be smooth and bare for the rest of my life."

"Wow," I said in awe. Of course, I was imagining some *Star Wars* type equipment shooting laser beams across the room.

"Dude! They didn't whack my hair off with light sabers," she said with a knowing grin. I loved how she already knew the paths my mind took. Which was why she opened her towel when she had my full attention, showing off the most beautiful breasts I had ever laid eyes, hands, lips, teeth, tongue, and cock on. I'm pretty sure I heard my spunk let out a victorious cheer when I painted her luscious tits the previous night. "Hurry along, Elijah. You won't want to be late," she said, swaying out of the room making it impossible for me to tear my eyes away from her toned legs and ass.

"Tease!" I yelled after her.

I refused to acknowledge or relieve my hard dick and plotting a revenge fuck later that night sure as hell did nothing to make it go down on its own. Remembering Lyric and Memphis were probably on the way and would be back later in the evening deflated my cock a little, and Maegan hollering from the bedroom that I had another random unknown call on my cell phone took care of the rest.

Maegan was already gone by the time I dried and dressed. I could hear her talking down below as I left our bedroom. I recognized the voices that responded to her greeting. Memphis and Lyric had arrived, and Lulu's delighted bark let me know the dogs were with them. Of course, Rascal nearly tripping me as he bolted up the stairs was another dead giveaway. "Sorry, little man," I said after he stopped long enough to hiss and give me the middle claw. I knew I could make it up to him with ear scratches later.

"I assure you our bakery doors will always be open to you," Maegan said to Lyric as I reached the bottom of the steps.

"Should I be jealous?" I asked. "All I've heard Maegan talk about since she sampled your baked goods is how skilled you are in the kitchen." Learning Lyric liked to bake as a hobby was surprising but more shocking was that he made some of the best muffins I'd ever had. We not only invaded Memphis's home on Sunday afternoon, but we also scarfed down half of the homemade muffins Lyric had baked for Memphis even though we'd just crammed our bellies full during brunch at Milo and Andy's house before setting off to rescue Memphis.

"*Kitchen* is the key word there, Elijah."

"I know, Freckles. I love giving you a hard time. I'm going to walk my lady out, and I'll be right back, fellas." I placed my hand at the small of Maegan's back and followed her out to her SUV. "You look beautiful in your white dress. People will see you and think what a lady you are, but I look at that dress and see it pushed up around your waist while I'm on my knees licking your pussy and sucking your clit until you come for me."

"You're evil," she whispered. "Deliciously evil."

"I've been planning my revenge fuck ever since you pulled that stunt in the bathroom."

"Yeah? Is she someone I know?"

"Huh?"

"Elijah, a revenge fuck is when you go out and fuck someone else to get even with a person who hurt you. People don't commonly use that term when having sex with their partner. I want to know whose ass I will be kicking after you exact your revenge." God, how I loved my blood-thirsty Freckles.

I backed her up until she was pinned between me and her SUV. "Well, from now on revenge fuck has a new definition for us. It means I will get even every time you taunt and tease and leave me hard."

"Okay," she said casually, but the soft tremble in her lips showed she wasn't unaffected by me. I placed my hands on her bare shoulders and felt her skin pebble beneath my touch. If I looked, her nipples would be furled into hard buds.

Maegan was expecting me to continue my sexual onslaught, so I switched it up on her by brushing my nose along hers and planting a gentle kiss on her forehead. "I love you so fucking much, Freckles. There will never come a day when I will want anyone other than you."

She promptly burst into tears. "Oh, I'm so sorry," she said when

I took a half step back in shock. "It wasn't what you said or did that made me cry. I love you too, Elijah. More than I ever knew I could."

"Then why the sad tears?" Don't ask me how I knew they were sad instead of happy; I just did.

"Lyric confirmed the ghost is Anthony," she said after a few minutes. "He also learned Anthony was the one who was locked in the attic. Elijah, if he died here, then Anthony never made it to San Francisco to be with Wallace."

"Freckles, we don't know they were actually lovers. Let's try not to be upset about facts we don't know are true."

"You're such a cop," she said then wiped at her tears with the back of her hand.

"I am," I agreed, lifting my hands to brush away her tears with my thumbs. "That doesn't mean I'm without feeling, Freckles. It simply means I reserve them until I know the right ones to feel."

"Oh, you're right." She waved her hands in the air like she was being silly. "I'm off to work now. I hope you have a great day and find out who is stealing chickens. Maybe you'll even answer one of those odd calls."

"They won't leave a message, so how bad do they want to talk to me?"

"Maybe they've worked up the courage to dial your number but are too afraid to leave a message." She clearly thought it was someone in my family who wanted to repair a broken relationship. She wouldn't be so eager for me to answer if she found out it could be a dangerous man who escaped prison because of corrupt cops and a broken system no one could fix.

"They'd most likely hang up if I answer."

"You won't know if you don't try," she added. "Now kiss me so I can get to work."

We started out with a chaste kiss, but I couldn't resist lingering longer until her lips parted for my seeking tongue. Every molecule in my body reacted to this woman, so I broke our kiss and stepped back before things got out of control. We softly exchanged words of love once more before she got in her SUV and drove to work.

Memphis and Lyric were still in the attic when I returned to the house. I wasn't due at the station until nine, but I would probably go in as soon as they finished because I suddenly was restless. I pulled my phone out of my pocket and checked out my incoming call log. I had more than twenty incoming calls from an unknown person since Captain Barker told me Axel Washington was a free man. They started out as once a day but had grown in frequency during the past week. Maybe Maegan was right, and I should answer the next fucking time they called me. Maybe it was another Markham finding the nerve to apologize or maybe it was one of Axel's henchmen. Wasn't it better to know than to keep guessing? If he was coming after me, I was only delaying his next move, not blocking it entirely.

"We're all set. Are you sure you don't mind us coming back tonight to record another EVP session?" Lyric asked. Hell, I hadn't heard them come downstairs because I was so lost in thought while staring at my phone like it contained the answers I sought.

"I'm positive," I replied, hoping I offered a friendly smile and not a grimace. "I was just kidding earlier."

"I know," Lyric said. "My traipsing through the attic is still intrusive. I would understand if you preferred to wait."

"Can I ask you a question about the investigation? Maegan seemed upset about something you said even though she tried to distract me with kisses." Well, first she brought up the calls then she got my mind off Anthony once my lips met hers.

"Man, I'm sorry. I should've just kept my mouth shut until I had some concrete answers."

"I'm not busting your balls, Lyric. I want to know what you suspect happened. It's the detective in me. I want to be the one to break it to Maegan when the time is right."

"You want to know what I suspect, or would you rather wait to hear when I have concrete answers? I don't want to put you in a position where you're keeping secrets from Maegan. I know you want to protect her, but I get the feeling she's not a shrinking violet, and I bet she has one hell of a temper."

I smiled because my Freckles was a real wildcat. "You can say that again." I blew out a breath because he made a valid point. "You're right. You can tell us at the same time. I'll be there if she needs me, but I won't treat her like she's helpless and can't handle bad news." It wasn't lost on me how ironic this statement was since I was keeping a pretty damn big secret from her. I reasoned the pros and cons again of telling her and stuck to my original decision. No good would come from worrying her needlessly.

"Good call, Elijah," Memphis said.

We agreed that seven was a good time then I invited them over to grill out before they started the video recording of their next interview with Anthony. After they were gone, I made sure all the doors on the first floor were secure and our pets had plenty of food and water before I headed to work. I had an idea how to find out who was stealing chickens from Blissville residents. It started out as a funny joke, but then I realized it had real merit.

Adrian was already at his desk when I arrived which rarely happened since he was the father of two small children. During the school year, Sally Ann's teaching position required her to be at work before Adrian, and he was responsible for taking the kids to childcare. Sally Ann was still on summer break for a few more weeks, so Adrian was able to arrive earlier. I could tell by the serious look on his face he was cooking up a chicken plot too. No pun intended.

"I have an idea," I told Adrian excitedly. "We need to set up a sting operation."

"A sting operation? Was there a bank heist I didn't hear about?"

"Are you no longer worried about Elvis, Aretha, and Gaga?" I wanted to know.

"You forgot Patsy, and no, I'm still worried about them. That's why I'm here early looking for solutions. So far, I've only come up with offering a reward and setting up a tip line like we did when the Christmas bandits attacked. Damn, that was pure chaos with every lunatic calling the number at all hours of the day. Want to take a bet on how many people would report seeing Henery Hawk in the area before the crimes occurred?"

I shook my head but couldn't wipe the grin off my face. Fuck, I loved small-town living. "I was thinking about a slightly more aggressive approach, partner."

"Yeah?"

"Decoys and hidden cameras," I said with pride. "What's the one thing all of these chicken owners have in common?"

"They love chickens?"

"They advertised they had free-range eggs for sale with a sign in their yard."

"Yeah, they did."

"Do you know who has chickens, access to video equipment, and hasn't advertised he has chickens on his property *yet*?"

"No way," Adrian firmly said, shaking his head. "You want me to invite criminals to the home I share with my family to steal our beloved birds?"

"Can you think of a better way? We could wire their pens for sound. Maybe put little tracking devices around their legs."

"You think the captain will go for something that extravagant?" Adrian asked.

"I think he might consider it if his best friend's prized birds were in jeopardy."

Before we could talk to Gabe, another citizen called to report their chickens were stolen. "Fine! We're going to do it your way even if I have to pay for this out of my pocket," Adrian said as he strode for the door. "There's a war on chickens in this town, and I won't stand for it."

A war on chickens? I managed to contain my laughter until Adrian lifted his hand and flipped me off once more. His crude gesture pushed me over the edge, and I had a pissed-off partner when I got to his car.

"You're lucky I even waited for you," Adrian said once I lowered myself to the seat and shut the door.

"Oh, what can I do to soothe those ruffled feathers?"

He wanted to stay pissed but couldn't in the face of my pun.

Chapter Five

Maegan

I COULDN'T SHAKE THE SADNESS I FELT AFTER HEARING ANTHONY was the one who'd been locked in the attic. My thoughts and emotions were on a riotous ride lately, soaring to the highest highs only to drop to the saddest of lows. I was ecstatic to learn Anthony was the ghost in my house but then felt guilty because it would seem he never made it to San Francisco after all. Everyone deserved to be with the ones who made their lives complete. Why would they lock him in the attic? Did Melanie Bliss find out about her husband's love affair with his best friend? Did Anthony die in the attic, lonely and heartbroken? What then? Did his family secretly bury his body on the land in the dead of night and report him missing?

By the time I got to work, I was an emotional mess. Instead of entering through the kitchen at Books and Brew like normal, I unlocked the rear door to Curious Things and hid in my office. I turned on the desk lamp and turned off the blindingly bright florescent light hanging above my desk. I hated that damn thing on a good day because it created a horrendous glare on my computer screen, but the harshness of it felt like someone took a whip to my already frazzled nerves. I should've let Milo know where I was so he wouldn't worry, especially if he saw my car parked outside.

I couldn't bring myself to do anything but cry. I propped my elbows on my desk, leaned my face forward until my forehead pressed against the tips of my fingers, and released my heartache. I cried for whatever Anthony and Wallace had gone through—the love, the hope, and the shattered dreams. Having finally experienced what love truly felt like made my sorrow more acute. I stayed that way until I heard the soft sound of someone setting something on my desk. I looked up and met the familiar blue eyes of the person who would always know me best.

"I thought maybe you could use a cup of coffee, your favorite peanut butter and jelly muffin, and a shoulder to cry on," Milo said. "Knowing you, you're probably about cried out. You're seconds away from pulling up your glittery, superhero boots and kicking ass. Whose ass needs kicking?"

"How'd you know I needed these things? You felt my sorrow through our twin link?" It's what we called our ability to feel one another's moods. Of course, I called it a twink link when I knew something was bothering Milo or if he wasn't feeling well.

"Well, I did feel a certain tingling in my spine."

"That was remnants from Andy's goodbye kiss," I teased.

"There will never be a goodbye kiss shared between Andy and me ever again," Milo said firmly. "I experienced the worst twelve years of my life after the last goodbye kiss we shared. We have see-you-tonight kisses and until-later kisses, but never goodbye."

"That's so sweet," I said then burst into tears again.

"Then why are you crying?" Milo asked gently, scooting a chair over from the corner so I could lean my head against his shoulder. "Is this about Anthony?"

"Did Memphis call you?"

"No, Elijah did."

"He did? I tried not to show how upset I was by my ghost's story."

That was the thing. I had stopped thinking of Anthony being the Bliss House ghost; he'd become *my* ghost and hearing about his fate felt so personal to me.

"Mae, you've loved that house and the mystery since we were little kids. The house and its ghost were always meant to belong to you." Milo was so full of sass most of the time that I forgot how tender he could be. "Memphis told me what they learned so far. The don't have any conclusive proof, so please try not to think the worst."

"I'm trying, Milo. You know how I can't stand an injustice."

"Boy, do I ever. You couldn't sleep for a week after Grace Atkins beat me for student body president our sophomore year in high school."

"She didn't win the election fair and square," I reminded him. "A person shouldn't win because they're skilled with their hands and use their mouth for things other than stating their positions on critical issues."

Milo snorted. "You know how rumors spread in high school. I'm sure her sucking and jacking activities were *blown* way out of proportion." We giggled over his blatant pun usage. "Why are you hiding in your dark office and crying when you have that sexy beast with the broad shoulders at home? Not that I mind lending you a shoulder."

"You know I don't like to cry in front of people, Milo."

"Maegan, I know that better than anyone. Don't you think I heard and felt your tears when you were so sick? You don't think the wall between our bedrooms was thick enough to drown out the sounds of your sorrow and pain, do you? I wanted to come to your room every time so we could cry together, but I knew you were trying to spare us by putting on a brave front. I wouldn't be the person to take that away from you. But you know what? There's nothing wrong with expressing your feelings and pain. Who better than Elijah to help ease those hurts? Don't hide from him, Mae. Let him see all the sides of you, not just the sexy, tough girl." Fresh tears threatened from hearing the anguish in Milo's voice. I had thought I'd fooled them all, and knowing I hurt him filled me with so much regret.

"You're so smart when it comes to relationships now," I teased, wiping the drying tears from my face. I sat up and kissed Milo's cheek before sitting upright in my chair again. "I know you're also right. I just don't want to add to Elijah's burdens." I took a sip of my salted caramel coffee and a bite out of my muffin. I admit I felt better when the familiar, favorite tastes hit my tongue.

"Something going on with him?" Milo asked, furrowing his brow in worry.

I wouldn't discuss Elijah's past or his estranged relationship with his family. I knew my parents and brother were curious since the only family he ever talked about was his grandfather who left him the old truck he drove every day and the cabin in Tennessee that Elijah cherished. Therefore, I couldn't mention the ever-increasing calls from an unknown caller since I suspected they were from a Markham family member. I was very tempted to answer his damn phone that morning, but it would've been an egregious breach of privacy.

"Earth to Mae," Milo said, waving his hand in front of my face. I hadn't realized I'd taken so long to answer him.

"Mostly it's the case of the stolen chickens."

Milo had just torn off a piece of my muffin and popped it into his mouth. It must've lodged in his throat because he started coughing and reaching for my coffee. Once he finally had himself under control, he said, "Excuse me? A case of stolen chickens? Like a box of frozen ones from the Sac-N-Save?"

"No, as in live chickens are being stolen from back yards in Blissville."

"Wait, how many people living in town have chickens?"

I shrugged and snatched back my coffee for a drink. "I don't know all the particulars, but Elijah mentioned it to me last night before bed. Raising chickens for eggs is a thing now."

"Huh," Milo said. "You ever feel like you're never in the loop when it comes to important things? I mean, I know Martin Sowden likes black coffee with no sweetener and has a foot fetish according to Edna Browner. We have some kinky widows and widowers in this town."

"Mr. Sowden and Mrs. Browner are a thing?"

"No, Mr. Sowden and Mrs. Ravenor are a thing. Mrs. Ravenor told her neighbor, Mrs. Browner, what Mr. Sowden was into after Mrs. Browner came right out and asked Mrs. Ravenor why Mr. Sowden was in her bedroom the previous evening."

"She just told Mrs. Browner he has a foot fetish?" I asked.

"No," Milo said calmly, but the wicked sparkle in his blue eyes let me know he was about to drop a delicious bomb of Blissville gossip. "According to Mrs. Browner, her exact words were, and I quote, 'Well, Edna, if you must know, he was licking my toes.' I guess there was a pregnant pause before Mrs. Browner asked her to close her bedroom blinds in the future."

"Oh, I bet Mrs. Ravenor had a witty comeback for that too."

"She told Mrs. Browner that she should close her own blinds if she didn't like what she saw."

Milo and I had a good laugh then thumb wrestled for the last bite of muffin. I won, of course, but I suspected he hadn't put his full heart into beating me. "How am I just hearing about this with Mrs. Ravenor and Mrs. Browner?" I asked.

"I just learned about it today. The two ladies had a showdown just this morning. I was trying to show how quickly that kind of gossip spreads but not a peep about the residents' stolen chickens. How long has this been going on?"

"I think he said a week."

"A week?" Milo asked. "That's equivalent to ten years in Blissville-gossip time."

I snorted. "True. Anyway, I guess stolen chickens aren't salacious enough."

"Well, I'll keep an eye out for chicken hawks or giant roosters running around saying, 'Boy's gotta mouth like a cannon, always shootin' it off.'"

His Foghorn Leghorn impersonation made me giggle. "Let's get back over to Books and Brew before our employees decide to kill us for leaving them alone during the morning rush." We both rose to our feet and headed toward the door. I stopped Milo by touching his sleeve. "Thank you, Milo."

"Always, Mae."

Staying busy always made the day go by faster and kept my mind off sad things, like my ghost and the stolen chickens, and gross things, like Mr. Sowden licking Mrs. Ravenor's toes. I had to convince myself that Mrs. Ravenor had only said that to get a rise out of Mrs. Browner so I wouldn't blush, cringe, or hide the next time any of the them showed up in our stores.

Elijah sent me a text late morning to let me know we were having guests for dinner. He told me not to worry he'd grill out hot dogs and hamburgers. Who did he think he was living with? I replied that I had dinner under control. During my lunch break, I made a quick trip home to put a pork roast in the smoker out back. I decided crockpot macaroni and cheese was easy and would go perfectly with the roast. Luckily, I had everything I needed for it and coleslaw. I set the crockpot on high, whipped up a batch of coleslaw, and returned to my store.

Not long after I arrived, one of my favorite people showed up to do a bit of shopping for her first grandbaby. "Any news, Mama Richmond?" I asked.

"Not yet," she replied, shaking her head. "I think Meredith is doing this on purpose because she knows how badly I want to get my hands on that baby."

"Come now, Mama," I teased.

"Okay, my baby girl is ready to welcome her baby girl into the world even more than I am."

"I thought Meredith didn't want to know the gender of her baby."

"She doesn't, but Mama knows anyway."

"I'm not about to argue with Mama."

Willa "Mama" Richmond was a retired school nurse who you could count on to dish up love or a verbal slap upside your head when you needed it. She and Meredith moved to town right before our freshman year of high school. Willa accepted the job at Blissville High after her husband passed away. I wasn't sure if she was trying to outrun heartache or just needed a fresh start. She would only say that Blissville High was ranked in the top one percent of all schools in Ohio, and her Meredith deserved the education the school could offer her. As much as I loved my hometown, we couldn't brag about our diversity with only one African American family and one Asian family living here. If Meredith was ever unnerved by being the only black student at Blissville High, it never showed. She had a warm smile and a loving personality that people were drawn to, none more than her best friends Chaz and Josh. The three of them were inseparable to this day even though they were married with growing families.

"My wise girl," Mama Richmond said, patting my cheek affectionately.

It reminded me of how gentle and nurturing she was when I returned to school after cancer treatments—bald, skinny, and lacking any self-confidence. I tried to hide the latter more than the former, but it didn't help when some people gave me a wide berth and acted like I was contagious. Mama Richmond, then Nurse Richmond, called me into her office on my first day back.

"You can come here anytime you need a break." She handed me a permanent hall pass that I could use whenever I needed a quiet place. Mama must've been able to tell that I had no intention of using it. "Save that brave face for a time when you need it. This is the time to take care of yourself and let your body heal. This office is your haven away from the little assholes walking the halls of this building. There are some great kids here, but there are some that should've been spanked more by

their mamas and daddies. I won't pressure you to visit my office, but I will remind you on occasion that I'm here for you."

I ended up using that hall pass more than I ever would've predicted. It did feel great to lie down for a bit and gather my strength. Mama would often sneak me a cookie or a cup of hot cocoa when I visited. I could lean on her in ways I didn't want to with my own family. I needed to put up a brave front for them, but I didn't do that with Mama Richmond. It was because of her that I was finally able to stop crying at night. I gave my tears to Mama, who dried them, and encouraged me to be brave and strong. I was more grateful for her kindness and tough love than I could ever express. Well, maybe there was something I could give her.

"I have a surprise for you," I said. "Follow me. I stashed it safely in my office."

"What is it?" Mama Richmond asked excitedly.

"I recently acquired some beautiful pieces for your granddaughter." I pulled out a gift bag from the antique cupboard behind my desk and gently placed it on my desk.

"Maegan Miracle, you shouldn't have," Mama Richmond said in awe before she even opened the bag.

"You don't even know what I've done."

"I can tell it's special by the reverent way you set it down. I'm almost afraid to look."

"Please don't be afraid. I wanted to do something truly special for a remarkable lady." My voice broke a bit on the last few words. *What the hell was wrong with me?* I hadn't cried this much in more than twelve years. I hoped it would be another twelve years after this crying jag moved the hell on.

Mama Richmond finally reached inside the bag, removed the tissue paper, and set it on my desk. She glanced up and gave me a nervous smile before reaching back inside the gift bag and removing eight small white boxes. Inside each one, she discovered a vintage Beswick England Winnie the Pooh porcelain figurine from the 1940s.

"These are numbered," Mama Richmond said breathlessly after she carefully turned Winnie over. "I can't accept these."

"I'll just throw them away then."

She gasped. "You'll do no such thing."

"There's more in the bottom. You might have to shuffle the rest of the tissue paper around." Inside were classic Winnie the Pooh books to complete the collection. I knew Mama Richmond planned to pass her love for books onto her grandchild.

"This is the loveliest gift," Mama Richmond said once she pulled the books out and set them beside the figurines. "I know Meredith will love them too. Those were her favorite books as a little girl."

"I'm so happy they're going to a home where they'll be cherished. I hope you're holding your granddaughter in your arms soon."

"Me too, love. Me too. I stopped by today to find a pretty little lamp for the nursery."

"I have just the thing."

Twenty minutes later, I helped Mama carefully load her car and received her warm, grateful hug before she drove off. I suspected she was headed straight to Meredith's house to show her the new things. I grinned fifteen minutes later when Meredith called and thanked me for the thoughtful gift. I was in a much better mood when I arrived back home than when I left. Of course, it helped that Elijah was waiting for me on the front porch.

"Hello, Freckles," Elijah said when I walked up the steps. The sultry, rumbly timbre of his voice let me know he was looking forward to teaching me a *hard* lesson about not teasing him.

"Let the lesson begin." I reached between us to cup his cock in case he wasn't sure about what kind of lesson I meant.

Chapter Six

Elijah

I HAD EVERY INTENTION OF HONORING THE SEXY THREATS I made to my lady that morning, but not as soon as she got home. I wanted to take my time and teach her a lesson, but the matching firm grips she had on my heart and cock overruled my brain. Thoughts like *we should wait until the fellas have left* and *I want to be able to take my time* started to fade and *make her come!* started to take over.

I pulled Maegan inside our home and backed her up against the door then dropped to my knees. Keeping my eyes locked on hers, I lifted the skirt of her dress and revealed the lavender lace panties beneath. Damn, she drove me insane.

"Let me help you with that," Maegan said, grabbing the hem of her skirt. "So you can have both hands free."

It was just the gesture I needed to slow down and truly make this a lesson she wouldn't forget anytime soon. Our eyes met and locked as I gently slid her panties past her thighs so they could fall around her feet still encased in her strappy, high-heeled sandals. I lifted one foot then the other to free the scrap of lace she'd used to cover her lady bits. I shoved them in the front pocket of my jeans.

Then I wrapped my hands around both ankles and slowly slid them up, reveling in the way her skin pebbled in response to my touch. Her vibrant green eyes shone with lust and need, and her pirate's smile said she expected me to please her. I would…just not yet. I had a point to make after all.

Revenge Fuck Lesson Objective: Make Maegan Miracle as needy and desperate as she made me that morning, leaving me with a raging hard-on and no time to do anything with it.

Step One: Make Her Tremble with Need

I pressed my nose to the cleft of her pussy and inhaled her scent deeply. I felt her legs tremble beneath my hands and knew I was ready to move to the next step.

Step Two: Make Her Moan and Cry Out My Name

I pulled my head away from her soft, silky flesh just far enough so I could purse my lips together and blow softly.

Maegan's breathy gasp was followed by, "Oh, Elijah." It wasn't a loud cry but said on a long, shaky sigh. Good enough.

Step Three: Make Her Pull My Hair

I slid my hands up from her thighs to part her lips with my thumbs, revealing her clit and center to my hungry gaze. Taking her to the edge of pleasure without pushing her over would send me to the brink of sanity. I'd be a stark raving lunatic the rest of the night, but I'd sure as fuck enjoy the journey. I leaned back in and delicately flicked my tongue over her swollen clit before sucking it between my lips.

"God, yes!" she cried out, fisting her free hand in my hair.

Step Four: Make Her Fuck My Face

I lifted her left leg and propped it on my right shoulder, exposing her even more, then speared her opening with my tongue, letting my nose rub and tease against her clit while I reached my left hand up to tease her hard nipples through the fabric of her bra and dress. I circled my thumb around one of them until it was hard and desperate then moved over and pinched the other nipple between my thumb and first finger.

I heard Maegan's head fall back against the door in a soft thud. Seconds later, she angled her pussy so it pressed tighter against my face. Almost there, but not quite. I slid my finger inside her silky heat, pressing against her G-spot.

"Don't stop," she cried softly, riding my finger and face. "Oh God. Please don't stop!"

Step Five: Pull Back Right Before She Comes

Maegan must've anticipated my move because she gripped my hair even tighter and snapped her hips faster. God, I loved how she didn't shy away from pleasure. She fucking owned it.

"Don't you even think about it, Elijah. I didn't learn my lesson, and I'm going to do it again. I like knowing you'll leave for work thinking about me, wanting me. Just like I thought about you and wanted you all day too. God! I'm so close. Right there! Yessssss!" I felt her clinch tightly around my finger and felt her get even wetter for me. "Fuck me, Elijah. Please."

I set her foot on the floor then released my cock as I rose to my feet. Maegan turned and faced the door, keeping the skirt of her dress rucked up around her waist and presented her perfect ass for me. It was the only invitation I needed to step up and sink balls deep inside her. Maegan's pussy was still spasming from the orgasm, and I knew her G-spot would be extra sensitive, so I aimed my cock head straight at it, taking no prisoners and not accepting that her orgasm was finished.

"I can't—" Her words broke off in favor of moaning. The hand she had pressed against the door balled into a fist as pleasure rolled through her body.

"You know you will." I kept one hand on Maegan's hips to steady her for my thrusting and unzipped her dress with the other so I could get my hands on her breasts. Maegan released the skirt of her dress long enough to help me shove the straps of her dress down her arms pooling it around her waist. I pulled the lacy cups of her bra down beneath her firm tits and cupped both swells while pounding into her from behind, rattling the door.

"Elijah," she cried. "Oh. Oh. Ohhhhhhhhh."

"That's my girl. Come for me again," I managed to grit out before I spilled inside her, rutting and marking my territory like a beast until I had nothing left to give. I collapsed against her, careful not to put too much weight on her since a door wasn't a comfortable place for a post-coital cuddle.

"I learned a valuable lesson after all," Maegan said. Her arms were folded on the door acting as a pillow for her forehead.

I nibbled a path down her neck and playfully nipped the delicate flesh where her neck curved into her shoulder. "Not to tease me again?" I asked.

Maegan snorted then laughed. "I need to leave you hard and wanting at least once a week."

"Freckles," I said in a menacing tone.

"You'll have to try harder to resist my…um…charms," she teased. "Now kindly remove your cock so I can clean up before the guys get here."

"No cleanup," I said. "You'll wear me all night long then I'll use my spunk as lube for backdoor action later."

"You mean you're going to fuck me against the back door after everyone leaves?" I knew if she were looking into my eyes she'd be batting her eyelashes playfully.

"I mean I'm going to start by getting my cock nice and wet from the cum I left inside you then I'm going to pull my dick out, press it up against that tight little rosette between your ass cheeks, and—" The sound of a vehicle pulling into our driveway cut off my words. "Our guests have arrived, dear." My dick was only semi-soft when I pulled it out of her tight clench since it started to react to the sexy image I described for our evening activities. I quickly pulled her panties out of my pocket then dropped to my knees once more to help her put them on before I stood up, fixed her bra, and zipped her dress.

Maegan was mostly presentable when I tucked my cock away and zipped my pants. That's when I noticed the cum splatters on the hardwood floor from after I pulled out. Maegan followed my gaze then hooked the sweater she'd dropped on the floor with her foot and dragged it over to wipe up our spill.

"Dry clean only," she whispered. "This is going to cost you, buddy."

We hauled ass to the kitchen to wash our hands and get a drink to quench the thirst we'd worked up before the guys came knocking on our door.

"How do I look?" Maegan asked.

"Thoroughly fucked."

"So do you." She gave me a quick kiss then headed back toward the door while I stayed in the kitchen.

I'd never had such an intense desire to smoke a cigarette in my entire life, not even after surviving harrowing gunfights with enemy combatants when we were ambushed in Fallujah. Jesus. The lady not only stole my heart, she wrecked my universe. I fucking loved every second of it.

I smiled when Maegan threw open the door and exuberantly greeted Lyric and Memphis. And by greeting, I meant she demanded to know what else Lyric learned.

"Mae, can we at least let the fellas in before you interrogate them, or are you planning on withholding their dinner until they talk?" I asked. It would just be the four of us for dinner because Andy was working late to finish a construction project and Milo had drag queen rehearsals for an upcoming charity event at Queen City Divas in Cincinnati.

"I guess you guys can come in," she grudgingly said, "but no dessert until you talk."

Lyric was hesitant to say much since he wanted to avoid upsetting her again, but he agreed to answer her questions since it was her home and her ghost. Okay, he said it was her home, but we both knew

Anthony was her ghost too.

"Do I want to know?" she asked, sounding uncertain.

"She wants to know," I told Lyric. I knew she wouldn't sleep if she didn't find out everything he knew, or at least suspected.

I will say this about Lyric Willows; he was a man who didn't settle for wild guesses. He slowly and methodically explained everything he had learned, making sure to emphasize what was supposition versus facts he could verify with articles or documents he found online. Maegan gasped when she heard the EVP recording they'd made the night before. Anthony hadn't spoken in complete sentences like, "Hi, my name is Anthony Bliss, and I'm the ghost living in your attic." He answered Lyric's questions with single-word responses. He confirmed he was Anthony and when asked what happened to him, he said, "Asylum." The only complete sentence he spoke was when he asked where Wallace was. Then Lyric set down a photo showing a man who looked identical to Wallace Bennington standing outside a building with a Blissview Hotel sign on the front. I couldn't see his face because it was turned away from the photographer, but Lyric showed pictures of the two men side by side and everything about them from their height to the unique way they stood told me I was looking at a picture of Wallace Bennington in San Francisco. Furthermore, the horse on the other end of the reins was Anthony Bliss's horse, Starlight.

"Oh my God," Maegan said softly. "You think Melanie Bliss had him committed because she found out about his plans to leave her? There's no way Anthony sent Starlight with Wallace if he wasn't planning to go too. I'm surprised the horse wasn't in the formal family photos."

"That's what I thought too," Lyric agreed.

"What about the asylum angle?" Mae asked.

"We've searched for anyone in the family trees, or even a friend of the family, who would've had the authority or connections to have him committed," Memphis said. "So far we're coming up with a big miss."

"What about someone bribing a person in charge at a facility? Let's be honest here, the doctors and administration at a lot of the asylums were not good people. For enough money, I could see them slipping a man in without a proper judiciary ruling."

"Damn," Lyric said, whistling between his teeth. "I didn't consider that."

"I'll look into that angle while you're in San Francisco," Memphis said.

"San Francisco," Maegan and I said at the same time.

Lyric told us he was flying to San Francisco in the morning to meet with the concierge of The Golden Gate Bridge Inn, formerly the Blissview Hotel. He said it was rumored the concierge position had remained in the same family since the hotel was first built, and he hoped to find out the stories passed down through the generations. It was a good strategy, and we were eager to find out what he learned.

I hadn't agreed with Maegan's opinion about the hamburgers and hot dogs until I tasted her smoked pulled pork for the first time. "Can we have this every week?"

"Next week, I'll show you what I can do with beef brisket."

"Okay," Lyric and Memphis both said. It was nice to know that Lyric might still be around a while longer. The way Memphis blushed while looking at him was too adorable for even me to miss. There was something special going on between the two men.

After dinner, Lyric and Memphis went upstairs to fire up the video cameras and conduct another interview with Anthony. I loaded the dishwasher while Maegan put the leftovers inside the refrigerator. She gasped suddenly, and I knew she saw the pastry box I stashed inside before she got home.

"What's this?" she asked.

"A little something to celebrate our anniversary."

Maegan spun around with wide eyes. "What?"

"We met six months ago today. I couldn't let the day pass without a little celebration."

"Do people celebrate six-month anniversaries? Is that a thing? I feel terrible I didn't get you anything."

"Freckles," I said, closing the distance between us, "you've given me *everything*. I just wanted to do a little something to show you how much I love you."

"Oh wow." She pulled the box out of the refrigerator and noted the name of the bakery. "You've been talking to my mother, haven't you? I bet that was an adventure."

"Jackie Miracle is an incredible woman who adores every freckle on my Freckles. She was happy to help me since I'm still learning all there is to know about you."

"Babe, I'm a woman. You could know me for a hundred years and still not know everything about me."

I threw my head back and laughed. "I look forward to trying then."

"This is a peaches and cream cake, isn't it?"

"Jackie said it's your favorite."

"It is." Maegan breathed in deeply, a lot like I had when my nose was pressed against her pussy. Of course, that reminded me of the second part of the *punishment* I had planned for her.

My phone rang as soon as I turned back to the sink to start hand-washing the crockpot. "Do you mind seeing who that is?" I asked Maegan.

She set the cake down on the counter and pulled my phone out of my pocket. "It's your mysterious caller again," she said. I could tell by her expression she was thinking about answering it.

"Please don't, Maegan. There's nothing I want to say to whoever is calling. They'll eventually get sick of being ignored and give up." I hoped but wouldn't hold my breath.

"Okay, Elijah," she said softly, slipping the phone back in my pocket. She rose on her tiptoes. "Thank you for the cake. It's the sweetest thing anyone has ever given me."

"You're welcome, Freckles." I leaned in for a longer kiss, but I could hear Memphis and Lyric coming back downstairs. They had some ivory and gold jar-like thing with them.

"Oh cool! A pipe tobacco humidor," Maegan said when she saw it. "That's a large one too."

"It smells like the tobacco wafting through the air whenever Anthony is around," Memphis told her.

"Really? I wonder if this is the item he's attached himself to."

"It would seem so," Lyric told her. "Especially since we think it holds his remains."

"Whoa!" I said. "His what now?"

Maegan slowly opened the lid like she expected something to pop out and get her. We peered into the humidor for a few seconds before she closed it. "Looks like cremated ashes to me," she agreed. "The question is: how'd they get here?"

"And when?" I asked.

"I hope to find those answers for you and more while I'm in San Francisco," Lyric said. "I'll be in touch when I find something out. In the meantime, what would you like to do with Anthony's ashes?"

"I'll put them in a place of honor on the mantle above the fireplace, of course."

"Whoa, Freckles, can we talk about this?" I asked, following behind her.

"We live with his ghost, babe. What's the harm in placing his ashes on the mantle?" She set him right in the middle of the mantle then rearranged other antique items belonging to Bliss House around it. I had to admit it looked lovely but still…

I heard Memphis say, "We'll just show ourselves out," but Maegan and I were too busy preparing ourselves for battle to respond, knowing we could apologize for our rudeness later. "Yeah, I know," I replied. I don't know why an urn sitting on our fireplace skeeved me. "How do you know Anthony wants them there? Maybe Anthony thinks my softball trophy should go there."

"I don't see a trophy to put on the mantle, Elijah," Mae said, turning to face me. She placed her hands on her hips, and the raised brow told me she wasn't going to compromise or budge about the placement of the urn. "Anthony, do you mind if I keep your urn on the mantle for now?" The answer to her question came in the scent of tobacco smoke floating through the air. "He approves, and you haven't even won that first-place trophy."

"Yet."

"Yet," she agreed. "We'll talk about it when you do." My cell phone rang again just then. "Babe, it seems to me that its past time you deal with some ghosts too."

Damn it. Whoever was calling me multiple times a day wasn't going away, nor would they leave a message. Before I could talk myself out of it, I answered the phone. "Hello," I said gruffly. No response came, and I thought about hanging up until I heard a familiar cough on the other end of the line. Smoking three packs of cigarettes a day took a toll on a man. It wasn't Axel Washington calling to threaten me; it was someone who could hurt me far worse. In fact, he already had. "Hello, Dad."

Chapter Seven

Maegan

I'D NEVER SEEN A PERSON LOSE THEIR COLOR AS FAST AS ELIJAH did after answering the phone. And his voice... I never again wanted to hear his voice shake with hurt and hesitation as it did when he spoke those two little words. I reached for him, but he stepped away from me, his deep brown eyes wide and skittish and mouth forming a stern line as he listened. It was like the last six months had faded away and we were standing at the curb on our old street. We'd recently met and rushed into a night of passion without care of the awkwardness that would come later. Of course, it was made worse when Elijah immediately disappeared for a few days. I later learned he'd retreated to his grandfather's cabin in Tennessee, but at the time, I just felt the sting of his rejection. After he returned, he was cold and aloof, signaling that whatever we experienced would never happen again.

Oddly, for as new as our relationship was, I rarely engaged in bouts of doubt. Elijah said he loved me, and I believed him. He wasn't the kind of man to whisper words of love just to get laid. But feeling his rejection again filled me with doubt as I retreated upstairs to lick my wounds in private. On my way to our master suite, I stopped at the door to my favorite room in the house. It was the bedroom tucked inside the turret overlooking the back yard with the amazing window seat and bookshelves built into the large bow window. As if drawn to the room by some invisible pull, I walked inside and flipped on the light switch, bathing the room in a soft, ambient glow. Whoever lived in this room would have a little reading nook and library.

I had big dreams for the room and had even imagined Elijah and myself bringing home our adopted child and placing them in a crib or, depending on their age, a toddler bed in there. I'd had Andy paint the room a soft yellow color that would act as an amazing back-drop for so many themes, like those vintage Beatrix Potter figurines I bought for the store but couldn't bring myself to list online or display. Why? I knew someone would gobble them up, and I finally admitted I didn't purchase them as an investment for the store; I bought them for the nursery I would have someday.

Instead of worrying that Elijah was downstairs resenting my pressure to answer the phone or fearing our relationship wasn't as solid as I thought, I began to design a whimsical mural that would look stunning in the turret and could spread out to encompass the walls around it on a smaller scale. The soft yellow walls on the in-side of the turret morphed into a quirky, hand-painted tree, and sur-rounding the room would be a picket fence with flowers, birds, and butterflies here and there. I knew just the artist to pull it off too. Our, or maybe my, child would sit there, and it would be as if they were in their own little treehouse overlooking the back yard. Andy's electri-cian friend could tuck rope or tape lighting under the bookshelves once the mural was complete to give the treehouse extra lighting. On second thought, I could string twinkling lights that would resemble fireflies. How perfect would that be for a kid? He or she would want some task lighting for reading, but I'd find a way to disguise it as best I could.

"Freckles," Elijah said softly behind me, startling me from my fantasy. "I—" His words died when I turned around to face him, and his eyes opened wide in shock. "Baby, why are you crying?" His voice was so tender which was completely opposite of the coldness I saw in his expression and body language downstairs.

"I didn't realize I was," I said, wiping at my face. I looked at my hand in shock. "I've become a leaky faucet today."

He crossed the room and pulled me into his arms. I didn't bother resisting him because it was exactly where I wanted to be. No games. No bullshit. I'd give him a chance to explain. Elijah placed one hand on my lower back and slid the other in my hair, lowering his forehead to mine. "I'm so sorry."

"Sorry you met me?" I asked. "Or sorry you listened to me and answered the phone?"

"God no, Maegan. I'll never be sorry I met you. I wasn't pulling away from you or rejecting you downstairs. I was just in shock and overwhelmed by all the memories and pain when I realized who was calling me. I'm so sorry for making you cry, Freckles. Please tell me you forgive me."

"There's nothing to forgive, Elijah. You had a terrible shock and you went into protective mode. I get it." And I did. I'd found myself doing the same thing many times over the years. I heard the sincerity in his voice and felt the love and adoration in his gentle touch. "You don't have to tell me about the conversation."

Elijah straightened to his full height and looked down at me. "I want to."

"Whenever you're ready." I knew he might need some time to organize and process his thoughts before he shared them with me. He was deliberate and methodical like that, and it made him a great detective.

Elijah nodded then changed the subject. "What are you doing in here? You looked all dreamy until I saw the tears on your face."

"I was just fantasizing about the mural I want to paint in here someday."

"You'll have your nursery, Maegan. I promise you. We'll paint any mural you want."

"We won't, but Vanessa will," I corrected him. "She is so much more than a tattoo artist, Elijah. She is so unbelievably gifted, and she already agreed to paint a mural here once I decided what I wanted."

"And now you know?"

I nodded. "And now I know."

"So, we can expect the mural complete by Christmas?" he teased.

"Halloween," I countered half-jokingly. Vanessa was like me when it came to putting plans into action, so it was possible she'd have it done by then. "Of course, we can help fill in the mural after she draws it on the wall. She numbers each section and puts a coordinating sticker on each one."

"Paint by numbers but on a much larger canvas?"

"Yep," I answered. "I've helped Van paint a jungle-theme mural before. She'll go back in once it dries to add shading and highlighting to give it an extra special touch."

"That sounds fun."

"It was," I admitted. "I'm in the mood for a hot shower and a big slice of cake. Care to join me?" There wasn't any suggestiveness in my tone or expression because this felt like one of those times where sex just didn't fit.

"Not a hot bath?"

"Well, I would, but our earlier activities kind of ruled it out." I loved Elijah, and I even loved the possessive ways he marked me with his cum, but I didn't want to soak in the tub while it floated around in the water.

"We'll take a quick shower to wash the sex off, and you can run a bath while I get a beer for me and a glass of wine for you."

Bathing in hot-as-fuck July should've sounded like a terrible idea, but it was just what I needed. I felt Elijah's hot gaze on me while I quickly cleaned myself, and I wasn't surprised to feel his hard dick pressed between our bodies when we kissed. I decided that I didn't want to waste a good erection, but Elijah dropped his hands from my waist and stepped back before I could reach between us and fist his hard length.

"I'll be right back," he said, exiting the shower and wrapping a towel around his hips. I didn't feel rejected by his actions because I saw the love and tenderness in his eyes and heard his desire in his lust-roughened voice.

I shut off the shower and wrapped a towel around my body before heading over to the large, clawfoot tub. Instead of fragrant bubbles or bath bombs, I dropped a handful of Epsom salt into the hot water filling the tub even though I knew it wouldn't provide the kind of soothing Elijah needed for a hurt that ran bone-deep.

He returned promptly with a glass of red wine in one hand and a bottle of beer in the other, highlighting our different alcohol preferences, although I did prefer an ice-cold brew with pizza or burgers. Waiting patiently for Elijah to share the details of his phone conversation went against my nature. I was a planner first then a hardcore doer. I was a woman of action, but there was nothing for me to *do* except show Elijah I loved him by giving him the space he needed. Luckily for me, he didn't want a physical distance because I loved resting between his parted thighs and reclining my back against his chest. I loved even more the sweet way he kissed my temple and trailed his wet fingers up and down my arms once we were submerged in the soothing water. We abandoned our drinks on the small, antique shelf that made the perfect bath caddy once Elijah laid a piece of glass over the wood surface of the table to protect it from water damage when we…um…splashed about.

"You give me greater peace than I have ever known, Maegan," he whispered huskily. "I can't thank you enough for it." He wasn't worshiping my body; he wasn't talking about the all-consuming desire that raged between us; he was showing his gratitude for the way I made him *feel*. It was the loveliest compliment I'd ever received, and I discovered being patient wasn't all that hard. A person just needed the right motivation and bringing peace to his riotous mind was all the reason I needed.

"I don't just love you, Elijah. I adore you." There was a difference.

"I adore you too, Freckles." Elijah wrapped his arms around my chest and held me even tighter. I felt tension creeping back into his body just before he spoke again. "My father has lung cancer." The words sounded rough and jagged like they were ripped from his soul. I wanted to turn and take him in my arms, but his hold around my chest didn't allow movement.

"I'm sorry, Elijah."

"That's what he said too after he dropped the first bomb. Not 'hello, Son,' or 'it's good to hear your voice.' Just 'I have lung cancer' followed by 'I'm sorry, Elijah.'" It seemed like such a cold, brittle way of delivering the news, but then again, Elijah's father picked the side of his older brother after he slept with Elijah's wife while he was overseas, knocking her up in the process.

"Was he apologizing for his horrible communication skills or for the way he treated you ten years ago?" I made no effort to hide the contempt I had for the man.

Elijah chuckled and kissed my temple once more. "I think both. He wants to see me."

"Do you want to see him?" I asked, softening my voice.

I felt the way his body trembled and understood the reason why he had me pinned against his body. He didn't want me to see his tears. Screw that. I squirmed until he loosened his hold then turned around until I kneeled between his thighs. "I thought I was all cried out when it came to this," he whispered.

I tapped on his thighs, indicating that I wanted him to close his legs so I could straddle them. I needed to get as physically close to him as I could. Once I was exactly where we both wanted and needed me to be, I said, "I don't think that's a real thing. Some hurts run too deep, and they sneak up and smack us upside the head out of the blue, causing tears of sorrow and grief to flow." I wiped his face before I leaned in and kissed him. "Did he say how advanced his cancer is?"

Elijah leaned forward, resting his forehead on my collarbone. "He only said that he has a good prognosis. He's completed chemotherapy already to shrink the tumor and is having surgery in a month or so. They want him to recover fully from chemotherapy first since it weakens the immune system. After that, he'll have radiation therapy."

"Do you want to go see him?" He never answered my question when I asked the first time. Elijah raised his head and looked into my eyes. I cupped the face I adored and said, "I'll go with you."

He didn't say anything at first, and I half-braced myself for him to refuse my offer. Then an expression of relief washed over his face seconds before he nodded.

"You just let me know when. Mom can cover for me at work."

"I—" His voice broke off, and he closed his eyes like he was trying to gather himself. I kissed his forehead, his eyelids, the tip of his nose, then finally dropped a soft kiss on his lips. The tension in his body lessened but didn't quite disappear, and his eyes looked less turbulent when he reopened them. "Tell me what you imagined for our nursery. I want to think about hopeful things tonight."

He made me feel hopeful all the time, and I wanted to repay that gift to him. "I would like to paint the bow window to look like the interior of a treehouse," I said then told him about the other details I envisioned. "I don't want to make it seem too feminine or too masculine."

"It sounds amazing, Freckles. I know you'll strike the right balance."

"Some time ago, maybe a year, I found these vintage Beatrix Potter figurines at an estate sale. They were in pristine condition, and I knew a collector would easily pay more than double what I gave for them. I could never bring myself to upload them to my site or even display them in the curio cabinet at the store. They felt like they belonged to me and any future children I might have."

"So, bring them home and place them on the bookshelf inside the future treehouse. It's obviously where they belong. Just like you belong here in my arms."

After our bath, we went downstairs to eat big slices of the cake Elijah bought as a surprise. I took Lulu out to do her final business while Elijah sat on the couch facing the fireplace. When I returned inside, I sat on his lap instead of sitting beside him.

"I have to admit that the humidor looks right on the shelf." We both stared at it quietly. "Two things occurred to me while you were outside."

"Yeah?"

"The Blissview Hotel logo is on the lid of that humidor, and there should be at least twice the amount of ashes inside it if they belonged to an adult male."

"Are you saying they belong to an animal or something?"

"I think they belong to Anthony, but I have to wonder what they're doing in a Blissview Hotel humidor and where the rest of his remains are?"

"Those are keen observations. I was too wrapped up in my emotions to notice those things. I can't wait to hear what Lyric discovers in San Francisco."

"I have a feeling he's going to solve the case," Elijah replied. "I'm also feeling optimistic about the outcome for the first time since the investigation started."

"It's only been a few days, but it feels like a wild ride nonetheless."

"That it does, Freckles."

Later in bed, Elijah opened up a bit more and told me stories about his dad and the way he viewed him as a little kid. "Earning his praise was my highest priority in life until I learned the cool thing my dick could do." I tried to squelch my snort before it escaped but wasn't successful. "My brother... He was my hero, Maegan. I'm not sure I can ever get over him sleeping with Brandy or forgive the rift it created between my father and me."

"I don't think you have to know all the answers tonight," I replied softly. "Maybe you should acknowledge that you're going to see your father in a few days and let that sink in. Let the words flow naturally when you see him again rather than prepare a speech in advance."

"That's probably sound advice." Elijah blew out a long sigh. "I just hope Jack and Brandy aren't there."

Well fuck. I hadn't thought about *her* being there. She was the first girl Elijah loved, emotionally and physically. They might still be together if she wasn't a faithless hag. I could feel my blood pressure rising just thinking about it. I wanted to go in there, wherever this meeting took place, all classy to make Elijah proud, but a big part of me wanted to tear those two up. "I'm sure they'll stay away," I said. Who was I trying to assure? Him or me?

Elijah didn't respond, and I realized why when I paid attention to his breathing. I was glad he fell asleep easily but knew it would be a while before I could shut down my brain and follow him to dreamland.

Chapter Eight

Elijah

I T TURNED OUT THAT DECIDING TO SEE MY DAD AND PUTTING A plan into motion were two very different things. He'd given me his cell phone number to program into my phone which I did after we disconnected our call Tuesday night. Hell, I was stunned to learn my dad finally broke down and got a cell phone after blaming them for society's downfall for so many years. I'd started to call him a dozen times between Wednesday morning and Friday night, but I hung up before the call could even go through. I expected Mom to call and lean on me a little since Dad made the first move, but she didn't. Mom had waited for this moment for ten years, and I knew she wanted her family put back together more than anything. I wouldn't give her false hope and make her believe we could go back to the way things were before our lives exploded because of two selfish assholes. Agreeing to see Dad was a decision only I could make, and even though I'd made it, I couldn't seem to take the next step.

On Friday night, Maegan and I went on a double date to dinner and a movie with Milo and Andy. We invited Memphis, of course, but he claimed he was working on a special project while Lyric was still out of town, but we suspected he was moping. Well, all except

Milo who thought Memphis's special project was manscaping for his reunion with Lyric the next day. Either way, it was just the four of us, and Maegan chose an awesome action adventure movie that we all enjoyed. I loved the action and plot while the rest of them drooled over one of the lead actors. Even I had to admit the guy was a sexy beast and pulled off playing a villain better than any of his nice guy roles.

Saturday morning rolled around, and Maegan went off to work while I hung around the house. I walked by the open door to the nursery, and that was when I finally worked up the courage to call my dad back and confirm I was coming to see him. I wanted to be the best father I could be to my children, and that meant I needed to unburden myself of the hurtful things of my past. No one said I had to forgive and embrace him, but I could at least find peace and move on with my life.

"Hello, Elijah," my father said, sounding exhausted and vastly different from the robust man I remembered.

"Did I wake you, Jack?"

A rough and tumble chuckle came from the other end of the connection. "You're back to calling me Jack again, eh?"

"Well, you caught me off guard when you called me the other night, and I said the first thing that came to mind."

"I guess I have your answer to my request then. Honestly, I didn't expect you to call me back. I appreciate that you at least heard me out."

"Not so fast," I firmly said before he could hang up. "That's not the kind of man you raised, Jack. I needed a few days to think about what I wanted to say to you. I guess I never really thought I'd have the chance."

"So, you're coming then?" he asked. Was that hopefulness I heard in his voice. *Couldn't be.*

"I'll be there tomorrow afternoon."

"That's great, Elijah. Your mother will be so happy."

72

"She's especially going to be happy when she meets the special someone I'm bringing with me." Mom had heard plenty about Maegan during our phone conversations, but there was no way she was prepared for the awesomeness of seeing my lady in person.

"I thought you sounded happier than the last time we talked." I knew he wasn't referring to the brief conversation from a few days prior.

"Jack, the last time we talked, I was in the hospital after a brawl fight at a bar. You wanted me to suck it up and soldier on after learning about Jack and Brandy."

"I vividly remember the encounter, Elijah. I have lung cancer, but I'm not senile."

"That's good because pretending it never happened won't fix anything."

"No, it won't," my dad said after a pause. "Do you know about what time we can expect you? Your mother will want to prepare food for you and your lady friend."

"We'll probably be there around four o'clock if that works for you. Please tell Mom not to go to any trouble though."

"I'm not going to waste my breath because you know how she is." I did know, but it was worth a shot. "Elijah, I'll be happy to see you and meet your lady."

Emotion rose up from the pit of my soul to choke me, making it hard to breathe or speak. "I'll see you tomorrow," I managed to say after a brief pause. I hung up before I could make a fool of myself by doing something like bursting into tears.

Sitting around the house was the worst thing I could do because it would give me too much time to think. I remembered Andy had said the night before that he was all caught up on paid projects and planned to work on his and Milo's house on Lover's Lane. I knew my way around a hammer and had plenty of experience painting, so I headed over to the new house.

When I arrived, Andy was jamming to rock songs that were

popular before either of us were born, but they called it classic rock for a reason. It wasn't his music choice I found interesting; it was the air guitar he played on the long pole attached to his paint roller while lip syncing.

"You're making great time with the renovations in here," I said, noticing all the hideous dancing pepper wallpaper and outdated cabinetry had been removed.

"Jesus fuck!" Andy shouted then whirled around to face me.

"I'm pretty sure he didn't fuck, but maybe I missed church the day they read that section of the bible."

"You scared the fuck out of me," Andy said, crossing the kitchen to turn down the radio. "I need to be less dorky if people are just going to pop in unannounced."

"Sorry. Would you like me to go back outside and text that I'm stopping by so we can start all over again?"

"Would you pretend to forget what you just saw?"

"Not in a million years," I said, grinning from ear to ear. "Hey, I know. Why don't you do a repeat performance tomorrow when we come over for brunch?"

"Why don't you kiss my ass?" Andy aggressively dipped the paint roller in the pan of paint on the floor then rolled it up and down the washboard-like grooves of the tray engineered to help spread the paint evenly on the roller.

"Aw, don't be mad," I teased. "I just stopped by to see if you wanted some help."

"How good are you at cutting in?"

"I have a steady hand," I said, holding them up in the air. "You want me to cut in these other two walls while you roll the ones you already did?"

"That would be great. The ladder is right around the corner, and there's a small paint bucket on top with the paintbrush I used."

I pulled the ladder into the kitchen and positioned it by the wall opposite to the one Andy was painting. "I like this beige paint color.

It's warm and inviting. I have to admit I expected Milo to pick out a bolder paint color for the kitchen."

"Nah," Andy said. "He tends to go for neutral backgrounds and bolder accent pieces. We are doing a charcoal gray accent wall in our bedroom as a contrast to our white headboard. The rest of the room will be a soothing, medium gray with a hint of blue undertone."

"You sound like you're the guy working the paint counter at the hardware store."

"Dare used the description when he helped me stage the flip house I bought earlier this year. I wrote down the name of the paint because I liked it."

Conversation trailed off as we focused on our tasks. Once I was done cutting in, I found a spare roller and helped paint the rest of the kitchen. "What next?" I asked when we finished.

"I appreciate your help, Elijah, but I sense there's an ulterior motive."

"I'm wounded."

"You're full of shit. I won't force you to talk, but I will accept your kind offer."

"You're so magnanimous."

"Is Milo talking about my condom size again?" Too bad I'd just taken a healthy gulp of the extra Gatorade Andy had in his cooler. I ended up shooting the orange drink out my nose which burned like hell.

"I believe that's called magnum," I said once I could speak, "and no, that's never come up in a conversation between us."

"There is something you can do to help me out," Andy said, leaning close like he was afraid someone would overhear him. "Tell me what Maegan has planned for the turret room."

"Hell no," I said, shaking my head. "I am not getting in the middle of their battle." The upstairs bedroom in Andy and Milo's new home had a window seat tucked into the dormers of the Cape Cod windows. The Miracle twins were locked in a battle to see whose room turned out the best. I assumed Andy and Milo were planning to use their room for kids too, but I didn't really know for sure. Maegan would kill me if I spilled our plans to the enemy. After all, Milo was just as tight with Vanessa as Maegan was, so it was likely he'd call on her to paint a mural if he found out what Maegan planned.

"It was worth a shot," Andy said, shrugging.

"Are you in the doghouse or something?"

"No, but it never hurts to gain some advantage over a Miracle."

We painted the living room and dining room before Maegan called looking for me. I couldn't believe how quickly the day passed when I was busy doing physical labor and seeing which one of us could do the best air riff to the hair band classics. I was by far the best air guitar player between the two of us, but Andy's lip-syncing skills far surpassed mine.

When I got home, Maegan was practically coming out of her skin with excitement. "Lyric solved the case!"

She went to throw her arms around my neck, but I stepped back in case some of the paint smears on my T-shirt were wet. That's when she really paid attention to my shirt and jeans. "Sitting around here wouldn't have been good for me today, so I decided to help Andy out. We got three rooms painted on the first floor."

"Do you know anything they have planned for their nursery?"

"No, and I wouldn't share any details with Andy when he asked me for some insider information."

"That scoundrel!" Maegan gasped.

"What did you learn about Anthony, Freckles?"

"Why don't you go shower and change clothes while I start dinner. Then I'll tell you everything I know."

"What are we having?"

"Stuffed pepper soup, salad, and breadsticks."

I took the steps two at a time until I reached the top. Oddly, I didn't like stuffed peppers, but I loved them deconstructed in a soup form. I showered, changed, and returned downstairs in less than fifteen minutes. By then, Freckles was cooking the diced onions, garlic, and red and green peppers in olive oil. It was one of my favorite smells, second only to Maegan's arousal. Speaking of which, I was in desperate need of my girl.

I came up behind her at the stove, wrapped my arms around her waist, and propped my chin on the top of her head. "I'm back."

Maegan pushed her ass against my crotch. "I can feel that. I'm happy you're home too."

"I better tell you my news before I get caught up in the ghost story and tangled up in your limbs. I'm a goner once I'm inside you, and there's no guarantee my brain will start functioning again before the morning."

"What's up?" she asked, although I suspected my Nancy Drew had a good idea.

"I finally called my father back and told him we were coming."

"Are you okay?" Maegan asked, setting her spoon down and turning in the circle of my arms to look into my eyes.

"I am okay, but I didn't want to stew about it all day, so I kept busy."

"When are we heading north?"

"That's the part that might upset you," I said, grimacing. "I told Jack we would be there by four o'clock."

"Memphis, Lyric, and I are getting the first crack at an estate up around the Columbus area, but we should be finished in plenty of time."

"Freckles, I can reschedule. I don't want you rushing around to accommodate plans I made without consulting you. I can go by myself if—"

"I want to go, Elijah. We can make this work. The guys and I are heading up after brunch, and we will be done in a few hours."

"My folks live on a farm in Madison County which is north of Columbus. Why don't I meet you guys at an exit off the interstate? You can ride with me to my parents, and one of the guys can drive your SUV back to Blissville."

"That sounds perfect to me. Are your parents expecting me?" Maegan asked.

"I told him I was bringing home someone very special to meet them."

Maegan squinted playfully. "Do I know this bitch?"

"Jack said he and Mom are both excited to meet *you*." I swallowed hard. "He also said he would be happy to see me again."

"Elijah, that's wonderful. He's making an honest effort."

"Because he has cancer."

"Or facing mortality gave him the courage to do what he's wanted to all along." Maegan reached up and caressed my cheek.

"Happier news," I declared. "Tell me what Lyric found out."

"Do you remember Lyric saying the concierge's great-great-great-grandfather worked for Denver Collins, aka Wallace Bennington III?"

"Yeah. Lyric was hoping some awesome stories were handed down through the generations."

"Anh Yang, that's the concierge, had so much more than stories. She had Wallace's journals and photos which have never been shared with the public before, and she also had a humidor just like the one on our mantle containing the other half of Tony Reid's ashes."

"Tony Reid? Was that Anthony's alias in San Francisco?" I asked.

Maegan nodded. "He made it there, Elijah."

"How? I thought he was locked in the attic or sent to an asylum."

"The story just keeps getting better. You won't believe what Lyric uncovered." She vibrated with joy which was exactly what I needed.

"I won't know until you tell me."

Maegan giggled happily then told me a story that I expected to appear in one of the historical romance books she loved so much. Anthony Bliss's mother came for a visit and discovered her son was having an affair with a man. Maybe she uncovered his plans to leave his family. She drugged him and locked him up in the attic with the intention of having him sent to an asylum. Maegan's eyes lost their happiness and humor when she got to that part. "Elijah, I will never abandon our children no matter what they do or who they love. I promise you."

"I know, Freckles." I couldn't wait to see her become a mother.

"Melanie Bliss sent a wire to San Francisco to let Wallace know what was happening. She turned the tables on Anthony's mother by slipping the same drug in her tea then helped Anthony escape with Wallace. She reported his disappearance to the police, and Anthony's mother returned to New York."

"Melanie Bliss helped her husband leave her to be with another man?"

"I guess it was an arranged marriage or at least one of convenience. Maybe Anthony and Melanie tried to make it work, but they were nothing more than friends. I wonder how hard it was for Anthony to leave his children behind?" she asked wistfully.

"How did the humidor with half of the ashes get here?"

"Wallace was convinced Anthony's spirit remained after he died because he was restless and would rather be in his beloved Bliss House. There was also speculation that he felt guilty for being the reason Anthony left his children."

"The children," I said. "There are probably Bliss heirs out there somewhere."

"Lyric's network will attempt to find them and see if they'd like to participate in the show."

"There will definitely be a show?" I asked

"As long as they can obtain permission from The Golden Gate Bridge Inn management firm to film. The network hopes to make this a big event with us taking our humidor to San Francisco to join the two spirits."

"Two spirits? You mean Anthony's ghost has a split personality?" I asked.

"Oh! In all my excitement, I forgot to tell you what else Lyric learned. Wallace Bennington's ghost lives in that hotel. Lyric thinks he can't rest until he knows Anthony is at peace."

"Did you say us?"

"Yes, we're going to San Fran to say goodbye to Anthony and wish him a peaceful journey to the afterlife with the man he loves. If the network can't get permission, then we'll still go and do it privately without the cameras running."

"What happens if the networks do get the approval?"

"Lyric refilms everything he has so far with his crew members."

"So, our home will be invaded by network people," I said, sounding as thrilled as I felt.

"Lyric said it wouldn't take long. Just a day or two of filming. There's no guarantee that Anthony will cooperate, so he might get stuck using the footage and recordings he already has."

"I'm not upset with that option," I admitted.

"Me either, but I'm willing to play nice and put up with a little bit of disruption to give Anthony the peace he deserves."

"I will do anything to see you happy, but I have one condition."

"Name it," she replied with a raised brow.

"No network people stay here overnight. I am not curtailing my sexy times with my lady or wearing a gag to keep from yelling out when I come inside you."

"You *are* noisy," she teased.

"And you love every minute of it."

"I do, and that love grows stronger every day." Maegan turned around toward the stove, put the cooked burger she'd already browned back into the pan with the vegetables then added two cans of diced tomatoes, one can of beef broth, and one can of tomato sauce into the pot and reduced the heat. "This soup needs to simmer for thirty minutes. Think I can make you yell and come in that amount of time?"

"There's only one way to find out."

Chapter Nine

Maegan

"**M**om, I'm nervous about today," I said into the phone as I drove to Memphis's house to pick the lovebirds up for our trip north. They couldn't rouse themselves out of bed long enough to attend Sunday brunch, so I wasn't even sure there would be a trip north.

"About rummaging through someone's belongings looking for a rare treasure? Honey, you've loved that since you attended your first garage sale at five years old," Mom said. "Do you remember trying to talk Mrs. Darling into lowering the price on that Care Bear?"

"Mom, I even knew back then there was a difference between merchandise in mint condition and those with wear and tear. I wasn't willing to pay a buck for that bear when it was only worth a quarter in the shape it was in. I bought it for a bargain, and you helped me get the stains out and repair the slight tear around the embroidered cupcake in the center of its belly."

"And you turned around and sold it for a buck twenty-five the following week. Boy, Mrs. Darling wanted to be pissed, but you convinced her there was no way your bear could be the same raggedy stuffed animal you bought from her."

"Hey, I didn't cheat her out of a cent. When I sold the bear, it was in much better shape."

My mom laughed warmly on the other end of our connection. It helped soothe my nerves. "I suspect your nerves have more to do with meeting a certain someone's parents."

Even though my folks had figured out Elijah's relationship with his parents was strained, they never pushed him or asked me to betray his trust. They knew a good man when they saw one, and the only thing they cared about was how Elijah treated me. I had told my mom about our plans when she texted me that morning to invite us to dinner. Just telling her "sorry, we can't make it," would never do.

"To be honest, Mom, I shouldn't care a damn what those people think about me."

"Except you do."

I did. There was always the chance Elijah would patch up the relationship with his parents, and I didn't want to be a source of contention between them. This meeting felt every bit as important to me as it did for Elijah, although for very different reasons. "I do," I admitted.

"Are you willing to hear some very sound advice from your mother?" she asked.

"Always."

"Here's what you do, my darling daughter. You go into their home, or wherever you're meeting up, with your chin up and shoulders back. Remember whose daughter you are and smile and be gracious even if it's the last thing you want to do. Know who truly loves you and where you're wanted, needed, and loved. And, Maegan, if you find yourself feeling overwhelmed, remember the one thing women have been doing since the beginning of time." Jackie Miracle paused for dramatic effect. "Fake your enthusiasm, darling."

"Mom!" I blurted out before laughter rumbled in my chest and spilled out of me, echoing loudly through the interior of my SUV.

"Darling, at thirty years old, I'm positive you've had to fake your way through something, although I suspect the skill has gotten rusty the past six months. Not everyone is as lucky as you and me, Maegan. Faking-it skills are useful in many situations and meeting Elijah's parents might be the most important one of all."

"M-m-mom, stop," I said, trying to catch my breath. I pulled to a stop in front of Memphis's house, expecting I'd have to knock on the door so he'd come up for air long enough to get in the SUV or tell me he wasn't going. "I need to get off here and let Memphis know I'm here."

"I bet he's forgotten all about your plans."

"Maybe, but—" My words cut off when the front door opened. "I'll be damned. They look exhausted, but apparently, we're still on."

"Drive safe and have fun. Call me tonight after you get home from meeting Elijah's parents."

"Will do. Love you, Mama." She returned the affection and blew kisses through the phone at me before disconnecting the call.

"Good morning, fellas," I whispered once they were inside the vehicle.

Memphis snorted and leaned over to kiss my cheek in greeting. "We're not hungover, Mae."

"Drunk on love, my dear. Same difference. You fellas look like you need a damn nap. You'll want to be sharp for our hunt this afternoon, Memphis. I have a good feeling about this one."

"It's probably a good idea," Memphis said before his face cracked open in a big yawn. He reclined his seat and Lyric stretched out in the back. They were both asleep before we crossed the town lines.

The quiet trip gave me plenty of time to think about how I wanted to approach the afternoon. I realized my mom was one hundred percent right. I didn't need to love Elijah's parents, and they didn't need to love me either. We just needed to be respectful of each other, which meant I had to keep my opinions to myself.

I sent Elijah a text once I arrived at the Gambini estate then woke Lyric and Memphis. I handed them both a piece of gum to

freshen their breath, and we headed to the front door. I wasn't prepared for some of the rare china and antiques I found inside the
house, and Memphis discovered records that made me question if I
should call an ambulance for him. Those high dollar items were way
out of our price range, and neither of us wanted Sonny to get taken
advantage of when it was obvious he wasn't familiar with their value.
Memphis and I promised to email him the contact information of
appraisers and auction houses who wouldn't try to screw him over.
There were many wonderful items we both could afford, including
an extraordinary Blue Libbey collection.

I realized I hadn't told them about my plans to meet up with
Elijah once we were loaded up and heading south. "I'm sorry, guys.
You were so tired, and my mind was preoccupied."

"It's no problem," Lyric said. "Memphis and I will grab a bite to
eat at the exit then drive back to Blissville."

"We'll even unload the SUV for you before we drop it off at your
house," Memphis added. "Is any of the stuff going home with you?"

"No, I'm going to sell all of it." I rarely kept the things I found at
estates. "Thank you so much for helping me."

It didn't take us long to arrive at the London exit where Elijah
waited for us in the parking lot of Long John Silvers.

"Mmmmm. Greasy fish, coleslaw, fries, and hush puppies,"
Memphis said. "I haven't eaten here in forever."

"I've never eaten here," Lyric said.

"You're in for a treat."

Lyric looked to me for confirmation, but I just shrugged.
Different strokes for different folks. "I get a basket that has fried
chicken instead of fish that's good."

"I'm up for new experiences," Lyric said, holding out his hands
for my keys.

"See you guys later," I said, dropping them into his open palm.

Elijah was waiting next to the passenger door of his old beat-up
truck. He smiled like he was seeing the sun for the first time in years.

"You always look so beautiful, Freckles."

I didn't normally wear a dress and sandals to rummage through estates, but I didn't want to wear just any old thing to meet Elijah's mom and dad. I had decided to skip any dark and dusty corners to stay clean and smelling good, but I worried for nothing. The Gambini estate was immaculately clean, and there was an order to the collections.

"This old thing?" I asked, looking down at my cream dress with lavender and yellow flowers on it.

"My mom is going to love you, Maegan."

"I hope so."

"I know so. Are you ready?"

"I'm ready to tackle anything with you by my side."

Elijah opened the door for me and stood behind me as I hoisted myself inside the cab of his truck in as ladylike a way as possible. The first time he did it, I thought he was waiting to catch me if I fell and assured him I wasn't a klutz. Elijah patiently explained he was blocking anyone from seeing my underwear if the wind caught my skirt and blew it up over my head. I adored his charm and caring mannerisms.

We didn't say much on the ride to his parents' house beyond me commenting on how lovely the old farmhouses and barns were. Since we were early, he showed me his high school and the field where he played football, the grocery store where he bagged groceries as a teenager, and a covered bridge that looked so old I held my breath while he drove through it.

"The community is a lot like Blissville, but more spread out because its rural."

"I love all the cows," I said wistfully. "There's only grain farms around us now."

"Many farmers have stopped raising beef and pork over the last few decades, but there are a few holdouts. Most of these guys out here are raising food for their own families and to sell to other people in the community they trust to pay when the time comes. They're just making enough money to cover grain and vet bills."

"I couldn't eat anything I raised," I told Elijah. "I'd want to make all the animals my pets."

"It wouldn't be easy."

"Your family never had livestock?"

"My grandpa did when I was really little," Elijah said. "I don't remember seeing cows on his farm, but there's pictures of me toddling around beside them."

"It sounds like a lovely way to grow up. Clean and wholesome."

Elijah snorted, pulling my attention off the fields and onto him. A wry smile had spread across his face. "Freckles, kids in the country have the same needs and desires as city kids. We just have to get more creative when going about it."

"Like how?"

"Well, say you're a young lad who wants to see his lady love."

"Lad and lady love?" I asked interrupting him. "Have you been reading my historical romances?"

"Yes, but that's not what I was thinking about right now."

"You're reading my romance books? When?"

"When you're having your book club meetings with the girls or whatever," Elijah said with a shrug. "I'm curious about the kind of men you like, so I pay attention to the title of one that makes you squirm and fan yourself. Then I read it when you're not around. I've discovered that none of them have a damn thing on me, so I'm neither jealous nor disapproving. Can I get back to my story now?"

I nodded my head, knowing I looked ridiculous with my mouth gaping open.

"Since you don't like my fancy, old-fashioned references, I'll try to bring my story up to the twenty-first century," Elijah said, looking at me briefly before turning his eyes back to the road. "When a horny teenaged boy wanted to see the teenaged girl of his wet dreams, he had to find inventive ways to sneak over to her house in the middle of the night since she most likely lived several miles away."

"And her daddy most likely kept a loaded shotgun behind his bedroom door for intruders and horny boys baying at the moon outside his daughter's window."

"You've read this book then?" Elijah asked.

"And saw the movie."

Elijah threw his head back and laughed. I was so happy to see no signs of tension in his expression or body language. It seemed like he'd resigned himself to accepting whatever came out of the day rather than trying to predict. "Freckles, if we weren't pressed for time, I'd take you to my favorite secluded spot overlooking the Oak Run River."

"Maybe next time," I said, reaching over and squeezing his thigh. "Tell me how the horny kids met up."

"Easy," Elijah said. "They stole their daddies' tractors and met in the middle of a field somewhere."

"Is that what you did to spend time with Brandy?"

"Me? No. Our families were great friends, so I never needed an excuse to go over there or have her over. Our families went on vacations together and everything."

"Oh." His love for her went back further than I had imagined. I didn't know why it bothered me so much, but it did. Maybe it was because she got parts of him I could never experience. I'd never be his first for anything. Not his first love, his first wife, and certainly not the woman who'd bear his children. Fuck! I suddenly felt on the verge of tears again which hadn't happened since I heard the great news about Anthony.

"Jack was the one who stole the tractor to meet his girlfriend." Elijah quieted suddenly, and I could tell what he was thinking. "Hell, maybe he was meeting Brandy, and I just didn't know it. Maybe he got a kick out of me playing lookout while he snuck off to fuck my girlfriend." I could feel Elijah pulling further inside himself while sick ideas played over and over in his brain.

"Elijah," I said gently. "Does that really matter now? Hasn't the damage already been done? Even if they had fooled around in high school, what they did as adults was way worse. Stupid kids do stupid things, but adults should know better."

"I'm so sorry, Freckles." Elijah pulled his truck over to the side of the road and reached for me. I unbuckled my seatbelt and slid across the bench until I was right beside him. "I used to think not having a center console in this old beast was a terrible thing until the time you rode me to a delicious orgasm behind the strip mall after hours."

"We're a little out in the open, so I'll just stay in the middle seat if that's all right with you?"

"Fine, but on the way home, I might be dragging you off to the river after all." Elijah placed his warm palm on my thigh. I pressed my legs together trying to calm the shiver of longing vibrating through my core. "I made my peace with losing Brandy a very long time ago. Our marriage never would've survived for more reasons than her unfaithfulness. What I resent more than anything was losing my brother and my father, two people I loved dearly. Jack and I weren't just brothers, we were best friends, just like Milo and you. That's the betrayal I can't get past, along with my dad siding with them. I really hope you believe me and know I'm with the woman I want, and my pain and humiliation are not an indication of wishing I could have someone else."

"I know," I said, twisting in my seat to cup his face. "There's no faking the love and adoration I see in your eyes. Trust me, baby; I know a thing or two about faking it."

"Excuse me?"

"Not with you," I said, rushing to clarify. "I've told you that you were the first man to give me an orgasm, and I've never had to fake anything with you. I guess that response just popped out after my conversation with my mom today."

"Do I want to know why you and your mom were discussing faking it in the first place?"

"It's nothing bad," I assured him. "In fact, it's quite hilarious." I recounted the story word for word while we were parked by the side of the road. When I was done, Elijah was howling with laughter.

"I love that woman, Freckles." He wiped the tears from his eyes. "I especially love the subtle way she worked in that your dad is good in bed."

"Oh God! I didn't pick it up until you mentioned it. Eww, Elijah!" I slid back to my original seat and buckled my seatbelt. "Let's get on with the show, so I can think about something else right away."

It turned out, Elijah had pulled over half a mile from his parents' house which was a lovely, two-story farmhouse like the ones I'd been admiring for the past hour. "It's so beautiful," I said in awe.

"It's not as grand as our home," Elijah said.

"I can still feel the rich history here," I told him. "Has this home been in your family for a long time?" I asked, following him up the steps leading to a wraparound porch. "This porch is amazing."

"It's been in the family for several generations. The porch is my mom's favorite place, so I bet she'll invite you to pull up a rocking chair later."

Just then, the front door opened to reveal a short, graying woman grinning at her son. "Elijah!" she said in a tearful voice. "I'm so happy you're home."

"I've missed you too," Elijah said, scooping his mother up into a hug that left her feet dangling off the ground. Then he set her down and placed his big hands on her dainty shoulders. "Mama, I've brought home someone very special to meet you."

Chin up. Shoulders back. Smile.

"Is this your Freckles?" she asked then turned to look at me with wide, hopeful eyes. Was she worried I would judge her for the past and find her lacking?

"This is Maegan Miracle," Elijah said proudly, wrapping his arm around my shoulders and pulling me closer. "My Freckles."

"It's nice to meet you, Mrs. Markham."

"I've waited for you for ten years, Maegan. Even longer if I'm being honest. It's so nice to meet you." She pulled me into a warm hug, and I knew I had at least one ally in the Markham homestead.

Chapter Ten

Elijah

"CALL ME BRENDA," MOM SAID TO MAEGAN WHEN THEY pulled out of the embrace. "You're every bit as beautiful as Elijah described."

Maegan's face turned a delicate pink shade, and she glanced at me briefly. "Thank you, Brenda."

"I wasn't just referring to your outer beauty either," Mom told her warmly. "You're a strong, confident woman. I can tell that by your posture and the way you carry yourself when you walk." It was true. Maegan might think she had to do that thing with her chin and shoulders, but there was never a need for her to fake anything. She was spectacular all the time. "I can see how much you love my boy when you look at him. That makes a mother very happy." My mom released a quick sigh and placed a hand over her heart. "Forgive my silliness. I'm just so overjoyed to have both of you here."

"Do I smell pot roast?" I asked, sniffing the air.

"Well, it is your favorite," Mom replied. "I don't usually cook something so heavy when it's this hot out, but this day calls for a celebration."

"Mom…" I let my words trail off because I wasn't sure what to say next. This wasn't necessarily a start to something special and meaningful.

"I know, Elijah. I didn't mean to put pressure on you; I'm just so grateful to see you and meet your special lady." Mom pulled open the door and gestured for us all to go inside. "There's no need to melt out here while the house is nice and cool."

"When did you get central air?" I asked once we entered the house.

"Um, I'd say it was five or six years ago. We resisted for so long, but this old woman can't take these humid summers. Hot flashes are the devil's work."

"I bet it was a big undertaking and a huge expense," I remarked. I was surprised she never told me about it, but I guess she didn't want to waste our infrequent phone calls to discuss something like that. Honestly, I missed the old house and would've loved to hear updates about the remodeling progress. "That's not the only thing that changed."

"Oh, we took down some old wallpaper and repainted the walls. It wasn't a lot."

Maybe not to her, but she lived through the renovations and saw the changes over time. For me, it was like walking into a totally different home which was both good and bad. I wasn't flooded with nostalgic and painful memories, because it didn't seem like the same house where they occurred. On the other hand, I feel like I lost my childhood home and no one told me about it.

"Furniture is new," I said cataloging other changes I saw. "You painted over Jack's and my growth charts."

"You both are in your thirties now, Elijah. Surely you didn't expect me to keep those up forever."

Maegan slipped her tiny hand in mine and squeezed my fingers to comfort me. "You have a lovely home, Brenda. Elijah told me it's been in the family for generations."

"Yes, this farm has been in *my* family for four generations dating back to the civil war," she said.

"Mom likes it known that the house came with her bloodline," I told Maegan. "Dad calls her Scarlett and the homestead Tara."

Mom smiled when she heard me slip and say Dad instead of Jack. "Your father sure as hell isn't Rhett Butler."

"I heard that, woman," a weak, gravelly voice said from the dark corner of the living room situated to the right of the foyer. I hardly recognized my dad's voice. "Rhett gave up too easily."

"Gave up too easily? Did we watch the same movie?" my mom said into the room. "Besides, everyone knows Rhett wasn't truly done with Scarlett."

My dad chuckled then said, "If you say so."

"I do."

"Is that Elijah?"

"No, it's Santa Claus," Mom fired back. "Of course, it's him."

My mom tipped her head toward the living room, indicating I should go in there. Maegan squeezed my hand to let me know she agreed. It felt like it took me five years to work up my courage to take the first step toward the living room, but circumstances often seemed to speed time up or stretch it into long, awkward pauses.

I heard rustling in the dark corner followed by a metallic click of someone turning on a lamp. Suddenly, there was a circle of light surrounding my dad's old, battered recliner. It seemed like not everything changed, and seeing that ancient, busted piece of furniture finally made it feel like I was home. I used to love sitting in that chair when Dad was out because it smelled of his aftershave and bore the shape of his body from many years of wear. That old thing couldn't be comfortable, but he was too stubborn to give it up.

Then I looked at him, and I mean really looked. He'd lost so much weight his skin hung on him paper thin and white as a sheet. Dad ran his hand over his bald head like he felt uneasy then pulled his blanket higher to tuck beneath his armpits.

"Have any trouble on your trip up?" he asked, breaking the

silent standoff.

"No, sir," I said, feeling like a kid who was being interrogated for being out too long. Some might say I was *away* for too long.

"Is this your beautiful lady your mom has been talking about these past six months?" I admit I was shocked to hear my parents talked about me or the things I discussed with Mom.

"Nah, she's just a hitchhiker I found along the way."

Maegan squeezed my hand then pulled it free of mine. She walked across the room and extended her hand toward him. "I'm Maegan Miracle. It's nice to meet you, Mr. Markham."

Dad sat straighter in his chair as Maegan approached and attempted a warm smile. I had to bite my lip to keep from crying when the hand he reached out to her trembled severely. Maegan covered their joined hands with her free one to steady him. Where was the strong, invincible man who had raised me? Who was this imposter who looked to be nothing but skin and bones? Mom placed her hand between my shoulder blades to comfort and steady me which was just what I needed.

"He's not going to die, Elijah," she whispered.

"Damn right," Dad said with a shaky voice he probably thought was full of bravado. "Jack Markham might bend, but he doesn't break." He waved me over with the hand Maegan wasn't holding. "Maybe the ladies can go in the kitchen and have a chat so we can have some time alone."

"Of course," Maegan said, gently letting his hand slide from hers. She walked to me, raised up on her tiptoes, and kissed my cheek. "If you're lucky, maybe your mom will share her pot roast secrets with me."

"And meatloaf," I said hopefully.

"Sounds fun," Mom said. "Then I'll get the photo albums out so you can see Elijah during his awkward phase."

"Even better," Maegan said, following Mom out of the room.

"Pull up a chair," Dad said.

I slid an ottoman over from a club chair that I never would have picked for my mom and dad. "I'm not sure what to make of the changes," I told him. "I never thought I'd be so happy to see your beat-up recliner."

"It's a good thing you like it so much because I've left it to you in the will." He tried to laugh but it turned into a cough. He regained his composure after a minute and said, "Don't be alarmed if I need to reach for my oxygen. It doesn't mean I'm dying."

"Yes, sir."

"Elijah, I'm not sure where to begin, but an apology seems like a good place to start."

Seeing him so sick and weak was horrible, and I didn't want to cause him any more stress. On the other hand, I needed to hear the words if there was a sliver of a chance for us to repair our broken relationship.

"There are many things I want to apologize for, but the most important one is that I ever made you feel that you weren't good enough the way you were. Allowing you to mold yourself into a soldier because you thought it's what I wanted was just wrong. I should've told you I was proud of you for more important things like when you won awards in elementary school for character and citizenship. I should have had tears of pride in my eyes when you were inducted into the National Honor Society and not the sports hall of fame at the high school." Dad paused to cough again, and I handed him the glass of water from the small table beside his recliner. "Would you look at how tiny this table is?" he said. "It's barely big enough for a glass of water and the TV guide, but Brenda had to have it because it matched the other pieces."

"I think it's pretty miraculous she let you keep the recliner."

"No one tells a man with cancer he can't have his favorite chair."

"There's that," I said, tipping my head to the side.

"The things I said to you in your hospital bed..." Dad's words drifted off, and he swallowed hard. I wanted to tell him he didn't have to apologize for every little slight against me, but damn it, I needed him to be sorry. Nobody had ever hurt me like he had, not even Jack who had slept with my wife. "I spoke unforgivable words that day, and I've regretted nothing more in my life. I never should've implied you needed to suck it up and move on. I was scared I would lose my sons, and I did lose one of them."

I had a snappy comeback about how he got to keep his favorite son, but I had to meet the man halfway. "There was no way I could continue on like nothing happened. I couldn't sit across the table from them without wanting to choke them both."

Dad took another long drink of water. "I know, and I had no right to ask it of you."

"Why the change? Why apologize now?"

"I know you think it's because of the cancer, and it is in part, but I've always known I was wrong. I've always missed having you here and hearing your voice." His chin wobbled, and a tear slid down his face. I rubbed a hand over my face to keep from doing the same. "I was a stubborn fool who thought you'd miss us and make the first move. How stupid is that?"

"I did miss you and Mom."

"Staring down death made me realize how foolish I was, and I didn't like the person I saw in the mirror. I don't mean because I'm skinny and bald now, I'm talking about my soul. It was ugly and mean. If my time was up, I didn't want to meet my maker without trying to patch things up between us. If nothing else, I wanted to give you the apology you deserved."

"Dad, I don't know what to say."

"You just said a lot right now." I looked at him in confusion for a minute until I realized I'd called him Dad. "If you ever call me Jack again, I will take a switch to your ass."

"Yes, sir."

"Tell me about your life, Elijah. I want to hear about your new job as a detective in a small town. Your mother and I hated you working as an undercover cop in Columbus. We worried about you every damn day. Tell me about your Freckles. That's what your mother said you call her."

I spent the next ninety minutes talking to my dad about my life and all the ways it had changed over the last six months. I told him about Adrian, Gabe, and the rest of the police force. He got a big kick out of the missing chickens and my idea for a sting operation. He laughed until he coughed then laughed until he cried. Mostly, I talked about Maegan. He got a twinkle in his eyes when he heard about how we met. Dad had always liked feisty women, and Maegan was the feistiest I'd ever known.

Mom called us into dinner, and I wasn't sure if I should offer to help him up. I didn't want to step on his pride, but I hated to see him struggle. I waited patiently while he pushed against the armrests of his recliner, but it appeared as if the chair didn't want to relinquish him. I extended my hand, and he stared at it for a few seconds before accepting my offer. I gently closed my hand around his and helped him up. His frailty and bony hands made me want to cry, but I held it together for him.

Dad sat at his usual spot at the head of the table and Mom sat at the foot like normal. Maegan and I sat between them on one side, with Maegan next to Mom and me beside my dad. Mom's pot roast was every bit as delicious as I remembered, and I asked Maegan if she found out why my mom's roast tasted different than everyone else's.

"I sure did," Maegan said. "I also got her recipe for these homemade dinner rolls."

"I can't wait to be your guinea pig while you try the recipes," I said, tucking into another bite.

"Maegan," my mom said. "Elijah told me you bought a historic home with a resident ghost."

Dad snorted. "Elijah doesn't believe in ghosts, Bren."

"I do now, Dad." That got his attention. "Tell them all about Anthony, Freckles."

"I'm not sure what I'm allowed to reveal right now," Maegan said. "The story might appear on *The Paranormal Whisperer*, and I've signed a non-disclosure agreement."

"Oh my," Mom said. "We wouldn't want you to tell us anything you're not allowed to."

"Why don't I tell you what's already been made public then you can see the conclusion for yourselves on the show."

"That sounds fair," Dad said, leaning forward and propping his elbow on the table. Mom never permitted any of us, including him, to prop our elbows on the table. It was a sign of how much they'd been through the last few months while he underwent chemo treatment.

Maegan wove the tale of Anthony Bliss establishing the town and starting a new life, hoping to outrun the curse on the Bliss family. She talked about how progressive her hometown used to be, and how Anthony and his good friend, Wallace Bennington III, helped make it happen. My mom and dad held onto her every word as she talked about Anthony's sudden and unexplainable disappearance.

"The other fella disappeared too?" Dad asked.

"Well, he sold all of his holdings and moved to San Francisco. I don't think anyone in the town ever looked for him after that."

"I have a theory," my dad said. "I bet those two fellas ran away together." I nearly choked on my hunk of roast. "What? You think I'm out of touch. You think I wasn't aware I served in Vietnam with men who were attracted to other men? It never bothered me beyond they had to pretend to be something they weren't. That's the unnatural part if you ask me."

"I've never heard you talk like this," I said. Had I mentioned to Mom that Maegan's twin was a gay man? I was certain I hadn't.

"Did you ever hear me say mean or nasty things about gays and lesbians while you were growing up?"

"No," I admitted.

"Parents didn't talk openly to their kids about things like that back then."

"Dad, I grew up in the nineteen eighties and nineties, not the eighteen eighties and nineties."

"I know, Son," he said, waving me off. "Listen, I guess we should've done a lot of things differently in this house when you boys were growing up. Maybe the events that led to our divide never would've happened if I'd been a better father."

"Dad, neither you nor Mom were responsible for what happened. I had a wonderful, happy childhood. You might not have been the kind of dad to read bedtime stories and watch Christmas shows with us, but you taught us by example. The first thing you did every night was kiss Mom hello and make her giggle before you'd rumple our hair and ask us about our day. You demanded that we show women respect at all times. You worked extra jobs when crop prices were down so we could have the things we needed. I've taken those lessons and applied them to my life. Jack's actions are all on him, not you."

"Knock knock," came a soft voice from the foyer. Maegan stiffened beside me, and I knew it was because she thought Brandy had stopped by. I reached for her hand beneath the table and brought it to my lips for a kiss.

"We're in here, Daphne," Mom said.

A petite brunette with big brown eyes and hair pulled back in a ponytail walked into the kitchen. "Hello. I'm so sorry to interrupt dinner. I just wanted to drop off the casserole dish I borrowed before it never made it back."

"No problem," Mom told her. "Are you hungry? We have plenty."

"Oh, heavens no. I'll just go set this on the kitchen counter and be on my way." She dropped a kiss on my mom's head then circled around to do the same for my dad before she left the room. Who the hell was this woman who knew my parents so well? I might've thought she was a homecare nurse until she kissed them affectionately. She popped her head back in the dining room when she was finished putting the dish back. "All done."

"Daphne, this is Elijah, Jack's younger brother."

"I figured as much," she said warmly. "It's nice to meet you, Elijah."

"Likewise," I said, although I had no clue who the hell I was meeting. "This is my girlfriend, Maegan."

"Hello," Maegan said cheerfully but looked as confused as I felt.

"Good to meet you, Maegan. I need to be on my way. Have a good night, everyone."

"You too," we all called out after her.

Mom and Dad went back to eating while Freckles and I shrugged at one another. "Um, who was that?"

"That's Daphne," Dad said.

"She's Jack's girlfriend," Mom added. "They've been dating for a few years now. The kids love her."

"You weren't the only Markham Brandy fucked over," Dad said. "At least you didn't have kids to tie you to her for the rest of your life like Jack does." Was I supposed to feel sorry for him? "He also learned that being a single parent isn't so great, but at least the kids are happy and cared for with him."

"Jack has custody of the kids?" I asked.

"She didn't even put up a fight because she'd found the next sucker who thought she was a prize," Dad fumed. "She moved to New York City. Good riddance, I say. That hateful woman has caused this family enough pain."

"Jack," Mom admonished.

Maegan set her fork down. "Don't sugarcoat it on my behalf, Jack. I've dreamed about scratching that bitch's eyes out every night since I learned about her existence."

Dad hooted with laughter. "I like your Freckles, Elijah."

"I'm quite fond of her too, Dad." The fierceness in her eyes showed her passionate nature.

After dinner, I helped Mom do dishes while Maegan helped my dad back to the recliner. "Mom, why didn't you tell me about Dad's cancer diagnosis? Did you think I wouldn't want to know?" I was careful not to use an accusatory tone. My mom wasn't a suspect; she was the woman stuck in the middle of a horrible situation.

Mom released a long, shaky breath like she'd anticipated the question all afternoon and was grateful it had finally been asked. "I should've told you, but I didn't want to use emotional blackmail to get you back home. I would've called you sooner if the doctor had given your father a bad prognosis. Your father was convinced from the offset that he'd beat it, and…" Her voice trailed off. "I don't think he wanted you to see him in his weakest condition. He wanted to feel better when he made his apologies. He didn't want or need your pity; he wanted and needed your forgiveness."

"I'm getting there, Mom."

She looked up from washing her pot roast pan and smiled brightly. "You are going to marry Maegan, right? There's something different in your voice when you talk about her. I can hear how much you adore her."

"I do adore her, and I'm absolutely going to marry her." There was no doubt in my mind.

"Good, because there's something special I'd like for you to have." Mom reached into her cardigan and pulled out a red velvet box I immediately recognized. I knew a two-carat antique ring carefully rested on a ring pillow inside.

"That's Great-Grandma's wedding ring," I said in awe.

"It is," she agreed, lovingly tracing her finger over the top. "This ring means the world to me, and I want you to have it. More importantly, I want you to give it to Maegan when you feel the time is right."

"Mom," I said in awe. I'd asked her if I could give it to Brandy, but she'd gently told me no. Here she was offering the precious ring so Maegan could wear it someday. "She's going to cherish this ring."

"I mostly care that she cherishes you."

"She truly does, Mom."

After we finished cleaning, it was time to head home. I couldn't say all of my hurt was gone after one visit with my dad, but I could say his apology went a long way to healing the pain I'd felt. We promised to return soon for another visit, and Mom assured me she'd keep me updated on how surgery went.

During the trip home, I had a ring in my pocket and a burning question on my mind. I just needed to find an occasion worthy of the woman who would wear the ring.

Chapter Eleven

Maegan

"**G**IRL, GET IN HERE," APRIL SAID WHEN SHE OPENED HER front door. "It feels like I haven't seen you in ages." It was her turn to host our weekly Tuesday night book club meeting.

"It's only been a few weeks, but it has seemed longer." I hugged April and noticed she held onto me a little longer than normal. She felt thinner and her long, dark hair didn't seem as lustrous. "I—we all—missed you." I exchanged a worried glance with Vanessa, who'd arrived before me. April smiled like she wanted to believe it, but I could tell she wasn't sure. Things between her and Violet were still a little strained, and I hated the heartache it caused them. "One of us missed you more than the rest and took your absence personally."

April's poor attempt at a smile slid off her face, making me want to kick myself. "I've tried, Mae. God knows how hard I've tried to fix things between us, but I can't reach her. I fucked up so bad."

"Honey, she just needs more time." I didn't know that for sure, but I hoped Violet would come around. I pulled April back in my arms and hugged her tight.

"I didn't want to be an experiment to her, Mae. That happens so much. You hear women say all the time that they've given up on men and think they'll give women a try. It's so fucking insulting. I didn't know she was serious. Fuck, if I knew…"

"You'd have done what?" asked a voice from the door. Violet stood in the open doorway with a bottle of wine in her hand. "You'd have taken me up on my offer?"

"Violet," April said softly. "I didn't think you'd come tonight."

"That makes two of us," she replied sharply. "Now I wish I hadn't." Violet turned to leave.

"Don't go, Vi," April said. "Please stay. I—"

"Are you done insulting my intelligence?"

"What? When?"

"Just now when you told Maegan you thought I hit on you because I was done with men. I knew what I wanted, and I wanted you, April."

"I didn't mean to—"

"And the comments you've made in the past about the alcohol," Violet said, cutting her off again. "Do you really think alcohol makes people do something they don't really want to do? Did you ever think that bottle of wine loosened up my inhibitions so I would take a chance and go after what I wanted? It's called liquid courage for a reason."

"Put yourself in my shoes, Vi," April said pleadingly. "I have loved you since I knew what romantic love was, and it took you getting drunk to tell me you were attracted to me. Can you possibly understand that I was hurt too?"

"Ladies," Candace said, entering the room. "Not this same old argument again. Fuck and forgive already." She looked April up and down then rubbed her forefinger over an artfully, arched brow that was the exact same shade of red as her long, wavy hair. "I'm so glad you dressed for company. I think you owned those yoga pants back in junior high. I know for a fact you got your New Kids on The Block T-shirt back then."

The T-shirt was baggy on her because she'd lost a lot of weight since we were kids. She'd also grown taller so the shirt now hovered just above her belly button. Violet seemed to have a hard time looking away from the strip of exposed skin that included a pierced belly button. The feminine, crystal hearts dangling from the belly button ring reflected prisms of light onto April's skin. It looked like she had mini disco balls dangling above her—

"Pizza is on the way," April said, steering the conversation back to where she wanted it to go. She closed the door and turned to face us. "I ordered everyone's favorite pizza or sandwich, including yours, Vi, because I hoped you would come."

Candace snorted because her mind had gone straight to the gutter. I glanced up at Vanessa who was doing her damnedest not to grin. She failed epically and started laughing hard enough that she had to lean against me for support.

April walked slowly toward Violet. She took the bottle of wine from Vi with her left hand then cupped Vi's face softly with the right. "I am sorry, Vi. You're the last person on the earth I'd hurt." She pressed in slow, giving Violet time to back away or meet her halfway. Instead of kissing her, April rubbed the tip of her nose against Violet's. When she stepped back, Violet looked glassy-eyed and dazed.

"Holy fuck," Candace said breathlessly. "Our girl has serious game."

"That's nothing," April said smugly. "The rest is for a private audience only."

"What's more private than your own living room?" Vanessa asked.

"My bedroom and three less people."

Candace pointed to herself, Vanessa, and me while counting, "One, two, three."

"You guessed it."

"Well, talking about a book after witnessing that seems kind of tame now," I said.

"Let's get caught up on each other's lives while we wait for dinner to arrive," Vanessa suggested. "Then we can talk about the book."

Everyone agreed except Violet and April who probably had forgotten we were still there.

"Maybe we should just go," I said, looping my arm through Van's and tugging her toward the door while giving Candace a look that silently implored her to follow my lead. She rolled her eyes at me but started walking toward the door too.

"Don't go," Violet said softly. "Not yet, anyway." She smiled sweetly at April. "How long before the food arrives?"

"Twenty minutes."

"Fine, we'll do a round of speed sharing where we each get four minutes to talk about what's going on in our lives. We eat pizza then have a thirty-minute discussion about the book."

"Then we get the fuck out so you can…" Vanessa let her words trail off.

"Do whatever we want," Vi finished for her.

"We might be down to three minutes each now," I said.

April, Violet, and I took the couch while Vanessa and Candace sat in the club chairs on either end that were turned to face one another over the coffee table.

"I'll go first," Violet said, tucking her feet under her and cuddling into April's side. There was nothing new about the position because the two of them were always touching. It had been that way since we were little kids. "I finally worked up the courage to tell my parents I have romantic feels for April."

"Whoa!" we all said while Violet grinned, nestling closer to April.

"We haven't even had our first kiss yet," April said. "What if you—"

"I'm aware that things will feel physically different with you than a man, but more importantly, it will feel different emotionally. I will feel things with you no man has ever given me because I've lived a lie for so fucking long. Everything I feel with you will be better; you've had my heart since we were ten years old. I'm tired of lying to myself. I'm tired of pretending my desire to touch you is platonic. I'm done running." April ran her hands through Violet's hair the entire time she gave her impassioned speech. "It's always been you, A."

"What did your parents say?" Vanessa asked softly.

I saw April tense like she was bracing herself for bad news. She should've known Vi wouldn't have started this conversation in front of us if her parents had been upset, but I suspected her emotions were all over the place and they greatly diminished her ability to rationalize.

Violet giggled and said, "Mom said it was past time I realized I loved you for more than friendship, and Dad said he'd be honored to welcome someone as kind, smart, and beautiful as you into our family."

"Wow," April said.

The rest of us said, "Aww."

"What about you guys?" Violet asked, diverting the attention away from them.

"Not much on my end," Vanessa said, holding my stare for a few seconds. For whatever reason, she still hadn't shared her wild, passionate weekend with the ladies. "Tattoos and reading books about fellas who love other fellas. Chaz Hamilton can write some seriously good books."

"No book talk yet," Violet said. "What about you, A?" Vi said, lifting her head off April's shoulder once more to look at her. "What's been going on with you besides all your traveling for business?"

"Like I can remember anything at this point," April said, sounding dazed. "Besides missing you, I worked out a bunch, traveled for work ten out of the last fourteen days, and I managed to eat and sleep some when I wasn't doing those things."

"Are the Hollingsworth Corporation takeovers going according to plan, Miss Chief Financial Officer?" Candace asked.

"You know I'm not allowed to discuss work."

"Can you discuss if that sexy beast of a CEO is single or taken?"

"I wouldn't know, Candy Apple. Mr. Hollingsworth is a very private man. The only conquests we discuss are the corporate kind."

"Speaking of conquests," I said, noticing the way Van stiffened. "Do *you* have anything to share, Candace? You seem to love asking questions about our love lives but are secretive about your own."

"I'm quiet because there's little to report. I found a delicious new toy that's getting the job done for now. Did you know they made ones that stimulate your G-Spot, clit, and anus?"

"Yes," we all replied.

"How the hell did I not know? These are the important women's issues we need to be discussing each Tuesday."

"Vibrators are now considered women's issues?" I asked.

"Equal rights to orgasms," Candace said boldly, reminding me of the mom on Mary Poppins fighting for voting privileges.

"I'll start making the posters," Vanessa said excitedly.

"I'll sew the sashes to wear across our chests," Violet said.

"I'll call the Blissville Daily News and let them know we're hosting a meeting at Maegan's house," April volunteered.

"Thanks a lot," I told April. "What will our slogan be?"

"Equal Rights to Orgasms," Candace said. "That's catchy enough."

"Nah, we need something that will stand the test of time," April said. "My rainbow community has the best ones."

"Yeah," Candace said. "We can't steal one of theirs."

"Instead of telling people to get out and vote, we'll be telling them to get out and come," Vanessa said.

"That's a good one," Candace said. "We could use the two together. Equal Rights to Orgasm. Get Out and Come."

We were laughing hysterically when the pizza delivery arrived. The young guy was too awestruck by April's tight yoga pants and exposed belly to pay us any attention. "Here's your pizza, Miss Uh..."

His eyes zeroed in on her breasts, and he stopped speaking altogether.

"Let me help you with that, Timothy," Violet said, squeezing between him and April. Timothy tried to look around her, but Violet moved every time he did. It was quite entertaining. Violet signed the credit card slip then handed it and the pen back to Timothy before she took the pizza boxes and carryout bags from his hands and shut the door in his face.

"So rude," Candace said. "And territorial." Candace made a roaring sound and swatted Violet on her butt. "And smoking hot."

"I'll say," April said, sounding like she was still in awe over how the night was turning out.

We devoured our food like starving animals and drank wine like it was grape juice which loosened up my lips to tell the girls about the situation with Elijah's family. I'd never shared the details of his past before, and I felt guilty as hell for doing it then. I just needed to vent to someone about how I felt, and Elijah wasn't the right one to hear what I had to say.

"She married and cheated on both brothers?" April asked to clarify.

"Women like her make us all look bad," Vanessa added.

"Poor Elijah," Violet said softly. "Thank goodness he found you."

"Maybe we can have Chaz kill her off in a book," Candace suggested. "I mean, it's really fun having a writer living amongst us."

"I'm sure he gets suggestions all the time," I said, but killing off Brandy was starting to sound good. "I guess there was part of me that wanted to have a showdown with her." Van started whistling the tune to *The Good, The Bad, and The Ugly.* "I really wanted to tell her what I thought about her and the way she treated Elijah, but I wanted to do it in a classy way and not full of shouty, rage-y curse words."

"With your chin up and head held high," Candace said.

"Have you been talking to my mom?" I asked when Violet opened the second bottle of wine and started pouring us each a glass.

"Not recently. Why?" Candace replied. I told them about my

mom's advice a few days earlier, and they had the biggest laugh.

"God, I love Jackie," Vanessa said.

"Me too," I said. I couldn't imagine life without her.

"I'm glad Elijah is trying to patch up his relationship with his dad," Violet said softly. "It's too bad it took a cancer diagnosis to get them there."

"Yeah," I agreed. "Men can be stubborn mules sometimes."

"You ladies have fun with that," Vi said, leaning into April.

"Like you two won't have issues," Candace snorted, taking for granted everything would work out for our friends. "Better hope your periods sync up, or you'll only have two weeks out of the month for sexy times."

"Does that happen?" Vanessa asked. "Some women swear by it."

"I couldn't tell you," April said. "The only woman I've lived with is my mother, and she had a hysterectomy at thirty-two which was many years before I started having periods."

"Report back to us," Candace said.

"None of you are driving away from here after two and a half glasses of wine. You all look like you're about to topple over," April said.

"I'll call Elijah," I said.

My knight in shining armor showed up fifteen minutes later. "Hello, ladies," he said. I nearly came from just hearing his voice. Candace sighed, and Vanessa giggled. His eyes landed on April and Violet then returned to meet my gaze where I waggled my eyebrows as if to say, "It's about damn time."

"Let's all pile into Maegan's SUV, and I'll escort you home." He looked at April and asked, "Mind if I leave my truck parked out front? We can pick it up in the morning before work?"

"That's fine by me," April said. "You all have a good night." Neither she nor Vi budged from the couch to walk us out.

"Hey, how are we getting our cars back?" Vanessa said.

"I'll come pick you gals up after I drop Elijah off to get his truck."

"That works," Vanessa said. "Make it early enough for us to see if Violet's car is also still in the driveway."

Once Elijah and I were finally alone, I confessed that I'd talked to my friends about his family. "I feel like I've betrayed you or something."

"It's perfectly normal that you told your closest friends. I know they only want the best for us, and I'm okay with it. I don't want to see it show up in that tacky gossip column in the Blissville Daily News, but I trust your friends." He paused for a second before continuing. "I'm curious what you discussed, but I'm okay not knowing."

"We've decided to ask Chaz to kill a Brandy-inspired character in a book."

Elijah snorted. "Is that a real thing?"

"It could be. Chaz once said he's always looking for a victim or villain. Your ex-wife is the vilest villain I've ever had the displeasure of hearing about."

"I love so many things about you, Maegan, but I think your loyal heart takes the cake," Elijah said when he pulled up to our house.

"Elijah, I'm so happy you love my loyal heart, but right now I want you to love my horny body."

"Your wish is my command, Freckles."

Chapter Twelve

Elijah

"**G**OD, YOUR SKIN IS SO SOFT," I WHISPERED AGAINST THE swells of her breasts popping up over the lacy cup of her bra. "You smell delicious too." I dipped my tongue beneath the lace and licked a path across her tits.

Maegan stretched in the center of our bed, arching her back and thrusting her breasts up higher. She didn't have a shy bone in her body when it came to her sexual needs, and I fucking loved it so much.

"Then eat me," she purred, slipping her hand down her stomach and beneath her underwear. I saw her fingers slide further under the lacy fabric until they dipped over the curve of her mound, inching ever so slowly toward her slick, smooth entrance. Maegan parted her thighs ever-so-slightly, and I watched her middle finger dip inside her pussy. My wildcat gasped in delight then clinched her thighs to keep her hand in place while rocking her hips to attain friction against her clit.

"Mine," I growled.

Maegan unclenched her thighs and removed her hand from her panties then held that middle finger up in front of her. She wasn't giving me a crude gesture; she was presenting her taste to me, and I engulfed the entire length of her finger inside my mouth. I sucked and licked her finger clean then let it slide from my lips.

"Tastes delicious too," I said, reaching for her panties. I'd learned to tame myself enough that I wasn't ripping them and leaving scraps of satin and lace in my wake. Tossing the scrap of lace over my shoulder, I positioned myself on my stomach between her parted things, drinking in the sight of her smooth, creamy skin.

Maegan released the front clasp of her bra then cupped and pushed her breasts together, teasing her nipples because she knew how much it drove me crazy. I wanted to clone myself so I could go down on her and suck her tits at the same time, but I'd be too jealous to let anyone, even another version of me, anywhere near my lady.

"Mine," I repeated, moving in and pressing a kiss against her mound. "All mine."

I went to work on her clit, sucking and flicking it with the tip of my tongue, lightly tugging it between my closed lips. I could make her come from that alone, but I wanted more. I parted her lips and teasingly darted my tongue inside her, making her gasp and plead for more. I waited until she fisted my hair before I plunged my tongue inside her heat as far as it would go, making sure my nose rubbed against her clit at the same time so I could breathe her in and work her closer and closer to climax from the friction.

"Oh, please, Elijah."

I lifted my head and looked at her flushed face and shiny, green eyes. "Please what, Freckles?"

"Make me come."

It would've been so easy to lower my head back down and make her climax with my mouth, but I wanted to feel her shatter while wrapped around my cock. I got to my knees, removed my briefs, and climbed up her delectable body.

"Now we're talking," Maegan said when the head of my dick inched inside her. "More."

I gave her what she demanded with her words and the hands she'd placed on my ass to urge me deeper inside her. I claimed her mouth in a feral kiss as I slid in and out of her, easy at first to gently stretch her then at a much quicker and intense pace when she slid her hands into my hair and wrapped her legs around my waist.

Maegan arched her neck and cried out my name at the same time her cunt clenched tightly around my cock. I fucked her through her orgasm while chasing my own. By the time I spilled inside her, I was incapable of words, barely able to breathe.

"Wow," Maegan said after I gently lay on top of her. "It just keeps getting better. I think I might've snapped a toe or two from curling them so hard."

"Should I apologize?" My voice was muffled against her shoulder.

"I think you should stand up and take a bow."

"I need strength in my legs for that." I wasn't a bit ashamed that I needed a few more minutes to recover.

"I like you right here anyway," Maegan said, squeezing her arms tighter around me.

A few minutes later, I found the strength to roll off her, and we headed to the shower to clean up.

"Did you discuss the book this time?" I teased while soaping up her back.

"Hey now," Maegan protested. "We normally discuss the book after dinner, but April and Violet put us on a time limit, and we had too much to discuss in the allotted time. Given a choice, we had to discuss what was happening to each of us instead of the book. I mean, those characters aren't going anywhere. Well, shoot," she said suddenly. "I forgot to discuss my idea for the next book."

"You can always send out a group text in the morning, Freckles. Hell, you'll see Candace and Vanessa when you take them to pick up their cars."

"I'm so excited for April and Vi."

"Going from friends to lovers sounds like it should be easy, but it rarely is. Both people feel like they have so much to lose if it doesn't work out."

"Nothing about love is easy, is it?" Maegan asked.

"I find loving you is pretty damn easy."

"It wasn't like that in the beginning though," she reminded me.

One night in her arms shook me to the core and fucked me up. I knew she wasn't just someone I could fuck and forget, and I resisted her until my duty as a detective threw us together again. I slid my arms around Maegan and held her against my body. "I was such a fool."

"Yes, you were." I swatted her ass playfully, but the sound of wet flesh against wet flesh echoed loudly in the bathroom. "Okay, you were scared of the way I made you feel. It wasn't foolishness; it was self-preservation."

"You're so sweet to give me a pass, Freckles. I'm sour about the time I lost with you though."

"Babe, at least it wasn't twelve years of stubbornness like my brother and Andy."

"True. Those two wear the title belt for stubborn jackasses."

Maegan snorted then stepped out of my arms so she could pick up the body wash she bought for me. Before Maegan, I used a bar of soap and didn't think about the condition of my skin, but I noticed a difference when she talked me into trying different products for it and my hair. My skin was softer and more supple instead of scaly and dry. My scalp no longer itched, and my hair looked healthier and shiny.

After our shower, we only went downstairs long enough for Lulu to do her business and grab ice cream to take back upstairs with us.

"One big bowl to share or two individual bowls tonight?" she asked.

"Depends what kind of ice cream you're planning to eat," I said, keeping an eye on Lulu as she sniffed at least fifty percent of the yard while looking for the perfect spot to pee. I started humming the

Batman theme song because she looked like she was wearing a bat mask. It seemed to make her happy, and she finally squatted down to pee.

"I'm thinking strawberry cheesecake tonight. How about you?"

"I'm kind of in the mood for chunky monkey."

"Two bowls it is," Freckles said.

"Great, now I think she wants to poop."

"Better out there than in here."

"True, but our show is starting in a few minutes."

"Elijah, is there something you want to tell me about your obsession with *Expedition Unknown*?"

"Like?" I asked, turning to face her.

"It sounds like you have a little bit of a crush on Josh Gates. Should I be jealous?"

I snorted. "Look, if I were into dudes, he'd be the kind of guy I'd pick. He's intelligent, has a thirst for adventure, a wonderful sense of humor, and a great smile. What else would anyone want in a guy?"

"Okay, now I'm crushing on him too," she said as if I didn't already know about her crush on the host.

I turned back to check on Lulu in the back yard and noticed she was gone. Fuck! I regretted that we hadn't put up a fence yet. "Freckles, your little darling has taken off through the woods surrounding the property again."

"You want me to go with you?" she asked, not sounding alarmed because this wasn't the first time Lulu got bold enough to dart off the second one of us wasn't looking. I'd find her easy enough with the flashlight on my phone.

"Nah, you go on up and start our show. Lulu and I will be there in a few minutes."

"I'll put your bowl of ice cream back in the freezer so it doesn't start melting," she said.

"Lulu," I called when I stepped outside. "Here, girl." I didn't bother whispering because we didn't have any neighbors to overhear us since trees surrounded us on all sides. Anthony planned the layout of his property very well; although, I'm sure he'd be surprised to realize how much his town grew.

I headed in the direction the little dog normally took but didn't find her sniffing the ground where I usually did. "Lulu?" I asked, starting to worry a bit. How far could she have run in the amount of time it took me to tick off Josh's attributes?

I stopped when I heard a foreign sound. It wasn't tree branches snapping as someone else walked through the woods or leaves rustling in the wind. It was a sound that didn't belong—chickens clucking.

I stood still so I could determine the direction the sounds came from, turned off my flashlight, and followed them as stealthily as I could. I had a feeling it was the chickens that drew Lulu out of the yard this time. Chickens that had no business being in the woods to begin with. I had a suspicion I knew whose chickens they were but no idea how they got there or who put them there. I wanted to call out for Lulu but didn't want to give myself away in case the chicken thieves were around.

There was a gap in the trees above allowing a sliver of moon to illuminate the ground, and I saw Lulu standing by a makeshift chicken coop wagging her tail at the new friends she'd found. I cautiously scoured the area and determined it was just the chickens, Lulu, and me out here. I dialed Adrian who answered on the second ring.

"Everything okay, partner?"

"I solved the case of the missing chickens," I said proudly. "Well, I found the chickens at least." Lulu barked as if to say she was the one who found the chickens.

"Where?" Adrian asked. I heard rustling in the background and suspected he was putting on clothes to rush out of the house.

"In the woods behind my house," I answered. "Do you think we should get the chickens and return them or set another stakeout for when the culprits come back?"

"Man, that's a tough call. I don't want the chickens to get harmed."

"They appear to be okay. This coop is a real DIYer, but the chickens don't appear to be distressed. There's food, water, and shelter from the elements here."

"You think you can get Lyric out there early in the morning to set something up like he did at my house?"

"I'll give him a call as soon as I get back home."

"How'd you even find them?" Adrian asked.

"Lulu technically found them. She must've heard them clucking and ran off to investigate while I was telling Maegan how hot Josh Gates was."

"Huh? The guy from *Expedition Unknown*?"

"I mean, he would be hot if I was into dudes," I said. "You know humor, smarts, and adventure."

"He has a nice smile too."

"Yeah, that's what we were discussing when Lulu ran off."

"That's a good girl," Adrian said. "Uncle Adrian is bringing her extra treats."

"I'll let you know what Lyric says."

"Thanks, partner."

I scooped Lulu up and jogged back to the house, taking her straight upstairs to our bathroom to check for injuries or dirt.

"You were gone a long time," Maegan said, making a beeline for her precious dog. "Where'd my girl go, and why is she so filthy?"

"Lulu solved the case of the missing chickens."

"You did?" Maegan asked her. "That's my good girl." Lulu wagged her nub for a tail and barked happily.

"Well, we know where they are, but not who placed them there or why."

"What are you going to do now?" she asked.

I repeated the conversation I had with Adrian, and she nodded. "I haven't seen a coyote or fox around here in years, but that's not to say there aren't any. That's your biggest threat to the safety of the birds while you set up your sting."

"What about Henery Hawk?"

Maegan snorted. "I think you're safe from him too. The person who took the chickens would've hurt them already if that had been their goal. They're trying to make a point or something."

"A political point? Like an animal rights activist?"

She shrugged. "Makes as much sense as anything else."

"Know of anyone who fits the description?"

Maegan tilted her head to the side. "No one comes to mind."

"Okay," I said, kissing her freckled nose. "Are you okay to clean Lulu up while I call Lyric?"

"Yeah," she said. "*Expedition Unknown* is a rerun tonight anyway."

I expected Lyric to say he'd be over in the morning, but he sounded eager to set up a few trail cameras equipped with night vision rather than wait until the morning. "There's a better chance of me getting spotted in the morning than there is right now. I'm used to walking around places in the dark."

"It's fine with me if you want to come over now." I sent a text to Adrian, letting him know that Operation Chicken Snatcher was underway.

Lyric and Memphis arrived exactly twelve minutes later, both wearing headlamps like miners use down in coal mines. Lyric had his ever-present bag of gear while Memphis carried a ladder. I didn't have anything quite as savvy and resorted to using my phone again, but it got the job done.

Lyric carefully surveyed the area to determine the best place to install the trail cameras and ended up setting up two adjacent to each other. One camera picked up the front and right side of the coop while the other picked up the back and left side.

"We'll catch those fuckers now," Adrian said, entering the small clearing and scaring the shit out of me. "What? You thought I'd let you have all the fun without me?" He slapped my back hard enough to rattle my lungs then counted the chickens.

"Yep, they're all accounted for."

I wanted to make a joke about counting chickens, but I was too damn tired. When we got to the house, Adrian said goodbye and headed home while Lyric and Memphis followed me inside.

"Is Maegan still up?" Lyric asked, sounding almost shy.

"Probably, would you like me to go upstairs and get her?" I offered.

"No, I'm being silly. I'll see you guys tomorrow for my first ever French toast brunch. I just wanted to ask if she was serious when she offered to hire me to do the baking for Books and Brew."

"She wouldn't have said something if she wasn't serious," I told him. "She's very impressed with your baking skills, and to be honest, your muffins are better than the ones they buy from the commercial bakery in Cincinnati. More importantly, she'll be happy you're sticking around." I extended my hand to him. "Welcome to Blissville, Lyric."

Lyric shook my hand and thanked me before they headed home. I took the steps two at a time to tell Maegan the good news, but she was curled up around Lulu sound asleep. Instead, I turned off the television and lamps, climbed beneath the sheets, and spooned up behind her. I thought it would take forever for me to fall asleep after all the chicken sting setup, but I drifted to sleep almost as soon as my head hit the pillow.

Chapter Thirteen

Maegan

TYPICALLY, THE MOST EXCITEMENT I GOT ON WEDNESDAYS involved a ride on Elijah's cock followed by French toast brunch. Afterward, I had the rest of my day to myself. I admit in the past that "me time" usually amounted to planning out the rest of the week, month, or even my life with a bubble bath and a good book thrown in. I also scheduled my hair, manicure, and pedicure appointments on Wednesdays, but Josh was out of town on vacation with his husband, Elijah's captain, so my usual eight weeks between hair colorings was stretched to nine.

My morning started out earlier than usual when I drove Elijah over to April's house to pick up his truck. I was disappointed neither April's black Audi nor Violet's dark blue Mustang were parked in the driveway. That didn't mean Vi didn't spend the night though. They both could've left for work already.

Candace and Vanessa eagerly awaited me at their prospective front doors.

"Was her car there?" they both asked when I picked them up.

"No one's car was there," I told them.

"I think it's pretty pathetic we didn't walk to get our cars this morning," Vanessa said.

"Speak for yourself," Candace said, running her hand over her sleek, red waves. "It's too humid for outdoor activities if you have naturally curly hair." I could see her glancing in my direction out of the corner of my eye and knew she was checking out my extra week of roots showing. "Besides, I've already been on the elliptical for an hour, showered, and styled my hair."

I returned home after I dropped them off at their cars, indulged in a long, hot shower then set about putting my weekly French toast brunch together. Most of the time, I stuck to making traditional French toast on the griddle, but I liked to try something new at least once a month. Last night while Elijah was romping in the woods, I put together a French toast slash cinnamon roll casserole dish that smelled scrumptious and had to rest in the refrigerator overnight. I had a feeling it would be a big hit, which was confirmed when my guests arrived and began salivating before the casserole was even out of the oven.

Elijah's schedule didn't always allow him to attend my weekly brunches and other times he popped in for a quick bite and a lingering kiss before he returned to work. On the latter occasions, Adrian always came with him. I loved seeing the two men ribbing each other and watching their bond grow. Besides, it was lovely to have another fan of my spectacular French toast and crispy bacon extravaganza.

Instead of praising my cooking skills as I was accustomed to, Elijah, Adrian, Lyric, and Memphis were gathered around Memphis's laptop to watch surveillance video from the woods around our house overnight. They were able to watch whatever the trail camera recorded overnight and also watch real-time videos. Even Andy and Milo were caught up in the sting operation.

"The chickens look well cared for," Adrian said while staring at the screen. "Someone is providing them with food and water on a regular basis, so we're going to find our snatcher soon. I feel it in my gut."

"That's the pound of bacon you wolfed down, partner," Elijah said, slapping him lightly on the back.

Adrian glanced up at me suddenly. "I've let this chicken snatcher sting take over my brain and have completely forgotten my manners. Pardon me, Maegan. Thank you so much for a delicious breakfast."

"You're very welcome." I looked at Elijah with a raised brow. "Is the chicken snatcher sting the reason why you forgot to thank me for brunch?"

"I'm sorry, Freckles. I admit I'm excited about making a bust. Can you forgive me?" Elijah's tone said he was pleading for forgiveness, but his smile and twinkling eyes said he wanted me to punish him—long and torturously slow.

"Maybe," I replied noncommittally. Elijah's dark eyes narrowed, assessing to see if he was really in trouble or not. Our arguments were few and far between, but they weren't nonexistent.

"Well, whoever is taking care of the chickens hasn't returned yet this morning," Lyric said. "So far, we've only seen a curious buck and adorable bunnies and squirrels checking out the enclosure."

Memphis shut the laptop and pushed it aside so he could return to his breakfast. "This fancy software Lyric's friend designed allowed me to set up a perimeter around the coop. I will get a notification anytime something steps inside the zone. We'll catch whoever this is very soon."

"Sally Ann said everything is quiet on the home front, so our snatchers haven't taken the bait."

"They may not if they're familiar with the residents. You are a police detective and acting captain with Gabe gone, so maybe they know better than to mess with you."

"If we haven't nabbed them soon, I want to take the birds back to their rightful owners. I don't want to take a chance the snatchers saw or heard us in the woods last night and will neglect the chickens to avoid capture," Adrian said.

"I agree," everyone around the large table said.

"Let's hope we wrap this up today so we can strut around like Foghorn Leghorn," Elijah said.

"Very funny," Adrian said. "Kiss your girl so we can get back to the station."

"With pleasure," Elijah said. He reached for my hand and pulled me down the hallway toward the library in the back of the first floor. "I wish I had time to show you just how much I appreciated brunch," he said once we were behind the closed door. "I love you, Freckles." He pressed a lingering kiss against my lips, making me sigh with need and want when we broke apart.

"I love you too. I'm looking forward to you nabbing the chicken snatcher today and kicking ass on the ball diamond tonight."

"I do have a game tonight, don't I? I can't believe I forgot."

"Me too. You never forget."

"I guess there's a lot on my mind."

I reached up and ran my fingers over the furrowed V of his brow. I knew he was worried about his dad and had called home every day since we returned from our visit. "Anything I can do to help?"

"You're already doing it. I'd be a fucking mess right now if not for you."

"Elijah, I haven't done anything special."

He opened his mouth to respond, but a firm knock sounded at the door. "Elijah, Memphis just got an alert on his computer."

Elijah dropped a quick kiss on my forehead. "I'll give you an update as soon as I can." He opened the library door and revealed a frazzled Adrian standing there. "Are they in the woods right now?"

"The alert is for my house. Sally Ann took the kids for their routine checkup which means they were watching our house. The alarm we rigged to the coop scared them off before they could nab Elvis, Patsy, Aretha, and Gaga."

"Let's get going, partner," Elijah said as seriously as if Adrian had said someone had tried to abduct his kids. His family was clearly attached to the rooster and chickens.

"Thanks again, Maegan," Adrian yelled over his shoulder as they disappeared down the hallway.

Everyone else left soon after so we could all get on with our day. My hair schedule might've gotten out of whack, but I still had my standing bi-monthly appointment for a manicure and pedicure. My mom often joined me, but she had made plans with friends to have lunch and see a rom-com movie my dad didn't want to see, so I settled into the pedicure chair with the next book for our book club. I'd have plenty of time to catch up with Dee during the manicure. I quickly got lost in the world of Kevin Kwan's *Crazy Rich Asians*. The film was scheduled to release soon, so I thought it would be fun if we read the book as part of our book club then went to see the movie in the theater to compare differences. The girls all seemed to be on board after I texted them in a group chat while I made brunch, so I decided there was no better time to start the new book than on my day off.

I chose a dark, sparkly purple nail polish for my toes and a pale lavender color for my fingernails. Who said your toenails and fingernails had to match? I planned to head back home after Dee finished, but her sister, Josi, stopped by and said she had a cancellation and asked if I was willing to try a new facial peel she'd recently purchased. She assured me my bravery would get me a full facial as part of the deal.

How the hell could I pass that up? Of course, I made *Fun with Dick and Jane* references which cracked Josi up while she went through her routine.

"I assure you this isn't a product testing session like the one in the movie. This peel has already gone through a rigorous testing process. I just need to get a feel for how it works on other skin types besides my own. It says it's made for all skin types, but I always look at a product sideways when it says that. I'm oily as hell, so how could any product that works for me work on someone with dry skin, or even combination skin like yours."

125

"What's the verdict?" I asked, looking up at her as she examined the texture and feel of my skin once she finished.

"I admit I'm very impressed. How does it feel to you?"

"Tingly, but in an invigorating way and not a scary, my-face-is-about-to-swell way." I raised my hand and touched my skin. "My face has never felt this smooth before, Josi. I'm so glad I agreed to be your guinea pig."

"The product information recommends you keep your face free of makeup for twenty-four hours. I probably should've stated that part up front."

"Not a problem," I replied. "I don't always wear it, and no events are occurring in the next day which require me to go full-on glam. Do you plan on selling this facial peel at the salon, or can we only get it by booking an appointment?"

"That's for Josh to decide, and I'll discuss it with him when he gets back. This product recommends monthly use only. There's a risk someone would buy it from our salon, damage their skin after not following directions, and sue us. For that reason alone, I don't see Josh selling it like we do other products. I'd think he'd want this service monitored to make sure we're doing it to the manufacturer's specifications."

"Makes sense, and I will gladly shell out the money to have a face that feels like this," I said then hugged her goodbye.

I left Curl Up and Dye feeling like a brand-new person with fresh nails and a vibrant, glowing face. I'd hoped to hear Elijah and Adrian had nabbed the chicken snatchers, but I didn't hear a peep from him as the late morning turned into mid-afternoon. I made a light lunch and took it out on the covered back porch to enjoy while doing more reading. I didn't worry about Lulu running off as long as there was a single piece of grilled chicken left on my salad.

My cell phone rang midway through lunch, and I debated whether I wanted to answer it when I saw unknown caller displayed on the screen. It reminded me of how Elijah ignored the calls on his phone then later worried he could've missed out on reconnecting with his dad.

"Hello," I said into the phone.

"Hello," a rich, baritone voice said. "Is this Maegan Miracle?"

"Yes, it is. May I ask who's calling?"

"My name is Theodore Rutledge," he replied, "although, I doubt my name rings any bells for you. Would it help if I said Edwina Bliss was my great-great-great-grandmother and the oldest child of Anthony and Melanie Bliss?"

I gasped. "Oh my goodness! Are you for real?"

He chuckled warmly. "As real as it gets. Our family attorney was contacted by the network that airs *The Paranormal Whisperer* and let us know about the investigation into Anthony's disappearance. The network seems convinced the mystery has been solved. Is it true?"

"We do believe so, yes."

"I spoke with Lyric Willows this morning, and I have to say he sounded very convincing. He was the one who provided your number. I'd hoped he would inform you I planned to call you, but I'm guessing it never happened."

"It must've slipped his mind." I suspected I knew exactly what he was up to since Vinyl and Villains was closed on Wednesday.

"Is now a good time to talk?"

"Absolutely. You've caught me at a great time."

"I know I'm a virtual stranger to you, but I would appreciate the opportunity to see Bliss House. I'm willing to provide character references or submit to a background check if it makes you feel better." His offer made me snort out a laugh. "Something funny?"

"My boyfriend is a police detective and will have no trouble looking into your background. He'll know your shoe size before you take one step inside this house."

"I think I'm going to like this guy. Why don't you and I exchange email addresses so I can provide him with any detail he'd like to do a thorough background check on me?"

"That sounds perfect." I rattled off my email address for him.

"Great, I'll start off with my full name and current address. You'll have my email address once I send this information to you. I'm looking forward to learning more about Anthony. Our family has been pretty tight-lipped about him over the generations."

"I don't think they had much to go on," I said. "I'm willing to bet Melanie took his secret to the grave. I sort of feel like we're exposing him, and it feels like a betrayal."

"Mr. Willows told me how much you love the house and how connected you feel to Anthony's *ghost*." I could tell by his tone he had a hard time accepting that part. I suspected he'd come around once he visited. My thoughts immediately turned to how Anthony would receive his flesh and blood back in the home he loved so much. "I'll send you an email in just a bit so we can put your detective's mind at ease."

"Sounds great. I'm looking forward to it," I said politely. As soon as the call disconnected, I leaped from my chair and did a happy dance. Lulu danced around and happily barked even though she had no idea why I was excited. Once I had it out of my system, I called Lyric.

"Oh fuck," he said instead of the usual greeting. "I forgot to give you a heads-up that Theodore Rutledge was going to call you."

"Technically, you forgot to ask my permission to provide my number in the first place, but I'm willing to let it slide this once."

"Fuck! I'm sorry, Mae. I won't ever do something so stupid again. Elijah is going to kill me when he finds out."

"Maybe we won't tell him you skipped that all-important step. Theodore seems like a standup guy, and to prove it, he's emailing me his personal details so Elijah can run a background check on him before he steps foot on our property."

"Whew, I feel so much better. I'm so excited one of Anthony's heirs is interested in taking part in the process. He sounded—" Lyric's voice cut off suddenly, and I heard Memphis speaking rapidly in the background. "I gotta go, Mae. The cameras caught our chicken snatcher in the woods. I need to call Elijah."

I don't know what the hell possessed me to do it, but I retrieved one of Elijah's ball bats from his equipment bag, locked Lulu safely in the house, and set off through the woods.

Chapter Fourteen

Elijah

"**U**M, ELIJAH," MEMPHIS SAID WEAKLY INTO THE PHONE. "I think we have a problem."

I had Memphis on speakerphone so he could give us live updates as we sped across town. It shouldn't have been a big deal, but we had to give way to the fire trucks as they went on a run, stop for a funeral procession which was longer than any I'd ever seen before, and a water main break on Main Street had closed down the primary intersections to get around Blissville. We had to take side streets and even two alleys as part of the detour which slowed us way down. Adrian couldn't tear through there and risk running over somebody on the way to my house, so he had to settle for blaring sirens and inventive swear words for people who didn't move out of his way fast enough to suit him.

"Oh no! Is he hurting them?" Adrian asked, his voice laced with panic. He stomped on the accelerator just as he cleared the two houses at the end of the alley and made a sharp left turn which nearly sent us careening into the path of an oncoming car.

"Slow down, Adrian!" I wanted to solve the case too, but damn.

"Uh..." Memphis hesitated. "Nobody is hurting the chickens.

I'm more concerned about the new arrival on the scene who has our chicken snatchers cornered against the coop."

"Who?" Adrian and I asked at the same time.

Then we heard Lyric say, "I should've been a bit more discreet when I talked to her on the phone just now."

Her? "My Freckles has the bad guy cornered?" I looked over at Adrian. "Go faster." It usually took a person less than five minutes to get across town but not when I needed it most.

"Bad guys," Lyric corrected.

"More like juvenile delinquents," Memphis said. "Now that she's forced them to lower their hoods, I can see their faces more clearly. I don't recognize the teenagers, so they must not come into my store."

"They are definitely miscreants then."

"That's so sweet. Thank you, Ric."

"You're welcome, Firecracker," Lyric returned huskily.

"Can we focus here?" I asked impatiently. "How many are we talking about?" Their age didn't matter if she was grossly outnumbered. "How is she getting them to submit?"

"Sorry, E," Memphis said quickly. "There are two boys and one girl. Maegan brought a wicked-looking ball bat for protection."

I'd seen my girl swing a bat during co-ed softball games and knew she could handle herself if they got too rowdy.

"None of them are exchanging calculating looks like idiotic villains typically do," Memphis added. "They look contrite."

"I'd even say they look embarrassed," Lyric said.

Adrian made a sharp right into our driveway and sped up to the house. I didn't wait for him to turn off the car and join me. I ran through the yard and the woods.

"Don't be mad," Maegan said when I came crashing into the clearing. "I saw the water main break earlier when I left the salon and knew it would delay you getting here."

"We'll talk about this later, Freckles." Then I turned to the teenagers who appeared to range in age between thirteen and seventeen.

"I'll have to take the three of you into the station so I can call your parents. I'm sure they'll want to be present when I question you or provide an attorney."

"Elijah," Maegan began calmly, "I think this has all been a big misunderstanding, and a misguided attempt on these kids' parts to save chickens from what they thought was animal abuse."

"You interrogated the suspects?" I asked in disbelief.

"I'm not a cop, Elijah. I'm allowed to ask questions without Mirandizing them and such."

"A judge isn't going to appreciate you questioning them while brandishing a bat."

"Do you mean the bat I dropped on the ground as soon as I realized I was dealing with kids?" She pointed to the bat which was a good fifteen feet away from where she stood. The kids could've easily fled the scene if they wanted to but chose to stay. Of course, Maegan's sharp tongue was probably enough to frighten them into staying put. "We're only having a conversation, and I think you should hear them out before you haul anyone into the station. Besides, I know every single one of the little troublemakers' names and who they belong to, so we can easily call their folks right now."

"Maegan, they stole property that didn't belong to them. Their actions can't go unpunished."

"That's right," Adrian said, finally catching up to me. Later, I would rib him about needing to work out more to keep up with me, but not in front of the chicken snatchers.

Maegan's green eyes beseeched me to talk to the kids, so I faced them with my arms crossed over my chest and a serious scowl on my face. "I'm willing to hear you out, but the chickens' owners will have a final say on whether or not juvenile charges are filed against you. One of you better start talking."

"We didn't mean to cause trouble, sir," the girl said softly. Her light brown hair was pulled into a ponytail high upon her head and adorable freckles covered her earnest face. I imagined Maegan looked a lot like the girl at that age. "We thought we were rescuing the chickens."

"How so?" Adrian asked.

"Holly Gundersen said the chickens were being raised as fighting chickens," she said in a rush.

"Fighting chickens?" I asked. All three kids nodded.

"Clay Morris said it was a bloody, fight-to-the-finish kind of thing," the girl said then promptly burst into tears. One of the older boys put his arm around the girl and tucked her beneath his armpit so she could cry into his chest. He had the same color hair, eyes, and freckles as the younger girl, so I figured they were siblings.

"We honestly thought we were saving them," the oldest boy said. His coloring was slightly different, and his skin was missing the freckles, but he had the same shape of eyes, nose, and mouth as the younger two. "We combined our Christmas and birthday money to buy the supplies to build this coop and provide food for the chickens."

Adrian and I both let out long sighs because busting these kids wasn't going to make anyone feel good. Still, they needed to learn a valuable lesson.

"Listen, cock fighting is against the law, and you should come to the police anytime you think a law is being broken or someone is planning to break it. You can't take matters into your own hands."

"Serious harm could've come to the chickens if you didn't properly set up their coop. You could've exposed them to deadly predators," Adrian added. "Not to mention the stress of taking the animals from their environments could've caused them not to eat or drink. I can see you had good intentions, but your actions might've had a very negative outcome."

"I'll take the responsibility," the oldest sibling said. "Let them go home."

"No," the young girl said. "This was all my idea. You two just can't tell me no."

A wry grin spread across the younger brother's face and warmed my fucking heart. Hell, I was ready to confess to stealing the chickens myself to spare them.

"Here's what we're going to do," Adrian said firmly. "The three of you are going home right now and telling your parents what you did. Detective Markham and I are going to return the chickens to their rightful owners and explain to them why you took the chickens. Rather than pressing charges, I'm going to ask if they're willing to accept community service instead. I know for a fact most of these are older women who rely on the egg money for their income. That means they could use help caring for the chickens and cleaning their cages." The three kids looked hopeful for the first time since we arrived. "And whatever else they need help with."

"Mowing grass," I suggested.

"Weeding the flowerbeds," Maegan added.

"Cleaning the gutters," Adrian tossed out.

"That sounds fair," the girl said quickly, but I could tell by her brothers' expressions they weren't very enthused.

"Better than picking up trash and cleaning sidewalks all over town," I told them, which was the typical starting point for community service in the county. I had to say it worked pretty well for most kids, especially when they wore those brightly colored vests with giant initials CCJCD on the back identifying them as part of the Carter County Juvenile Correction Department. I saw the dawning of awareness wash over the boys seconds before they vigorously nodded in agreement.

"Should I walk you home?" Maegan asked. "I do have the rest of the afternoon off."

"It won't be necessary, Cousin," the oldest one said. I knew I recognized those freckles.

"See you at the family reunion on Saturday," the girl said to Maegan.

"You can count on it," Maegan told them. "I will be calling your parents this evening to make sure you confessed to your activities, and Detective Markham will discuss the arrangements he made with the chickens' owners and when he expects you to be at their homes to begin work."

"We'll tell them when they get home from work, Mae," the middle sibling said.

I never asked their names, but it wasn't necessary after seeing the resemblance to Maegan and her familiarity with them. I'd get the names out of my Freckles even if I had to tickle it out of her.

"Adrian, do you mind if I head to the house for a chat with Maegan? I'll grab Lulu's puppy crate from the garage so we can transport the chickens back to their owners. I'm hoping the joyful reunions soften them up, and they'll consider the alternative arrangement to filing official charges against the kids."

"No problem, partner," Adrian said, exchanging a look with me which said I could take my time. He saw how unhappy I was when I found out Maegan had decided to intervene.

Maegan knew she was in for an argument, but it didn't stop her from sliding her fingers between mine and holding my hand. She wasn't doing it to soften me up or manipulate me; she understood our pending, frank discussion changed nothing between us.

She dropped my hand once we stood inside our home and turned to face me. "Let me have it."

"That was a risky move, Maegan. You assumed the criminals were as seemingly harmless as the crimes they committed. Your assumption could've gotten you hurt. Many people would never harm an animal but wouldn't hesitate to kill a person." I saw this firsthand with Axel Washington. The man adored animals but would kill a person who he perceived as a traitor without batting an eyelash. "It reminds me of the night we met when you saw I held a gun in my hand and you charged toward me instead of running."

"I know, and I am sorry."

"Promise me you won't do it again."

"Um..." She bit her bottom lip and briefly broke eye contact to study her feet before returning her ornery green eyes to mine. "I can only promise that I will try not to do it again."

"Fair enough." I hooked an arm around her waist and pulled her tighter against me. "I like those sparkly purple toenails." I liked the image of her lying naked in bed while I rubbed lotion into her feet so she could return the favor by massaging my cock between her arches and tease my taint with her big toe.

"Later tonight," she said, reading my mind. "I have something else important to tell you."

I listened to the story of Theodore Rutledge calling her with mixed feelings. She was so excited for a Bliss heir to step inside Bliss House again, so I was happy for her even though my protective and possessive instincts were triggered. Then she came to the part where he suggested she obtain a background check to make herself feel better about his interest. That relieved the protective part but did nothing to diminish my urge to pound my chest like an ape.

"Forward the email to me as soon as you get it. I'll run him through the system right away."

"Thank you, Elijah."

"You're welcome, Freckles, but what exactly are you thanking me for?"

"For loving me the way you do. I knew you were mad about me rushing into the woods to play vigilante, but I didn't fear you because you'd never lay a hand on me in anger. I also knew you wouldn't like the idea of a strange man in our house but would do everything within your power to alleviate those concerns because it would make me happy. I trust you with my heart, health, and happiness."

Her words moved me more than any she'd ever spoken. It felt like the perfect time to run up to our room and grab the ring box I'd hidden in my dresser. Then my phone beeped with an incoming text from Adrian, reminding me I had a different type of duty to perform.

"You better grab the cage and head back to the woods before Adrian thinks we're fucking." My dick twitched at the thought.

"Maybe I'll come home for a furious fuck on a Wednesday when Adrian isn't waiting for me in our woods."

"So, lunchtime next Wednesday?" she suggested.

"It's a date, Freckles."

I kept my goodbye kiss shorter and more innocent than I preferred then hustled back to Adrian. I was prepared for some good-natured ribbing, but instead, all his mirth was directed at our police captain whose vacation wasn't going according to plan.

"Did you tell him we caught the chicken snatchers?" I asked.

"No way," Adrian said, shaking his head. "I didn't want to give him an excuse to cancel his trip and come home early."

"He and Josh aren't getting along?" I asked.

"No, they're doing fine. He was having a great time with Josh until the other guests started arriving for the murder-mystery event they have going on." Adrian started laughing. "Let's just say some of the guests have an alternative lifestyle." He gestured his hand back and forth in a swinging motion. I had no idea what he was trying to say. Swing? Sex Swing? Oh!

"Swingers!"

"Among other things. It sounds like a whole lot of fuckery."

"Better him than me," I said.

"Me too. Ready to start transporting these chickens back to their rightful owners?"

"Do we take them back to the station so the owners can identify them?" I asked.

"Nah," Adrian said, tapping an icon on his phone. "The owners provided pictures of their stolen chickens, so I can easily match them up. These eggs will need to be discarded because there's no telling how long they've been sitting there. You need to be careful handling the chickens and their eggs because of salmonella. Those kids could've gotten very sick if they weren't following proper hygiene."

I would've teased Adrian about having those pictures on his phone if it weren't so damn handy. We delivered all of the chickens

137

back to their overjoyed owners. All of them heartily accepted the alternative punishment we planned, except for the final stop.

"Come now, Mrs. Blankenbauer," Adrian said softly. "These are good kids who thought they were saving the chickens from an illegal fighting ring."

"I want to see them go to jail for the fear and grief they caused me." She then started telling us about the world she grew up in and how that kind of thievery would never be tolerated under any circumstance. "They must pay."

"Mrs. Blankenbauer, the county judge is only going to assign community service to kids this young, but it will be cleaning up the little park in the center of town or cleaning sidewalks. As nice as it sounds, wouldn't it be better for you to personally benefit from their service?"

"Are there limitation to what kind of work they perform?" she asked.

"I suspect their parents will insist there be limitations. I think lawn work, cleaning gutters, and caring for the chickens is fair punishment for the crime."

"Well, they appear to have taken good are of Jezebel, Betty, and Gloria during their captivity, so I will accept your offer."

"Thanks, Mrs. B," Adrian said. "You won't regret it."

"If I do, I'm taking it out of your hide, young man," she told him.

Afterward, we stopped by the Johnsons' house to speak to Tom and Cyndi, parents of Stephanie, Brian, and Steven Johnson, aka the chicken snatchers. The parents were expecting us and were appalled by their kids' activities and so grateful they wouldn't have a juvenile record. They agreed each of their kids should serve a minimum fifty hours of community service. Hell, I was thinking two hours a day for the next two weeks, but who was I to argue with them? We decided two hours a day for four weeks, for a total of fifty-six hours for each of them.

Adrian dropped me off at my truck afterward, and I quickly

dialed my parents' house so I could tell my dad the chicken snatcher sting operation was a success. The phone was answered on the second ring, but not by my mother or father. I would've had a hard time telling the two Jack Markhams apart if it weren't for Dad's voice sounding weaker after chemo.

"Hello?" Jack asked again. I closed my eyes as a wave of misery and something else washed over me. I finally identified it as longing. The part of me that didn't hate my brother's fucking guts ached so much for his absence. Ten years ago, the ratio was nine to one in favor of hate. Slowly, the scale had shifted without me even being aware until I realized there was more longing to reconnect than there was hate in my heart.

"May I speak with Dad, please?" I said when I could find my voice.

Jack sucked in a sharp breath then said, "Sure. I'll take the phone to him, Elijah."

I heard murmured voices as Jack told Dad I was on the phone. When Dad came on the phone, he sounded better than he had the day before. In fact, every day was an improvement, and I knew it wouldn't be long before I wouldn't be able to tell the difference between the two men when they answered the phone. I wasn't sure how I felt about it, so I pushed it aside for the moment.

"I have great news, Dad. We caught the chicken snatchers."

Dad gave a great big whooping laugh then urged me to tell the story. "You and your partner did the right thing for those kids. I bet they'll learn a valuable lesson."

"I hope so," I told him. "I gotta run and get ready for my softball game tonight. I just wanted to bring you up to date."

"I'm glad you did. Tell Freckles I said hello."

"Will do. I'll call you tomorrow."

Talking to my dad got easier every time, but I wasn't sure what to do about my feelings toward my brother. My thoughts were consumed by happy memories of the two of us growing up on our farm.

For the first time in ten years, I wasn't willing to accept the current status of our relationship was the best we could hope for. I was eager to discuss it with Maegan, but I found her fast asleep on the couch with Lulu and Rascal.

I knelt beside the couch, brushed the riotous curls away from her face, and kissed her forehead. She made adorable little sighs that made me want to keep kissing her until she woke up, but I didn't. Maegan wasn't a nap taker, so she must've been really tired. Instead, I went into the kitchen and started dinner. My skills were limited, but Maegan seemed to love my spaghetti, and I had plenty of time to digest it before destroying my competitors on the diamond.

The only bad thing was the silence allowed me too much time to think about the complexities of families and the tangled relationships arising from them. I recalled my conversation with Maegan about Theodore Rutledge and checked my email to see if she sent the information while I was busy returning chickens, and I saw she had. I knew the background search could wait until the morning, but I had promised Maegan I'd get right on it, so I dialed Wen's number.

"Wen, can you do me a favor and run a background check?" I explained the situation and forwarded the email to him after he agreed. "Thanks. I'll owe you one."

After I hung up, I smelled tobacco smoke and knew Anthony was near. I wondered how he would react to his heir stepping inside Bliss House after so many years. We'd find out soon if Rutledge's background check came back clean.

Chapter Fifteen

Maegan

THE BACKGROUND CHECK FOR THEODORE RUTLEDGE CAME back crystal clear, and I learned the apple didn't fall far from the tree, regardless of the generation gap between Theodore and Anthony. Perhaps the hereditary markers in their DNA included a special strand for entrepreneurship. Theodore Rutledge was the founder and CEO of a Fortune 500 software and technology development company located in Northern Kentucky, and due to his busy schedule, our meeting kept getting pushed back until I started to think maybe he'd changed his mind and didn't want to upset me.

"I think he's the next Steve Jobs," Memphis said gleefully when we were crawling through the dust and debris in an attic after Sunday brunch one hot, humid day at the end of August looking for treasures we didn't know we needed until we cast our eyes upon them. "He's one of the largest employers in Northern Kentucky and has a great reputation. He offers benefits other corporations don't. People fight for a chance to work there."

"You know I'm standing right here, don't you, Firecracker," Lyric said from behind us. For whatever reason, he loved tagging along to help us look through other people's stuff. I think he took great joy in seeing the way Memphis lit up when he found something that excited him. I glanced over my shoulder to see if Lyric was really jealous about the awe he heard in Memphis's voice, and he winked playfully at me.

"Not to mention his charitable contributions," Memphis continued. "I believe I read someplace he donates nearly half of his salary to worthy causes. Anthony would be very proud to know many of them are LGBTQ+ causes to promote education and raise suicide prevention."

"Maybe Maegan can erect a statue of him and put it in the front lawn," Lyric said. "Or better yet, you can create a cartoon hero in his honor."

"No one is erecting anything, and I'm not putting him into a comic book, Ric," Memphis said, finally acknowledging his boyfriend's displeased grumbles.

"Are you sure? You sound kind of *erect* over there."

Memphis turned to look at his boyfriend with an impish grin. "I can admire a man's character without wishing he was in my bed or putting his likeness in an illustration. There's only room for one man in my bed and in the pages of my comic book."

"I hate to interrupt this tender moment—" I began.

"Then don't," Memphis interjected.

"We only have thirty minutes left to dig through the attic," I continued.

"Later, Ric," Memphis said, returning to dig through boxes. "Aha! A Michael Jackson *Thriller* album still wrapped in cellophane."

I started to pout because I hadn't found anything exciting until I came across a box with very little dirt and dust on it, indicating it had been there only a short time. The bare bulbs hanging in the attic weren't bright enough to illuminate the corner, so I switched on my small flashlight and knelt to see what was inside the box. I pulled out the packing slip lying on top. It identified the object as a soldier's foot locker from Vietnam and said it was shipped three weeks ago to Mr.

Betson who was the winning eBay bidder. I set the packing slip aside and opened the metal box inside. What I found made me gasp.

"Did you find something good, Mae?" Lyric asked when he joined me.

"Possibly," I said, pointing to the contents. "It appears to be the personal property of a soldier. There are letters, a bible, clothes, photos, and even a pack of cigarettes. There's no telling what else is inside."

Lyric picked up the packing slip and read it. "I wonder why Mr. Betson purchased the foot locker belonging to an unknown soldier?"

"I'll talk to his daughter and see if she knows. The box was recently placed up here, possibly as soon as it arrived." I looked over at Memphis who was the one who found this lead. "When did you say Mr. Betson died?"

Memphis came over and knelt beside me. "Why do you ask?"

"Mr. Betson won this item from an eBay bid three weeks ago, and it was shipped a few days later. There's no telling how long it took to arrive. I was just curious if he saw it before he died." It suddenly made me sad to think he died without knowing the contents of the foot locker."

Memphis pulled out his phone to study the notes he's made about the estate. "He died two days after the auction closed which was the day before the package shipped."

"That's really sad," Lyric said.

"I'm going to ask his daughter about it. Maybe she knows why her father wanted it."

I left the guys upstairs and found Dawn sitting in a recliner I presumed was her father's due to its large size and scruffy appearance. It reminded me of the recliner Elijah's dad refused to part with. Dawn was staring out the large picture window with tears rolling down her face, unaware I had entered the room. I could tell her mind was a million miles away, and I didn't want to intrude upon her grief, so I tried backing out of the room. I stepped on a creaky floorboard in the process, jerking her out of her daydream with a startled gasp.

"I'm so sorry," I said softly. "I didn't mean to interrupt."

"I'm fine," she said, shaking her head. "Well, I'm not fine today, but someday, I will be. Did you find anything interesting to either of you?"

I told her about the foot locker and asked, "Did it have significant meaning to him, do you think?"

"I know the foot locker you're talking about. It arrived after he passed away." Dawn drew in a shaky breath before continuing. "My dad is—was—a Vietnam veteran, and I think the idea of someone selling a soldier's personal belongings to the highest bidder would've greatly insulted him. Knowing him, he'd decided to track down the soldier's family and return the items to them."

"That's what I would try to do if I were him," I said, nodding in agreement. "Are you willing to sell the locker to me?"

"Will you do everything you can to locate the soldier's family and return it to them?"

"It might take time before I can work the research into my schedule, but I promise to do everything in my power to find the rightful owner. I have some contacts at our local veteran's affairs office. I'm willing to hire a private investigator if I need to."

"Then you can have it," Dawn said.

"I can't accept it for free."

"You'll probably be paying out-of-pocket expenses to locate the owner, and I know my dad would be pleased with my decision. I only ask one thing."

"Name it."

"You let me know when you find the family." *When* not if.

"You have yourself a deal."

In the end, I did buy a complete set of china that had belonged to her great-grandmother. She already had one set from a different grandmother and didn't have room for a second one. Memphis negotiated prices with her over a few items then Dawn and I loaded the foot locker in the back of my SUV.

"I'm excited about all the possibilities the search could uncover," I said to the guys once we were on our way back to Blissville. "Lyric, are you willing to lend me your investigative skills while we wait for the networks to work out a deal for our show?"

"I'd be happy to help you. Just let me know when you're ready to start," Lyric said. After a pause, he added, "There's another type of partnership I was hoping to discuss with you but lacked the courage to bring it up." I glanced at him in the rearview mirror and saw uncertainty stamped across his face. I suspected I knew what he wanted to discuss, but thought it was better to wait to hear him out first.

"Were you serious when you said you'd like to hire me to do the baking for Books and Brew?"

"I was," I said, trying not to get my hopes up too high. I heard the subtle sigh of relief escaping from Memphis. "What did you have in mind?"

"I just need something to keep me busy until I figure out what I'm doing with the rest of my life." It was the first time Lyric had confirmed he had no intention of returning to the show. Even if he decided to go back into television at some point, he could use Blissville as a home base just as well as anywhere else. "I don't want you pissing off the commercial bakery currently supplying your goodies now if this doesn't work out."

"You let me worry about my contractors," I said. "They're a business, so they should be used to clients trying other vendors or seeking other options. Even if they do get pissed, there are other commercial bakeries I could use."

"If you're sure—"

"I'm sure you bake the best cakes, muffins, and desserts I've ever had. If you're willing to give this a go, then so am I. Why don't you meet with Milo and me at my office tomorrow? We'll do lunch and discuss terms and come up with a plan we can all be happy with."

"Sounds perfect to me."

For the rest of the drive home, the conversation remained light and fun. Lyric talked about the recipes he planned to make later for us to sample as if we didn't already know how lucky we'd be to have him work for us. Memphis talked about the comic book he was creating with Lyric's encouragement. I started weaving wild guesses as to the reason Mr. Betson might've bid on the trunk. His daughter's assessment was probably right, but how did he even stumble across the auction?

"Good point," Lyric said. "Maybe it was something he frequently searched for, so they sent an alert when the auction went live."

"Yeah, it's a strong possibility. He did have an extensive collection of military items," I agreed.

As fun as our day was, I was looking forward to getting home and seeing Elijah. He came out to greet me when I pulled into the driveway. "There's my Freckles. How was the hunt?"

"I think it went well, but I might've volunteered for a project beyond my capabilities."

"What do you mean?" he asked, so I took him around to the back of the SUV so he could see the locker for himself. He opened it up and looked inside. "Did this stuff belong to the man who recently passed away?"

"Kind of, but not in the sense you're thinking." I reached into my purse and pulled out the packing slip I found inside the shipping box. "He bought it from an eBay auction then died before he received it." I told Elijah about Dawn's theory and waited for his input.

"It's possible he wanted to return it to the soldier's family, assuming they weren't the sellers. I think contacting the seller would be your best bet. Find out how these items came to be in their possession." Elijah looked quietly into the box then picked up the thick stack of letters wrapped with twine. "Those letters probably hold many clues. The return address would be a good place to start if the seller can't give you any promising leads."

"Name and rank of the soldier might help someone at the VA

locate an heir," I said.

"True, but it might be hard getting someone willing to search for a family simply to return clothes and letters."

I blew out a long breath. "Help me get this inside, and I'll start my search after I clear a few other things off my plate."

"I wasn't trying to discourage you, Freckles," Elijah said, grabbing the right handle while I grabbed the left.

"I know you're not, babe. You're being practical like always, and I need it sometimes. How was golf with Andy?"

"Interesting."

I glanced over when I heard the humor in his voice and saw he was trying to suppress a grin. "Why? Was he sharing stories about my brother?"

"Well, there were some funny Milo stories, but I was mostly thinking about your parents who joined us on the course today."

"Oh boy," I said, snickering. "I assume they were in a heated competition."

"Very much so."

"I feel like I should apologize for not warning you, but then again, I had no idea you'd invited my parents."

"Andy invited them, but I was glad to have them along. We had a fun day. Very enlightening."

"How so?"

"I see where you and Milo get your competitive streaks," Elijah said mildly, but I could tell there was something else he wasn't sharing with me. But what and why wouldn't he... I screeched to a halt which jerked Elijah back a step when he had continued walking.

"Oh my God! Andy is about to ask Milo to marry him, isn't he? That's why he invited Mom and Dad on the outing. Andy is surprisingly old-fashioned sometimes."

"Um..." Elijah's panicked look gave him away more than anything else.

"Don't even bother denying it!" I set the trunk down and began

147

jumping up and down like a lunatic for a few minutes. "How's he going to do it? Big extravagant proposal?"

"Um…"

"He probably hasn't thought it all out yet. I wonder if he wants help. Should I call him?"

"No!" Elijah said suddenly. "He has everything under control, Freckles. He's already come up with the proposal idea, but he isn't sharing it with anyone just yet. Not even you." Elijah kissed the tip of my nose, hoping it would soften the blow of his words. It helped a little. "I know how much you love Milo, and I know it's killing you not to be involved in the planning of one of the happiest days of his life, but Andy wants it to be a huge surprise for everyone."

"Apparently not you," I said with a slight pout.

"Freckles, I only know he asked your parents for their blessing. I wouldn't have known if your mom hadn't burst into tears and your dad hadn't shouted 'hallelujah.' It didn't take me being an ace detective to figure out what made them so damn happy."

"I can't believe my mom hasn't called me yet."

"Would you want your mom calling Milo and filling him in after I expressly asked her to keep it quiet so I could surprise you?"

"No, I wouldn't want your plans to get ruined by Milo's big mouth. He'd never be able to keep a secret like that from me."

"But you will manage to keep it from him, right? Andy and your parents will never forgive me if they find out I let the cat out of the bag."

"You didn't," I reminded him. "I guessed."

"That's right, Nancy Drew. I need you to promise me you won't let this slip."

"Of course, I won't." I had much better control than Milo did. Elijah stared at me as if he wanted to believe me, but worried about the competitive streak running through my blood. "Besides, I'll get a secret thrill every time we talk because I know something he doesn't."

"That's my Freckles."

Chapter Sixteen

Elijah

I'D KNOWN ALL ALONG JACKIE AND DENNIS WERE JOINING ANDY and me for golf while Maegan went digging for treasures and Milo went to drag rehearsal. The Queen City Divas were putting on a charity event to raise money for an HIV transition home owned by Milo's friend, Archie. It seemed like the perfect time to put our proposal plans into action. Andy had become my best friend, so of course I told him about my mom giving my great-grandmother's ring to me to give to Maegan. Andy confessed he was planning to ask Milo to marry him too. That's when we started planning our proposals so they wouldn't overlap or take away joy from each other.

Lying and keeping secrets from Maegan felt wrong, and I didn't enjoy doing it, but I couldn't tell her Andy and I purposely invited her parents so we could *both* ask them for their blessing to marry their children. I also couldn't tell her I knew how far Andy was going to give her twin brother a proposal he'd never forget. I had never planned to tell her anything about Andy's proposal, but my body language or tone of voice must've given something away. So, I threw poor Andy under the bus. At first, I worried Maegan wouldn't be able to keep the secret from Milo, but then I realized my fear was unwarranted. She'd go to any lengths to see her brother's dreams come true.

On Wednesday, instead of our usual French toast brunch, Maegan and I headed to The Ohio State University Hospital for my dad's surgery. I was nervous for many obvious reasons like something going wrong during my dad's surgery or finding out the cancer was more progressed than they thought. The biggest cause for my tension was knowing I would see my brother for the first time since I kicked his ass in his front yard after finding my wife in his bed pregnant with his baby.

Maegan and I arrived a few minutes after Dad checked in. Mom was sitting by herself looking calm and serene as she waited to be called back in to see Dad before surgery.

"Oh, Elijah," she said, hugging me tight. "Thank you for coming. He will be so happy to see you."

"I'm where I want to be," I assured her. "Well, maybe not in the hospital but with you and Dad."

"Maegan," Mom said, holding out her arms for the girl I wanted to spend the rest of my life with. "Thank you for being here with us today."

Maegan slid her hand inside mine after hugging Mom. "There's nowhere else I'd rather be."

Out of the corner of my eye, I saw Jack and Daphne approach. I reminded myself to breathe and remember I wasn't there for Jack; I was there for Mom and Dad. Maegan and I stepped back so Mom could greet them too. Maegan released my hand and slid her thin arm around my waist and pressed into my side. I raised my hand and rested it on the back of her neck because she loved the weight of my hand there. If we were alone, she'd lean into my touch more and practically purr from pleasure.

"Hello, Elijah," Jack said calmly, but his expression gave away how anxious he was. "I hear you've both met Daphne."

"Hello again," she said sweetly.

Maegan and I returned her greeting, and I knew I had two choices: introduce Jack and Maegan or pretend he didn't exist. My mom had been through enough and didn't need for me to act like a child.

"Hello, Jack," I said coolly. "This is Maegan."

"It's nice to meet you," Maegan said pleasantly.

"Likewise."

The pager in my mom's hands lit up and buzzed, signaling we could go back and see Dad for a brief visit before he was rolled into the operating room. A calm hush settled over us as we followed the nurse through the corridors as a Markham united front for the first time in ten years. Some of the players were new, and past transgressions weren't suddenly forgotten, but in that moment, we only wanted to give Dad peace of mind.

"Mercy me," Dad said when all five of us stepped inside his little curtained cocoon. Mom went to the right side of his bed and slid her fingers through his. I saw him squeeze her hand to assure her he was fine. "I didn't expect all of you to get up so early." His eyes searched mine, looking for signs of distress, but I'd be damned before I showed any. "I hate that you took time off for this. I'll be right as rain in no time at all." His voice shook just enough for me to detect he wasn't as calm as he wanted us to believe.

I walked to the left side of his bed and took his other hand in mine. "You took the day off when I had my tonsils removed."

"Of course, I took the day off. You were a frightened little boy having surgery for the very first time."

"And you're my father who's having surgery for the first time. There's no other place I should be." Tears formed in my dad's eyes, and one slid down his cheek. It was going to take some time to get used to seeing my dad express emotions this way. The man I grew up with wouldn't have cried if he cut his arm off with a chainsaw. He would've told my mom to stitch it up so he could get back to work clearing the fence line. "Everything is going to be just fine, Dad." It had to be.

"I know."

I stepped aside, and Maegan took my place briefly to give Dad a kiss on his cheek. "We'll see you when you come out of recovery."

"I'm liable to be grouchy and not the charmer you're accustomed to seeing."

Maegan giggled. "That's understandable. I won't hold it against you." She patted his hand and joined me in the corner so Jack and Daphne could wish him well too. Daphne was as sweet as Maegan, but when it was Jack's turn, Dad crooked his finger for him to lower his head then whispered something in his ear.

Jack lifted his head to look into Dad's eyes, nodded, and said, "Yes, sir." Dad squeezed Jack's hand like his actions and words pleased him greatly. Jack and Daphne moved to the opposite corner of Maegan and me so Mom could have all of Dad's attention.

Dad reached up and cupped Mom's face with his free hand. "You won't be rid of me yet, Brenda. Forty-five years of marriage to you just isn't enough."

"I'm not worried," she said serenely. "You're too ornery for heaven, and the devil hasn't figured out what to do with you yet."

Dad let out a loud guffaw then pulled Mom into a hug. When he pulled back, he looked into my eyes and said, "Would everyone give me a few minutes alone with Elijah?"

"Sure," Mom and Jack said at the same time. Mom rose from her chair and headed in our direction. She patted Jack's arm and smiled reassuringly at him as she walked by. She slid her arms around my waist and hugged me before taking Maegan's hand and leaving the room with everyone else.

I wasn't sure how much time Dad had left before they were going to wheel him back, so I headed straight for the chair Mom vacated. Dad, never one to mince words, got straight to the point. "This might seem like I'm taking advantage of the situation, but I'd like for you to make me a promise." I tensed because I knew where he was going. "Now, don't do that, Elijah. You think you're reading my mind, but you're making assumptions instead. I can't blame you, but I'm asking you to hear me out."

"Okay, Dad."

"I'm not asking you to pretend Jack didn't do a terrible thing to you, Elijah. I'm only asking you to talk to him and allow him the opportunity to apologize. He has missed you every single day you've been gone, and the look I saw in your eyes a few minutes ago makes me think you've been missing him too." I nodded because words weren't possible right then. "I'm not saying the two of you could ever go back to the way things were, but I know they can be better than they are right now. Will you at least give him the chance to talk? I'm not asking for me; I'm not even asking for him; I'm asking for you, Son."

I swallowed hard and took a shaky breath. "Yeah, Dad. I will do it for…all of us."

"I'm proud of you, Elijah. And before you go making assumptions again, I'd be saying the same thing had you told me no just now."

The curtain opened again, and a smiling nurse entered the room. "It's time, Mr. Markham."

"Okay. Let's do this," Dad said, sounding upbeat and confident. "I'll see you in a few hours, Elijah."

"I love you, Dad."

"I love you too, Son."

I had to stop in the hallway to get my shit together before I returned to the waiting room. They all stood up when I walked in, and the range of emotions on their faces ran from encouragement to anxious. I went to my mother first and hugged her.

"He's going to be fine. If I know him, he's telling them to skip the anesthesia so he can supervise." Mom giggled against my chest.

"Don't clip *that* artery, clip *this* one," Jack added, making Mom laugh harder.

"Make sure you wash those tools before you put them back," Mom added.

Our laughter and ribbing caused the others in the waiting room to look at us with various reactions, but we didn't pay them any mind. This was how Dad would want us to behave. I knew my mom wouldn't be interested in eating in the cafeteria, but I thought she could use a nice cup of coffee or a hot chocolate.

"Chamomile tea sounds lovely," she said after I offered to get her something to drink. "Do you think they have that?"

"I'll track some down if they don't."

"Elijah, please don't go to any trouble."

"It's no trouble." I looked at my brother, and I mean really looked at him for the first time in ten years. I noticed the age lines around his eyes and mouth and the few gray strands in his black hair. He was different, yet his warm brown eyes were the same. It was the oddest feeling, realizing I hadn't been around to see these changes slowly over time. It kind of felt like waking up after being in a coma for ten years, and the analogy wasn't far off. I had existed during our ten years apart, but I hadn't really lived. Not until I found Maegan. "Join me?" I asked him.

Jack quirked a brow in surprise but nodded. He kissed Daphne on the cheek and asked if she wanted anything. I turned my attention to my lady and didn't hear Daphne's response.

"What about you, Freckles? Can I bring you back anything?"

She raised up on her tiptoes and gave me a quick kiss on the lips. "Just yourself." Then she leaned toward my ear and whispered, "I'm so proud of you."

I saw the same emotion echoed in Mom and Daphne's expressions too before we left them sitting in the waiting room. I wasn't sure what to say, or even if I should be the one to start the conversation, but I had asked him to come with me. I guess Jack accepted the invitation as the opening he was looking for, so he broke the silence by speaking first.

"Elijah, I'm not sure where to begin, so I'll start with an apology."

I held up my hand to stop him because my emotions suddenly

felt too raw, and I didn't want to have this conversation in front of a bunch of strangers. I saw the sign for the chapel and nodded my head for Jack to follow me inside.

"I've already asked God for his forgiveness," Jack whispered when we walked inside the quiet chapel. "I can ask him again at the same time as asking for yours if it makes a difference."

A soft chuckle rumbled from my chest which loosened some of the tension gripping me. "It's a good start." I sat down on the rear pew once I confirmed we were alone and slid down so Jack could join me. Rather than look at the altar, I turned and angled my body so I could see Jack's face, and he did the same.

Jack released a shaky breath. "I apologize for the horrific way I treated you. I have no excuse for what I did; therefore, I won't be making any. What I did was—"

"Jack, I need you to say out loud and acknowledge exactly what you did to me. Otherwise, you could be talking about the time you took the tires off my bike so I couldn't compete against you in the bike race in elementary school."

Jack snorted. "It hurts so much to even remember what I did, let alone say it out loud, but you're absolutely right." He sat straighter and looked me square in the eyes. "Elijah, I am sorry I had an affair with Brandy while you were overseas. There is no excuse for disrespecting you and destroying the trust you placed in me when you asked me to look after her while you were gone. I take full responsibility for the affair and everything that happened afterward."

I had the urge to snipe "how big of you," but I breathed through the kneejerk reaction. Dad was right. I did miss my family, and although it felt like scaling a mountain would be easier than patching my relationship with Jack, we were offering one another a foothold toward a better future. Instead of a snappy comeback, I said, "All of the responsibility doesn't land on your shoulders, Jack. Brandy chose to have sex with you, so she equally shares the blame and shame. I just need to find a way to consign what happened to my past and try to forge a new relationship with you as part of my future."

Jack's lip trembled, and he briefly looked away. "I don't deserve it. My therapist says people can earn forgiveness, but I don't see how. Not in this case, anyway." I tried to hide my shock at hearing Jack had sought counseling. "I not only broke your heart and destroyed your spirit and self-worth, I nearly ruined our parents' marriage. They fought all the fucking time." Jack's eyes widened when he remembered where we were and the language he used. "The next few years were both the worst and happiest of my life."

"Your kids," I said softly.

He nodded. "They're my whole world and proof beautiful things can come from horrible deeds. Then again, I gave my children a mother who can't be bothered with them. I feel like they're paying for my sins, and it kills me. Things got really dark for me a few years ago, and I thought everyone would be better if I was gone. I knew Mom and Dad would do a much better job of raising Isaac and Will than I ever could." Tears flowed freely from his eyes, and all I wanted to do right then was stop him from saying anything else. Just the thought of Jack harming himself was enough to make me physically ill and sever the last threads of resentment I'd clung to.

"Jack—"

"I need to come clean, no matter how hard it is for me to say or you to hear." I nodded. "I tried drowning my despair in alcohol, and when it no longer worked, I decided to turn to pills. Then, one night, Will spiked a really high fever and needed to go to the hospital. I was a fucking loser, but I wasn't so far gone I'd put my kids in the car and risk their lives. I had the good sense to call Mom to come get us. The nurse on duty took one look at me and hated my guts. I just knew she was going to report me to children services and I'd lose my only reason for living, so I followed her out into the corridor after she assessed Will. I promised her I'd check myself into rehab the next day. I could see she wanted to believe me, but her life experiences told her I couldn't be trusted. I begged her for a chance. She finally looked at me and gave me an ultimatum. She would make arrangements for me at a facility she trusted right then and there. I could either show up the next day or she'd file a report with children's services, so I went to rehab."

"The nurse saved your life," I said to Jack.

"She restored my faith in people and healed my broken heart too."

"Ah, the nurse is Daphne." She seemed to have a nurturing personality, and I wasn't surprised to learn she was a nurse.

"I didn't tell you any of this to try to sway you, but I wanted you to know everything just in case we could…"

"Start over?" I asked.

Jack nodded. "There's no possible way to go back and change things, so the only way is—"

"Forward," I said, recalling our father's words. "I'd like to try, Jack. We'll start with family suppers and see where things go. I'd like to get to know Daphne better and meet Will and Isaac."

"Do you mean it, Elijah? I worried you'd only see them as a painful reminder of the things I did to you."

"They're innocent children. I could never blame them."

I did the only thing that felt right, I opened my arms and hugged my brother. Jack sobbed against my shoulder while silent tears slid down my face. Once we regained our composure, we left the chapel and went in search of chamomile tea for Mom while Jack entertained me with stories about his ten-year-old and seven-year-old sons. They sounded every bit as ornery as we were at their age.

The ladies looked up anxiously when we returned but smiled when they saw our relaxed expressions. Of course, our swollen and red-rimmed eyes gave away that our conversation wasn't an easy one.

"Hiya, Freckles," I said, holding her tight against my chest after handing Mom her tea. "Miss me?"

"Always." She searched my eyes to make sure I was truly okay. She must've liked what she saw because she blessed me with one of

157

her beautiful smiles.

It felt like we sat there for days instead of hours as we waited for the pager to go off again to let us know Dad was in recovery and the surgeon would be meeting with us. We crowded in the small consultation room and listened as Dr. Chen explained the surgery had gone well, but not entirely without complications. He assured us Dad was awake in the recovery room and we would get to see him soon.

It took another hour before we were led back to his recovery room. Dad opened his eyes when we walked in, and he cracked a tired smile. "I told you, Brenda." He looked at where I stood next to Jack, and he must've been able to read the situation even though I suspected he was still buzzing high from anesthesia.

"I've finally got my boys," he said.

Jack and I smiled at each other as we both gained a higher foothold on the climb to a happier future.

Chapter Seventeen

Maegan

"**I**S EVERYONE READY TO DO THIS?" VANESSA ASKED, standing before us wearing a pair of faded denim overalls over a white tank top, showing off her toned arms and vibrant tattoos. She brandished a dry paint brush around like a sword. "You all know the rules."

"Pay fucking attention to the numbers in the mural and match them up to the ones on the paint cans," Candace said dryly.

"Excellent start. What else?"

"Don't fuck it up," Violet suggested.

"That too, but to be fair, I can fix your screwups. None of you have mentioned the most important rule of them all."

"Don't tell Milo a fucking thing," I said firmly.

"Bingo!" Vanessa said. "Those drag queens kept a tight lip about what they painted in Milo and Andy's future nursery, and so will you."

"Will there be a big reveal where we vote on the winner?" April asked.

"There are only winners in this situation," Vanessa said. "First, it's my artwork so we can't go wrong. Second, their visions are…

159

Never mind. You'll know when they reveal the murals."

Was she going to say different or similar? It could go either way because we were very alike in some things and complete opposites in others. If anyone thought it was odd that the Miracle twins were painting nurseries prior to weddings, or even engagements, they didn't remark on it. They were used to us marching to our own beats. We knew what we wanted and didn't wait for approval or permission.

"Does it matter where we start?" Violet asked. "Do you want us all to complete one wall before moving onto the next?"

"It's up to Maegan."

"It doesn't matter to me," I told them. "Pick whatever you'd like to work on, and we'll see how far we get to day. This is a big undertaking." It took Vanessa weeks to draw it on the walls.

"I'll take the treehouse if you don't mind," Van said to me. "It's where most of the detail and shading is needed to give it a life-like appearance."

April chose the woodland critters, Violet started painting picket fences, Candace decided to work on fluffy clouds and blue skies, and I decided to go with the whimsical tree swing suspended from flower vines. Vanessa had created the design on her computer then showed it to me so I could make changes to the color scheme.

"I'm reporting for duty too," Elijah said from the doorway. He walked up behind me and slid his arm around my waist then lowered his mouth to my ear. "Where do you want me?"

"Wherever you're most comfortable."

"Freckles, mind your manners in front of our friends." I loved how he referred to the ladies as his friends also. They all adored him too, but who wouldn't?

"I meant pick the section that appeals to you the most. Just make sure you—"

"Pay attention to matching the numbers on the wall to the ones on the paint can and don't blab to Milo," Elijah said.

I took a rare Saturday off from Books and Brew so we could get as much done in one day as possible. Elijah and I would chip away at what was left over, and Van planned to come in at the very end to add shading and highlights or to fix our fuckups. We decided to order sandwiches and pizza for our friends to thank them for giving up their free day also. When the doorbell rang in the middle of the afternoon, Elijah assumed it as the pizza delivery boy and went down to answer the door while the rest of us took turns washing our hands in the Jack and Jill bathroom between the nursery and the bedroom beside it.

April and Violet went first while Candace, Vanessa, and I huddled up to shamelessly talk about our friends.

"They're keeping it close to the vest," Candace said, looking over her shoulder to make certain the door was shut. "Those two have waited so long for one another, and I expected a big announcement by now."

A sweet smile spread over Vanessa's face. "I think their old-fashioned dating is adorable."

Over the past six weeks, the ladies had insisted on experiencing all the things they wanted to do together in high school but didn't because neither of them was out. "It's the most beautiful love story I've ever witnessed," I said wistfully. I was humbled and awed to be a part of some of their special moments and surprises they'd planned for one another.

"Is it safe to come back in the room now?" April asked through the closed door.

Violet giggled then asked, "Or do you need more time to whisper about us and speculate about the state of our relationship?"

"It's safe," Vanessa called out. "We've already placed our bets." The door slowly opened to reveal our friends standing in the doorway wearing bemused expressions.

"For how long we'll last?" April asked then scowled.

"I may be cynical about love and happily ever after, but I'm not blind," Candace replied dryly. "*If* we were placing bets, it would be which of us you'll choose as your maid of honor at your wedding."

Violet blushed prettily while April looked embarrassed that she'd assumed the worst.

"Oh, um…" April stammered.

Violet leaned over and kissed her cheek, easing her jitters. "We'll get there when we get there and not a minute before we're ready, ladies." She looked at her watch. "Speaking of which, we have big plans tonight, so we better grab a quick bite to eat and get back to work."

April leaned over and kissed Violet's forehead before they linked hands and left us standing there in the center of the room exchanging sappy grins. "You heard the lady," I said, gesturing to the door they just exited.

When we got downstairs, a man wearing dark denim jeans and a pressed, black dress shirt stood beside Elijah. The sexy guy oozed success, privilege, and power. This was no pizza delivery man; it was Theodore Rutledge. I recognized him from the Google search I performed after learning of his existence. Elijah had his methods, and I had mine.

"I started to think you weren't coming, Mr. Rutledge," I said, walking toward him.

"Please call me Theo. I'm very sorry for all the delays and even more appalled I didn't call first. I can see you're very busy." His eyes swept over the women who came down the stairs behind me, jerked to a stop then swept back the other direction. His piercing blue eyes widened in surprise then narrowed, but not in a menacing way. I turned around to see who'd caught his attention and saw Vanessa was blushing and refusing to meet his eyes. Vanessa didn't blush. Who was this man to garner such a reaction from her. Then it hit me. Oh. My. God! Her weekend-of-wild-sex must've been with Theodore Rutledge because I knew everyone else Vanessa had hooked up with or dated. "Hello, Vanessa. It's good to see you again." I looked at my friends to see if I was the only one who noticed the man's voice drop a few octaves? Their wide-eyed expressions said they'd noticed too.

I expected he used the same voice to get her back to his condo and keep her there all weekend long.

Van squared her shoulders, lifted her head, and boldly looked into his eyes. "It's good to see you too, Theo." Then her eyes perused his tall, muscular body from top to bottom. When she finished, she aimed a man-eater smile at him.

I turned my attention back to Theo and said, "Would you like a grand tour?"

He finally peeled his eyes off my friend and focused on me. "Are you sure? I could come back another time perhaps."

"Don't be silly," I said, dismissing the idea. "Let's get started in the back of the house where the library is located." And the furthest away from Vanessa so she could retreat if she wanted. "I have several of your grandfather's items on display there."

"It sounds like the perfect starting point."

I was glad Elijah and his knuckle-dragging mentality followed behind Theo and me, hoping it would discourage our guest from asking me personal questions about Vanessa. Ha! He wasn't the owner of a Fortune 500 company because he waited for the appropriate time to do something. He was successful because he seized every opportunity to get what he wanted.

"I didn't expect to see Vanessa here," Theo said casually.

"How do you know Van?" Elijah asked before I could respond. My man crossed his big arms over his broad chest and gave the billionaire a don't-fuck-with-me look. Oh lord, he was fucking hot.

"I'm not sure it's your business," Theo returned, not looking the least bit intimidated by Elijah.

"It is my—*our*—business when you come into our home and start probing for information about one of our friends."

Theo's mouth tilted up on the right side in a wry, half smile. Elijah's protectiveness seemed to relax him even if he was the one Elijah was shielding Vanessa from. "I only remarked that I was surprised to see her here. I forget how small this world truly

sometimes. What are the odds the lady who bought my grandfather's home is friends with the woman who..." His words trailed off, and he looked truly surprised about what he had revealed or almost said. "Anyway, I'd love a tour then I'll get out of your hair."

"This is the coolest place to start," I told him. "Look at the incredible craftsmanship that went into building those floor-to-ceiling bookshelves."

"Incredible," Theo agreed. He walked over to one of the shelves where I displayed several pictures of the family I'd found in frames.

"I think you resemble him greatly," I said. "You have the same square jaw and aristocratic nose. It's hard to tell what color his eyes were since the photos are in black and white, but it's obvious they were a light color like yours."

"I've been told I have the Bliss blue eyes."

"You look taller and broader—" My words died off when I smelled pipe tobacco.

"Are you implying I should hit the gym more often?" Theo asked with a quirked brow. He stilled when he smelled the invisible smoke drifting through the air. He looked around the room and saw no one in the room was smoking a pipe. "I don't believe it," he said in awe. He held up his right arm and the dark hair on his arm was visibly sticking up where he'd rolled his sleeve to reveal thickly muscled forearms. "Oh, that's fucking weird."

"Good of you to join us, Anthony," I said. "This is your grandson, Theo."

"You talk to him?" Theo whispered, making Elijah snort.

"He doesn't answer back," I assured him. "Unless you count him slamming a door upstairs or romping around in the attic."

"He was very demonstrative when we picked out paint colors during remodeling," Elijah told him. "Maegan gave in every time he expressed his displeasure."

"He loved this house, and at the time, I thought he'd be here long after I died," I said with a shrug. "Happy ghost, happy life."

"I don't think that's how the saying goes, Freckles." Elijah then looked at Theo once more. "The logic applies just the same though."

"Do you really believe in all this?" Theo asked me then shook his head. "You're talking out loud to him, so you obviously believe."

"I knew there was something special about this house when I rode by it on my bicycle as a kid. I also knew someone truly special resided here too. I couldn't explain it then, and it sounds ridiculous to say as a grownup, but this place just felt like pure magic to me."

"It was the turret," a new voice said, entering the library. I turned and raised a brow at my brother. "She was obsessed with fairy tales, fair maidens, and dashing princes. The turret represented a tower where the fair maiden was locked away until her dashing prince showed up to rescue her."

Elijah puffed out his chest reminding me of Gaston from *Beauty and the Beast*. "I'd say the fair lady did well for herself. She has her castle and her dashing, heroic man." His deepened, dramatic voice made me giggle.

"I noticed there are a lot of vehicles in the driveway when I drove by. Are you having a party and forgot to invite me?" Milo laid the garment bag he'd had slung over his shoulder on a club chair and approached the three of us. "You must be Theodore. You have an uncanny resemblance to Anthony Bliss. You'd think genetics gets watered down over the generations, but it's like Anthony is standing right here."

"Maegan says I'm fatter than him. Please call me Theo," he said, thrusting his hand toward my brother.

"Please forgive her," Milo said, shaking his hand. "She can be so gauche sometimes. Our mother tried so hard with her, but there was no help for it. I'm Milo by the way."

"Milo, you just happened to be in the neighborhood?" I asked in disbelief.

"Maegan, you act as if we live in a metropolis. Everywhere you go in Blissville is 'in the neighborhood.' I came by to get your opinion on the dress for tonight. You know how much I love Dolly Parton, and I mustn't wear just any ole sequined dress. I notice how you deflected my question. Are you having a hen party of some sort? What are you ladies into these days? Kinky toys? The latest kitchen gadgets? Kitchen gadgets that also act as kinky toys? You know I love all those things too."

"None of the above, and you can cut the act. You know exactly what the girls are doing upstairs."

"Oh, is this the day you try to outdo the magnificent nursery Andy and I planned?" Milo snorted. "Good luck with that."

"I don't need luck because I'm positive my vision is grander than anything you can comprehend."

"We'll just see about that, won't we?"

"Will we also have a race to see who adopts a baby first?" Elijah asked, drawing disbelieving looks from us both. "Will we encourage knock-down, drag-out fights between toddlers over Easter eggs?"

"Not even we're *that* competitive," I told Elijah.

"We might playfully compete against one another, but we'd never pit our children against each other. Unless there's serious cash involved," Milo said.

Theo threw his head back and laughed until tears streamed down his face which was when Vanessa walked into the room to let us know our food was delivered. Milo didn't miss her tight voice, pale face, and stiff posture as her eyes locked on Theo.

"What's wrong, Van. You act like you've seen a ghost." Milo's eyes widened when he put two and two together and came up with ten. "Oh!" Milo looked back and forth between them. Theo looked like he was intrigued to know if Van had talked about him, and Van looked like she was seconds away from skinning Milo alive.

"Well, I should probably get going," Milo said dramatically. "I'm about to give the performance of my life tonight, so none of you better miss it."

"We'll be there," I assured him. "I thought you wanted help

picking out a dress."

"I lied," he said, snatching up his garment bag and tossing it over his shoulder. "I wanted an excuse to see what you were up to." Milo winked playfully before exiting with a flourish.

"Let's go eat," Elijah said, rubbing his hands together. "We have plenty of food, Theo. Would you like to join us?"

"I should probably get going," he said, staring at Vanessa. He didn't sound a bit convincing.

"Oh, come on," Elijah said. "Have a few pieces of pizza then Maegan can show you the rest of the house."

"Okay," Theo said with a calm shrug. He followed Vanessa out of the room, leaving me and Elijah alone.

"Andy is popping the question tonight, isn't he?"

"Freckles," Elijah said in a warning tone.

"Oh, all right. Keep your secrets." I gave him a quick kiss then headed into the dining room where lunch awaited us.

The tour with Theo thankfully finished quieter than it began. He appreciated the craftsmanship and the way we lovingly restored the home so it kept the vintage feel but with modern twists here and there. After he left, I joined everyone else in the nursery. I stood shocked in the doorway because I hadn't expected us to get so far in a few hours, but I could already tell Vanessa's mural would exceed my wildest imagination. I burst into tears, pulling everyone's attention to me.

"Freckles," Elijah said, pulling me into his arms. "We can change anything you don't like, right, Van?"

"It's perfect," I said into his chest. "It's so beautiful it moved me to tears. I have no idea why I'm crying at the drop of a hat anymore."

"As long as they're happy tears," Elijah said, kissing the top of my head.

Later that night, happy tears streamed down my face once more when Andy walked out onto the stage at Queen City Divas dressed as Kenny Rogers to perform a duet with his Dolly Parton in front of both families and all our friends. "Islands in the Stream" had never sounded so sweet, and my brother smiled brighter than I'd ever seen when Andy dropped to his knee after their performance and proposed. Milo had waited for this moment for so long, and my heart swelled to bursting with love on the happiest day of his life.

I curled into Elijah's side, noting the smug look on his face. I was tempted to torture him with pleasure later to see what other secrets he hid but decided I'd rather not know ahead of time the treasures life had in store for us.

Chapter Eighteen

Elijah

"**O**CTOBER IS THE BEST TIME OF YEAR TO HEAD TO Grandpa's cabin," my mom said wistfully. I imagined she was wearing her serene smile, and I wished I was sitting across the kitchen table from her instead of talking over the phone. "The leaves are changing, and the weather is perfect."

"How's Dad *really* doing with his radiation treatments?" I wanted to check in before we left for Tennessee in the morning.

A month had passed since his surgery, and he'd just started radiation therapy. I wanted to take Maegan away for a long weekend in the middle of the month because the end of October was a hectic time for her. I wanted this four-day weekend to be something special she would remember for the rest of her life, not a few days squeezed in between Halloween and birthday celebrations. On the other hand, I wanted to be there for my dad too.

"Elijah, your father isn't lying just to make you feel better. He's doing okay right now. As the weeks go on, the radiation will take its toll. Right now, he's just a little tired. You need to have this time away with Maegan, and you need to do it without worrying about us. I promise I will call you if something comes up, but I know it won't.

Give Freckles our love. And, Elijah," Mom said softly, "I cannot wait to see my grandmother's ring on her finger."

"How'd you know I was—"

"I'm your mother," she said, cutting me off. "Mothers know these things. I don't want to hear anymore conflict in your voice. Dad and I are doing just fine. Oh! Here he comes now. He's holding out his hand, so he must want to talk to you. I love you, Elijah. I hope you have an amazing weekend."

"I love you too, Mom."

"Son," my father said by way of greeting. "You aren't asking your mother about my health after I already told you I'm doing fine, are you?"

"No, Dad."

"I promised myself I'd be a better man if I ever got a second chance to be your father, and part of that is being honest and not trying to pretend I'm Superman. I'm flesh and blood, not a superhero."

"Really?"

"Don't get smart," he said, but I heard the humor in his voice. "I'm trying to make a point here."

"My apologies."

"I will be honest with you about how I'm feeling throughout radiation, Son. I'm only two weeks in, and right now, I'm mostly tired. The doctor warned the next five weeks will take a harder toll on me. I want you to have the weekend away you planned with your Freckles because I will need your strength and her smiling face soon. Will you do that for me?"

I had to swallow a few times before I could speak. "Yeah, Dad."

"That's my boy. Now, it's time for you to hang up this phone so you can finish getting ready for your trip."

"Yes, sir. I love you, Dad."

"I love you too, Son. You have a safe trip."

We said our goodbyes then hung up. I sat on the bed I shared with Maegan for several minutes staring off into space. My relationship with my father had changed so much since we reconnected. It was everything I'd always wanted as a kid and young adult, but I wished it hadn't taken a serious illness for us to patch things up. In the end, did it really matter why he took the first step? It didn't. The only thing that mattered was the result. I felt lighter and happier than ever before in my life. I not only had the girl of my dreams, but I had my family back. My future had never looked brighter than it did right then on the cusp of asking Maegan to be my wife.

I heard the front door open and close below. Maegan had gone to work even though she was off on Wednesdays to make sure Bonnie didn't have too much on her plate while we were gone. Jackie was also helping out wherever she was needed which was a big relief to Maegan. She'd texted me to say she was going to the store after work to get the non-perishable food items we needed for our trip. The general store closest to the cabin had the fresh meat and perishable items we'd need, but Maegan refused to pay their jacked-up, tourist-trap prices for boxed and canned goods we could bring from home. My lady was a shrewd businesswoman and negotiator.

"Elijah," Maegan called from downstairs. "I brought home the fried chicken you like from the deli." I almost made it to the kitchen before she finished her sentence. She laughed when she saw how eager I was to get my hands on the chicken. "How are your parents?"

"How'd you know I was going to call them?"

"I know you," Maegan said. "You wanted to make sure your dad wasn't lowballing his pain level so you could keep your plans. So, how is he?"

"Tired but otherwise good. He said the next five weeks will be hard on him."

"Then we'll make sure we get there as often as we can to give him the support he needs and your mom a break."

The chicken was forgotten when I pulled Maegan into my arms and looked into her adoring eyes. She'd change our plans in a heartbeat if she thought my parents needed us which only made me love her more. I ran a finger over the freckles on her forehead I loved so much.

"Our lives have been a bit hectic lately, so I'm glad the two of us are getting away for the weekend."

"And they're about to get even crazier now that the network has worked out all the arrangements with the lawyers for The Golden Gate Bridge Inn." A door slammed above. "Excuse me, Anthony," Maegan said dramatically, "I meant the Blissview Hotel."

"At least Anthony has prepared us for when our kids become petulant teenagers," I suggested.

"You make a very good point," Maegan said.

"I'm glad Lyric's crew is coming this weekend to do the bulk of the filming," I confessed then waggled my eyebrows. "Especially the nighttime stuff."

Maegan giggled and patted my chest. "There are definitely things bumping in the night around here that don't need to be recorded. Let's eat the chicken while it's still hot then we can finish packing."

"I'm all packed and ready to go," I boasted. "I'm willing to help you pack the essentials if you want some help."

"Elijah, I'd end up with a bag full of lingerie and nothing else."

"Not true," I said, shaking my head. "I was thinking you'll only need a toothbrush."

"You're going to keep me naked for four days?"

"Well six hours of the first day will be spent driving, so three and a half." I dodged her quick hand when she tried to pinch my nipple. "Okay, I plan on taking you on my favorite hiking trails, so you'll need appropriate clothing for hiking and a toothbrush."

"Different trails than the ones we took in the spring?"

"Yes and no," I replied. "Some of the trails are the same, but they will look completely different now that fall has arrived. There is one trail I saved especially for this trip."

"You were sure there'd be another trip back then, huh?"

"I hoped," I replied, smoothing the curls away from her forehead then cupping her face. "The cabin is my favorite place on earth, and you're my favorite person. Plus, I made some secret upgrades to the cabin since we were last there."

Maegan narrowed her eyes. "I'm not sure what to think about your ability to keep secrets from me."

"Freckles, the only secrets I keep from *you* are surprises for *you*. You've seen all my skeletons." My brain chose that moment to interrupt my happiness by reminding me Axel Washington was still out there, and I wasn't falling for his "going clean" act. It was a matter of time before he returned to his old ways, and I could be at the top of his revenge list. I trusted my former police captain to let me know when, or if, I needed to go on high alert. Until then, I wanted Maegan to have maximum joy in life because there was no need upsetting her about something that hasn't happened and may never happen.

"I'm just teasing you. I can't wait to see my surprises," Maegan said then rubbed her hands together. "Okay, dinner then packing."

Dinner went off without a hitch, but things went a little sideways when I followed Maegan upstairs to help her pack because her newest delivery of lingerie had arrived in the mail. She wanted to wait and show it off at the cabin, but I didn't want to wait another day to know what she received.

"You have your surprises, and I have mine," she teased, tossing the unopened package into the bottom of her small suitcase. I wanted to snatch it out of there and rip it open, but she had a point. Then she went to the closet and carried out an opened box she'd apparently hid in there.

"What's that?" I asked.

"More surprises."

"Can you at least give me a hint?"

"Only if you give me a hint first." Maegan raised her chin to challenge me.

We stared each other down like two gunslingers squaring off in the center of town. I expected a tumbleweed to roll by and a familiar tune from one of the old western movies to play. "Are we practicing a scene for The Hot, The Hard, and the Horny?"

Maegan was the first to blink, and I was on her in a flash. "I'll tickle it out of you," I said, wrestling her onto the bed and gently digging my fingers into her ribs, making her shout with laughter as she tried to wiggle free.

"I'll never tell my secrets," she said dramatically like she was performing in one of her mother's favorite soap operas. "There's nothing you can say or do to make me talk."

I raised my head and smiled into her twinkling eyes and daring smile. "Yeah?"

"Yeah."

Maegan's packing was delayed for quite some time as I took my time trying to wheedle the secrets from her with my mouth, tongue, hands, and cock. I still had no idea what secrets her luggage contained but neither did she know about mine nor the surprises awaiting her at the cabin.

The next morning, I woke up earlier than Maegan which was completely abnormal. She could easily be cast in a Disney princess role with woodland critters dancing about her feet or flying overhead as she made her way to the coffee pot while I grumbled and growled until I consumed a second cup of coffee. Maybe I was anxious to get on the road to avoid traffic or excited about being one day closer to making Maegan mine forever.

I kissed Maegan's nose, and she wiggled it in irritation. "More sleep," she whispered, rolling over and burrowing deeper in the covers. "Just fifteen more minutes."

"Okay, but then you have to get in the shower or you'll be late for school, dear."

Maegan rolled back over and cracked open her eyes. "Not funny. I wouldn't go back to high school for a billion dollars. Just fifteen more minutes, Elijah." It was so unlike her to lounge around in bed, but we were on vacation, and fifteen minutes really wouldn't cause much of a delay.

I ended up letting her sleep for another thirty minutes which threw her into a panic. "I can't believe you let me sleep so late," she said, running for the bathroom. "I had a shower before bed, so I only need to brush my teeth."

"Freckles, relax. You looked like you needed the sleep. This is our vacation, not a precise military mission." Although seeing her stand there in nothing but a lace thong and a barely there tank top made me think missionary-style sex. Making love to her was my favorite way to start the day. I could start by dropping down behind her and pulling the thin scrap of lace aside so I could lick a path…

"No way," she said firmly, pulling my attention away from her pert ass to meet her gaze in the mirror. "We don't have time for that now."

"I can be really fast, baby."

"That's just what every woman wants to hear," Maegan said sarcastically, replacing her toothbrush in the holder.

"Tell me you're not already turned on by knowing what I was thinking. Tell me you aren't fighting the urge to rub your thighs together to get a little bit of friction where you need it. Don't bother lying because I can see how hard your nipples are in the mirror."

"Okay, fine. You make me horny, but it doesn't mean I have to act on it right this second. I rather like the idea of you staying semi-aroused while plotting and planning all the ways you can make me come during the six-hour road trip. I'll be doing the same thing, looking at the beautiful scenery while wondering if your cock is as hard as the mountains we're driving toward."

"Be ready to leave in ten minutes," I said gruffly. "Do you need to toss any last-minute items into your luggage, or can I carry them down?"

Maegan's response was to turn around, pull her tank top over her head, and toss it at my chest. I caught it and held it up to my nose. I loved the sexy combination of flowers, vanilla, and something darker and sexy that clung to her skin and everything that touched it. "Everything is packed and ready to go. I just need to put on some comfy, travel clothes."

"What about your toothbrush?" I asked, looking to stall so I could keep looking at her glorious rack.

"I packed a new one in my suitcase."

"I guess I should take these bags downstairs and pack the SUV."

When Maegan walked by me, she made sure to rub the side swell of her breast against my arm. "Guess so." Of course, I turned and watched her head to the dresser where her outfit was folded neatly waiting for her. She hooked her thumbs in her thong and looked over her shoulder at me. "My bags are right there by the bed."

I wanted to stay and act out some cheesy bellboy porn that ended with an epic orgasm, but I wanted her to suffer as much as I did. Instead, I rearranged my aching hard-on so she would know what awaited her later and picked up our bags.

"Eight minutes now, Freckles."

"I only need three." Her happy laughter followed me down the hallway.

Chapter Nineteen

Maegan

IT DIDN'T TAKE ME LONG TO FIGURE OUT WHY ELIJAH LOVED the cabin so much when we visited the first time. However, the late spring beauty paled in comparison to autumn's splendor spread before us as we hiked through dewy grass late Friday morning.

"You might want to slow it down a little, big guy," I said. "It's a miracle I can hike at all after we christened the new copper bathtub last night."

My heart nearly burst when I saw it sitting in the master bathroom. I'd wanted one for Bliss House but couldn't justify the expense when one of the fiberglass clawfoot replica tubs was a fraction of the price. I was torn between elated joy over my surprise and horror over how much he spent. Elijah assured me he hadn't paid full price for it because a nearby contractor had custom ordered it for a new construction home, and the homeowner didn't like it. The contractor, Hal, couldn't return the tub, so he sold it for a deeply discounted price just to unload it. Luckily for me, Elijah was the first person he thought of since he'd done previous work at his cabin and knew how good it would look in the space.

He stopped and waited for me to catch up to him. "I do believe that was the best purchase I ever made, Freckles."

Of course, we didn't stop with the bathtub. We had to christen the large antique replica bed he'd found on sale. For an extra fee, the company delivered and set up the bed for us. Hal was also our nearest neighbor and someone we could rely on to supervise deliveries or keep an eye on the place.

"I think I owe Hal a pie," I told Elijah, sliding my fingers through his to hold his hand.

"Maybe two," he teased.

I noticed Elijah matched his pace to mine, and he seemed content to go at a slower pace, but there was something buzzing beneath his skin. Outwardly, he seemed calm, but holding his hand felt like I was holding onto a live wire.

"Too much coffee?" I asked him.

"Huh?" he said, turning to look at me suddenly. That was the other off thing about him. His mind seemed like it was a million miles away. Was it because our cell phones didn't work well out here? Our families had the phone number to the cabin's land line, so they knew how to get ahold of us if there was an emergency.

"You're practically buzzing," I said, circling my thumb over his erratic pulse in his wrist.

"I'm just happy to be here with you and excited to show you my favorite place in the entire world." He looked at me with a quirked brow. "Favorite place that's not a part of your body, I mean."

"You're so corny."

"Let's not forget horny."

I snickered. "That's all day, every day."

"In addition to making a delicious breakfast while you slept late, I packed us a lunch too."

"Lunch? I won't be ready to eat again until dinnertime," I told him. "The huge breakfast you cooked is enough to last all day."

"You'll feel differently by the time we reach our destination."

It was hard for me to imagine, but he had a lot more experience at hiking than I did, especially in this terrain. By the time we reached the clearing at the top of our climb, I knew exactly why it was Elijah's favorite place in the world. I was also glad I hadn't bet him about being hungry because the climb burned away every calorie we consumed. My legs felt like noodles by the time I sat down on the blanket Elijah spread out for us. He wrapped his arm around my shoulders, and I nestled into his side.

"I've never seen anything more beautiful in all my life," I said, looking over the deep valley nestled between the base of the ridge we climbed and the mountain range across from us. The tree leaves were various shades of oranges, yellows, and reds everywhere you looked. "It almost looks like the mountain is on fire."

"Now it's the most beautiful place on earth." Elijah's voice was thick with emotion and pulled my eyes away from nature's splendor to look into his warm brown eyes. "I didn't know what this spot was missing until now." He cleared his throat then offered me the wide smile that never failed to steal my breath. "You make everything you touch more beautiful. I have a confession to make, Freckles. I didn't just bring you up here to gaze at leaves and eat peanut butter sandwiches."

"This isn't where you confess to being a sociopath and push me off the ridge, is it?"

Elijah snorted and grinned. "Not hardly, and maybe you and Milo are watching too many shows on the ID channel."

"Then you brought me up her for sex?"

"No, but that guess is closer than a hidden desire to push you over the ridge." Elijah moved away from me, but only so he could sit in front of me and look into my eyes. "I have something very important to ask you, and I wanted to bring my special girl to my special place to ask it." Elijah swallowed hard and reached for his backpack. I shook all over when he pulled out a ring box and held it up between us. "I had this perfect speech planned, but now that I'm looking in your eyes, I can't remember what I was going to say."

"I don't need prepared speeches," I said through trembling lips. "I just want to hear what's in your heart."

"I love you, Maegan Miracle, with everything I have and everything I will be." Elijah turned the box around and opened it. I gasped when I saw the vintage ring nestled in the velvet. "This ring belonged to my great-grandmother who was fierce, passionate, and loving just like you are, and I know she'd be honored for you to wear it."

"Elijah," I whispered, placing my trembling right hand over my racing heart as tears rolled down my face. I cleared my throat but still couldn't speak above a whisper when I said, "It's so beautiful." Then again, I could've been yelling and wouldn't know it because the pulse pounding in my ears muffled the sound of my voice.

"Maegan Louise Miracle, will you be mine for the rest of our lives? Will you raise a family and grow old with me? Will you be my best friend and the person I always turn to when times get dark, and will you allow me to shelter you from the storms life throws at us in return?"

"Yes," I said, nodding and sobbing. "This is the happiest day of my life." My left hand shook when I raised it until Elijah held it gently in his big, strong hand and slid the ring on my finger. "It's the most beautiful ring I've ever seen."

"And it fits you perfectly because it was meant for you." Elijah kissed the knuckle above the ring I would wear until my dying breath.

"They don't make rings like this anymore," I said in awe.

"I happen to think you're a rare gem too." Elijah brushed the tears off my face, and I leaned into his palm. "Can we seal this engagement with a kiss?"

I pounced on him then, knocking him onto his back so I could straddle his hips. Elijah smiled up at me as I slowly leaned over him. "We will only have one first kiss as a newly engaged couple, so we must do it right."

Elijah reached up and pushed my hair away from one side of my face then cupped the back of my head and guided me down the rest of the way until my lips hovered just above his. I'd heard and read the phrase about tasting someone's smile but didn't fully get it until my smiling mouth met his. Then our lips molded to each other's in a few chaste pecks before lingering and finally parting to deepen our kiss. His tongue boldly entered my mouth, claiming and possessive while I met him stroke for stroke.

I felt Elijah's body responding to the urgent desire growing inside mine. Suddenly, we had way too many clothes on for either of our liking. The mountain air wasn't cold, but it was cool enough I was grateful for the plaid blanket Elijah had packed in his backpack. My hunger for lunch was replaced with the need for Elijah to claim my body as surely as he did my heart. We kissed while we stripped each other bare, our hands and lips touching and kissing every new inch we revealed until there was nothing between us. We'd surely had sex more than a hundred times since we started dating each other nine months prior, but there was no doubt that time, on top of the ridge wrapped up in a blanket cocoon, was different. There was always a possessive tenderness in Elijah's eyes when he slid his dick inside me, but the look was hotter and fiercer and so fucking delicious it made my toes curl.

I slid my hands into his hair as he began to move inside me with sure, even strokes. The sunlight caught the diamonds on my ring finger and prisms of light danced around my vision, but it was the look in Elijah's eyes which held me spellbound. His dark, glittery gaze burned in intensity, consuming me and ratcheting up the physical and emotional pleasure inside me until he was all I saw, all I heard, and all I felt.

Elijah gripped my hips tighter and rocked harder in and out of me, nailing the pleasure spot inside me over and over until my toes curled tight enough to break, but even then, I couldn't look away from him. Our lovemaking was usually peppered with dirty talk and sexy banter, but the only sounds on the ridge besides skin slapping as our bodies came together were our thundering hearts and choppy breaths. I didn't need Elijah to tell me I was the only girl for him or that my body drove him wild. I felt it.

He lowered his head and captured my lips once more in a passionately fierce kiss when he sensed we were both close to climaxing. Maybe he didn't want my shouts of joy bouncing off the mountains and echoing through the valley below, giving away our activities to every hiker and park ranger in a twenty-five-mile radius. I dug my fingers in his ass which was my signature move when I wanted him to go harder and faster. I heard the echoing growl of pleasure in his chest and braced myself for the ferocious fucking I wanted.

My orgasm hit me like a fucking tsunami, and Elijah captured my cries with his mouth. I felt his ass tighten beneath my legs seconds before he grunted and spilled inside my body. Afterward, Elijah lowered his forehead to rest on the blanket beside my head to catch his breath while I kissed his shoulder and massaged his scalp with one hand and traced the line of his spine with the other.

"This is the happiest day of my life too, Freckles," he said, echoing the words I'd said earlier. Elijah raised up and braced himself on his elbows above me. "We talked about marriage and kids, or at least assumed it would happen, but nothing prepared me for the way it feels to see my ring on your finger."

"Maegan Louise Markham," I whispered. "I love the sound of that."

"I'll be Mr. Maegan Markham," he replied, drawing a snort from me. "What? Like I don't know who's really in charge."

I giggled. "As much as I'd love to lie here cuddling with you, I think we better get dressed before someone stumbles upon us."

"I've never encountered another person in all the years I've been hiking this ridge. A few bears and other—"

"Bears!" I practically threw Elijah off me. He lay there sprawled on his back, laughing his ass off while I scrambled for the clothes we'd tossed about haphazardly. He was still having a good time at my expense when I cleaned myself with the wipes he'd stowed in his backpack. I narrowed my eyes at him as I wiggled into my undies but turned the tables on him when I put some extra sway and wiggle in my hips while I pulled my jeans on so my breasts would bounce enticingly.

"Don't be in such a rush," Elijah said, crawling toward me as I put my bra back on. "I was teasing about the bears. All the noise we were making would scare them off rather than entice them to investigate."

"Forgive me if I don't take your word for it." I pulled my long-sleeved shirt back over my head and reached for my vest.

"Suit yourself, but—" Elijah's words died suddenly, and he sucked a huge breath into his lungs before bellowing, "SNAKE!" He jumped to his feet faster than I'd ever seen him move.

"Where?" I said, looking around for a timber rattler or something that escaped from a zoo someplace and had been hiding out in the Great Smoky Mountains eating unsuspecting critters and horny couples who were too busy fornicating to notice the danger until it was too late because the giant, man-eating snake was right on them. Then I saw a small, brown snake slithering off into the woods. "That?" I asked pointing. Elijah's respond was a hard shudder, and it was my turn to laugh at his expense.

"Mock me all you want, Freckles. I saved your life just now."

I laughed even harder. "Elijah, I've seen bigger snakes in our yard."

"What? When?"

His panic only made me laugh harder until he stood there, buck-ass naked with his hands on his hips, looking at me through narrowed eyes. "I'm starting to rethink my proposal."

If he expected me to capitulate and stop laughing, then he was going about it the hard way. I held up my forefingers on both hands to indicate how little the snake was because I was laughing too hard to speak. Of course, I deliberately downplayed the snake's size so it resembled the length of an earthworm.

"My cock is way bigger than that, Freckles."

"Not if you don't put some clothes on," I said once I could speak again. "It's a bit nippy out here." I tossed his briefs and jeans at him then wiped the tears from my eyes as he put them on.

Elijah had just sat down to put on his socks and shoes when I heard the sound of twigs snapping and grass rustling. I whipped around expecting to see a bear, but a man stepped out of the clearing instead.

"Howdy, folks, I'm Ranger Nelson. I was in the vicinity when I heard shouting and decided to come investigate." His shrewd eyes roamed over our embarrassed flushes and Elijah's partially clad body, quickly surmising what we'd been up to. "Ma'am, are you here of your own free will?"

"Yes, Ranger Nelson. I'm with my fiancé who got frightened by a snake. That's what all the yelling was about." *Fiancé.* I knew I was going to find a way to work the word into every conversation.

"Sir?" Ranger Nelson asked, verifying my statement with Elijah. It was good he didn't take for granted that I, as a woman, posed no threat to a big, strapping man.

"Our cabin is at the base of the ridge, and I wanted to show Maegan how beautiful the area is in autumn. We hiked up here to have lunch."

"I agree," the ranger said. "I'll let the two of you get back to your…um…lunch."

"Thanks," I said, feeling my blush from head to toe. Thank God he hadn't arrived a few minutes earlier.

After he left, I looked at Elijah and said, "Never encountered another person, huh?"

"You're never going to let me live this down, are you?"

I shook my head. "Nope."

I wished I could slow down time to draw out the weekend a little longer, but it seemed to pass by in the blink of an eye. Elijah must've tipped off my parents that I'd said yes because they threw a barbecue to rival all others to celebrate the Miracle twins getting engaged.

Later that night, tucked away in the peace and quiet of our bedroom, I alternated between watching Elijah sleep and staring at the gorgeous ring he placed on my finger.

"I'm the luckiest girl in the whole world, and my life couldn't possibly get any better," I whispered.

Chapter Twenty

Elijah

THE FOLLOWING SUNDAY, MAEGAN AND I HEADED NORTH after brunch to see my parents. As predicted, the radiation was starting to take its toll on my dad, and he was often asleep when I called home to check on him. Mom assured me the radiation oncologist said it was normal and good for him to rest as much as he could. I also knew Dad couldn't fully rest knowing there were things around the house that needed done to prepare for oncoming winter, so Jack and I agreed to do all his usual chores around the house.

"I'm not too proud to accept your help, boys," Dad said when we showed up ready to work.

Of course, Mom was only interested in seeing the beloved ring on Maegan's hand. "Oh my goodness!" she exclaimed. "It looks perfect. If I didn't know better, I'd say it was meant to be yours all along."

"I can't tell you how much your trust means to me, Brenda." Maegan choked up a bit then giggled to cover it up. "I will treasure it forever."

"It's *your* ring now, Maegan. Maybe someday you'll be giving the ring to Elijah's and your son to give to the woman he loves."

Maegan smiled, but only those who knew her best would

recognize it didn't quite reach her eyes. "That would be lovely," she said.

Maegan's inability to produce biological Markham offspring wasn't something that came to my mind unless she brought it up. We said we would have a family, and we would, but not in the way my mom was dreaming for us. I should've told her sooner when I knew I had fallen in love with Maegan and wanted to build a life with her. Not because I needed my mom's blessing or understanding, but to save Maegan from uneasy moments like this one. Accepting she wasn't going to carry my child was one thing, but openly discussing it with people she didn't know very well was totally different. I placed my hand on the back of Maegan's neck and felt her relax beneath my touch. I would make this right and have a private conversation with my mom before we left. I knew without a doubt my mom and dad would accept and love any child we adopted.

"As for you," Mom said, turning toward me, "since you boys so lovingly volunteered to do things around the farm today..." Her words trailed off as she pulled a folded piece of paper from her apron pocket. I groaned, and Dad cackled in his recliner. "I thought of a few things I'd like done," she paused for dramatic effect, "if it's not too much trouble."

"Of course, it's not too much trouble," Maegan said, patting my shoulder. "Elijah would love to help out."

"Freckles," I said under my breath but loud enough for Mom to hear, "you've never seen my mom's lists, so you have no idea what you're signing me up for."

"Pooh Bear," Maegan said sweetly, "we both know you and Jack are going to cross off every item on the list to make your mama happy, so you might as well stop grumbling and get to work. The days are getting shorter and shorter."

Dad cackled harder and slapped the arm of his recliner. "Keeper!"

"Pooh Bear?" I asked, hooking my arm around her shoulder and pulling her against my body so I could kiss the top of her head.

"That's new."

"It's absolutely precious," Jack said, entering the house. "I'm never letting you live it down either."

I groaned because he wasn't joking. From that point on, he would find a way to call me Pooh Bear and wouldn't stop until one of us died. "Where are my nephews?" I asked.

"They had a birthday sleepover last night. Daphne is picking them up in a few hours and bringing them over." Jack smiled crookedly. "Which means we can get a jumpstart on Mom's list without you using my sons as an excuse to dodge work."

"Hey, I'm appalled you view me tossing the football with your sons as anything other than me bonding with my nephews. Such a cynic, Jack."

"I'll take the list, Mom," Jack said valiantly. "As oldest, I'll divide the chores up evenly."

It was my turn to scoff. "You're not fooling anyone, Jack." I looked at Mom and gave her the smile I used as a kid when I hoped to get myself out of trouble. "I'll take the list, Mom. You can trust me to make sure everything gets done to your standards." The smile didn't work then, and it sure as hell didn't work for me as an adult.

Mom handed the list to Maegan. "There's a new sheriff in town, boys."

"Let's see what we have here," Freckles said, unfolding the to-do list. "Oh, I know how much Elijah loves cleaning out gutters." She was loving every second of the power Mom gave her. "I bet Jack can't wait to power wash the siding on the detached garages." Maegan pressed her finger over her pursed lips briefly and hummed. "I think raking leaves is too big for either one of them to finish by themselves."

"I agree," Mom said. "They can start raking them together after they finish their solo tasks."

"It's always best to admit defeat, fellas," Dad said cheerfully from his chair. "Brenda, I think I'm going to have a whole new appreciation for the wraparound porch on this old house."

"So you can move around to enjoy the warmth of the sun?" Mom asked him.

"No, so I can move around and supervise our knuckleheads," Dad said with a snort. "I remember how chore days went around here. All that goofing around when you didn't think I was watching you."

"Come on, Dad," Jack groaned. "We're not little kids anymore."

"I think there are some things men never outgrow." Dad smiled crookedly. "The love of a good woman, and the desire to make mischief now and again." He had a point, so there was no reason to argue.

"To reward your hard work, I'm going to be making homemade applesauce," Mom said then looked at Maegan. "Would you like to give me a hand?"

"I'd love to." Maegan walked over to Dad's recliner and handed the list to him. "It looks like you're in charge of making sure the work gets done to your standards." Jack and I grumbled even more, making Dad laugh harder.

"This is going to be a great day," Dad said cheerfully as he slowly stood up.

He seemed to really enjoy barking out orders from the porch, sounding more and more like himself with every remark. I pretended to grumble and gripe, but I was loving it on the inside. The weather was perfect, and I couldn't ask for better company either. I especially had fun when I accidentally dropped leaves and dirt on top of Jack's head when he was stacking bales of hay around the foundation as added insulation against the oncoming cold weather.

"No gaps between the bales, Jack," Dad called from the porch. "I don't want frozen pipes this winter."

"Yes, sir," Jack said, stifling the grin trying to spread across his face.

"Elijah, I think an eight-year-old could trim the shrubs

straighter than you're doing right now," Dad teased from the porch when I'd finished one chore and started another.

"I was thinking about shaping them into animals," I fired back. "Snarling lions or something."

"You want to go to bed without supper?" Dad asked.

"No, sir," I replied humbly.

"Then less yapping and more cutting."

I glanced up to see him grinning from ear to ear, and it helped ease the ache in my heart whenever I saw how weak he'd grown over the past few weeks. Jack got ribbed for not being able to handle a screwdriver properly when he fixed the screen door on the side of the house, and Dad teased me after I nearly tripped over my own feet when a snake slithered out from under the porch.

"Haven't outgrown that, huh?" he asked.

"No, he hasn't," Maegan said, stepping onto the porch carrying a tray with three glasses of iced tea on it. "Did Elijah tell you about our recent hike in the woods, Jack?"

"No, he didn't," Dad said, patting the rocking chair beside him. "And call me Dad." I couldn't hear Maegan's soft voice, but I knew the instant she told Dad about my bellowing the word snake like the dumb jock you know will be the first to die in a horror movie.

I was so fucking grateful when Daphne finally arrived with my nephews. All joking aside, I couldn't wait to toss the football with them in the yard. Both boys played peewee football with seasons starting soon. Maegan and I had talked about coming to as many of their games as we could fit into our schedule.

I pretended to go down easy when they ganged up and tackled me. Okay, I didn't have to pretend much because I was sore all over from climbing the ladder and working around the yard. It was the absolute best kind of ache because I could look around and see the fruits of my labor. When we went inside to wash up for supper, I was overwhelmed with the scents I associated with home—cinnamon, apples, and fresh bread. It smelled like love.

"You look beat," Maegan said, stepping into the bathroom just as I was drying my hands. She closed the door and walked into the circle of my arms.

"What's wrong?" I asked, hearing her sniffle against my shirt.

"I broke the news to your mom that I wouldn't be bringing any little Elijah's into the world."

"Freckles, I should've told her months ago." I held her tighter, rocking her back and forth. I wanted to believe my mom was caring and compassionate when she heard the news, and Maegan's tears had nothing to do with something Mom said.

"No, I'm glad you didn't so I could judge her reaction for myself. Now, I won't have to wonder if she's just making nice to cover her disappointment."

"Maegan, you couldn't disappoint anyone if you tried." I tilted her head back and looked into the face I adored with everything I had. "What did she say?"

"It wasn't what she said so much as the look on her face," Maegan told me. "Her eyes and smile were filled with compassion and love, not pity and disappointment. Then she said, 'Thank God your treatments worked, and we're standing here together.' Then she told me biology didn't always make a family which reminded me of how you'd said there was more than one way to become a mother. It reminded me how lucky I am."

"These are happy tears then?" I asked, brushing them away with my thumbs. "I admit I haven't learned to read tears as well as I thought, and before you get sassy with me, women's tears should be classified as a language all their own."

Maegan giggled then buried her head against my chest. "I love you, Pooh Bear."

I groaned. "Really, Freckles. That's what you're going to call me? Not something representing my manly prowess?"

"I prefer to think about your cuddliness, and I don't want other women to be thinking about your 'manly prowess.' I'm a bit of a cavewoman myself, Pooh Bear."

"You're telling me to get used to the silly name."

"That's what I'm telling you."

"Okay," I said, looking into her eyes. "I'll put up with just about anything for you, but don't abuse my soft heart when it comes to you."

"Never," she replied, crossing her heart.

We were the last ones to enter the dining room, and I felt curious eyes volleying between us as we made our way to the table. It was obvious Maegan had been crying, and everyone besides Mom thought I was to blame.

"Do I need to take him back behind the woodshed, Freckles?" Dad asked.

Maegan giggled and leaned into me where I sat beside her at the table. "We weren't fighting, Dad. These are tears of joy, not sorrow." I thought it was only partially true, but I wasn't about to argue with her. "I'm such a lucky girl to have all of you in my life."

"I think we're the lucky ones," I told her.

Dinner was a delicious beef stew and homemade rolls with homemade applesauce that was still warm, just how I liked it.

"I will never be able to eat applesauce from a jar again," Maegan said in awe after her first bite. "The process was easier than I thought it would be too."

"It just takes time, patience, and love," Mom said with a warm smile.

"Maegan, have you guys picked out a wedding date?" Daphne asked.

"Not yet," Maegan replied.

"Having second thoughts?" Jack teased.

"Never," Maegan said seriously, shaking her head. "My brother is also recently engaged, and we don't want to encroach on one another's special day."

I snorted. "For once."

Maegan laughed then told my family about her rivalry with her twin brother. "So, you can see Elijah isn't exaggerating."

"Your mother must be so excited, Maegan," Dad said.

"She is ecstatic and claims to be the luckiest mother in the entire world because she will have the most amazing sons-in-law."

"I can't wait to meet your family, Freckles," Dad said. "They sound like a hoot." I expected my dad to be a little hesitant about Milo's drag queen alter ego, but it only made him laugh. He thought the Dolly and Kenny duet was an awesome touch.

After dinner, Jack and I somehow got roped into doing dishes too. When we were finished, I went looking for my lady because it was time we headed home to prepare for the next week. I found her fast asleep in Dad's recliner while the rest of the family enjoyed the crisp, cool air.

I heard the front door open, but not as loud as it was before Jack greased the damn thing with WD-40. "Elijah, can I see you in the kitchen?" Mom whispered.

I ran my hand over Maegan's hair then followed my mom out of the room. "I'm sorry I didn't tell you sooner, Mom," I said, guessing the reason for our chat. "I should've spared Maegan the heartache of having to tell you."

"Maegan isn't the kind of girl who wants or needs you to fight her battles for her," Mom said gently. "I didn't call you in here to give you a hard time. I wanted to say I am so proud of you. To hear how Maegan speaks about you just makes this mother's heart swell with pride."

"I don't see it as doing anything spectacular. I just love her."

"That, my son, is why you're so damn special."

Mom bagged up containers of leftovers for us to take home with us while I woke up my sleeping beauty. She looked surprised she'd fallen asleep in the recliner when Dad told her she could give it a test drive.

"No wonder your dad won't part with this thing," Maegan said, stretching. "One minute we were talking and the next thing I know, you're shaking me awake."

"Ready to go home?" I asked.

"Pooh Bear, I am home anytime I'm with you," she said adoringly while accepting my outstretched hand to assist her out of the chair.

Okay, maybe the new nickname wasn't so bad.

Chapter Twenty-One

Maegan

MY ANNUAL CONSULTATION WITH MY ONCOLOGIST WAS scheduled for after the first of the year, but my lack of energy and exhaustion drove me to call and move it up. I could chalk up my symptoms to having a hectic summer and the excitement of solving the mystery of Anthony's disappearance, but in my heart, I knew something else was going on. My life was always hectic, and not only was I used to the chaos, I loved it. I thrived on it. Lately, it was all I could do to stay up past 9 p.m. Falling asleep in Jack's recliner was the deciding factor. Sure, it was surprisingly comfy, but I wasn't the kind of person who could easily fall asleep away from home.

I knew Elijah noticed my growing fatigue, and I knew he was afraid to say something because speaking it out loud made it a real problem. It's why I called Dr. Lovett's office on Monday morning and snagged the first available appointment which luckily was Wednesday afternoon, so I didn't have to ask anyone to shuffle their plans to accommodate me. The request would've been met with questions I didn't want to answer.

I had many people in my life who would've come with me to

offer moral support, but it was something I wanted to do on my own rather than worrying people needlessly. Fatigue didn't mean my cancer was back, it just meant my body was going through changes. Dr. Lovett was the best person to work up a full blood panel to help determine what I might be facing. I'd only been under her care for a few years, but I really liked the time she dedicated to her patients. I never felt rushed when I had questions or concerns.

My first stop was the lab where they took blood samples to run various tests. In most cases, Dr. Lovett had results before she entered my room. On some occasions, she had to wait a day or so for additional results to come back. I hoped I fell into the former category rather than the latter. A wave of nerves made me nauseous, and I regretted not telling anyone about my visit. I considered myself to be an independent, strong woman, but I wasn't ashamed to admit I'd love to be holding Elijah's hand right about then. Luckily, Dr. Lovett swept into the room before I could get too worked up.

"Maegan," she said in her typical cheerful voice. Her red curls bounced as she crossed the room to shake my hand. "I didn't expect to see you for a few more months. Is everything okay?"

"You tell me," I said wryly. "By now you probably already have my blood test results."

Dr. Lovett sat down at the computer and wiggled the mouse to wake it up. "Let's see what we have back," she said while typing quickly. "In the meantime, tell me what prompted your visit."

"It's mostly fatigue and lack of energy," I told her. "I'm sleeping eight to nine hours each night and waking up feeling as tired as when I went to bed. I'm taking naps on days off when before I never needed to, and it just feels like I'm chasing my tail."

"Changes to your diet?" she asked while searching the screen.

"Nothing drastic."

"Your sodium levels are a bit high, potassium looks to be a little low, but other than that everything looks really good. Your blood counts look wonderful, so I'm confident you don't have so much as an infection right now. Are you in any physical pain?"

"Pain? No. My breasts feel achy and tender though."

"Like you're ovulating?"

It felt like she'd stabbed me in the heart. "It's been so long I can't remember, but I don't recall breast pain or tenderness. Besides," I said, releasing a shaky breath, "that's not really a concern I would have now."

"Says who?"

"The doctors who told my parents I'd never have children," I said slowly.

She got a screwed-up look on her face as she clicked the mouse, typed, and looked at the information on her screen.

"My chemo drugs threw me into menopause when I was seventeen," I told her. "The doctors told my mom it meant my ovaries were no longer functioning."

Dr. Lovett sighed. "Thank goodness we've come a long way in the past thirteen years. Maegan, while I don't doubt the chemotherapy threw you into menopause, it is not uncommon for ovaries to start working again years later. There are a lot of factors to consider when telling a young lady she might never have children. The first thing is knowing which chemo drugs cause permanent infertility and which ones lessen or delay your ability to have kids. The second thing is the age and overall health of the patient prior to treatment. You were a healthy, vital, seventeen-year-old young lady. The drugs you took back then were newer, and the long-term data wasn't available. I think it's quite possible your ovaries are at least partially functioning."

"What?" I asked in shock. "You mean… I could be pregnant? I haven't taken birth control all these years. I mean, until Elijah, I never had unprotected sex, but… Oh my God. Is that really a possibility?"

"Well, it very well could be, so I'm going to hand you a little cup in a minute to see if that's the case. If not, I'm going to run additional tests on the blood we withdrew to see if there's estrogen in your blood. If so, I'm going to recommend you see your gynecologist. There are many places you could fall on the spectrum between fertile and in-fertile, and I don't want to give you bad advice. Okay?" I nodded. "I won't have the estrogen results today, but I will have them back by to-morrow evening. I'll call you." I nodded again because speaking was beyond my capability. "Time to pee in a cup." Dr. Lovett reached into a drawer and pulled out the plastic cup and sanitizing wipes.

My hand shook so bad when I accepted it from her, and I nearly dropped the cup in the toilet when I sat down to give the sample. I managed to pull myself together while waiting for the results.

"Well, I don't know if this is good or bad news, but you are not pregnant at this moment."

"A bit of both," I said honestly. "I want very much to have a baby, but I want to plan and prepare for the pregnancy."

"Maegan, if you don't want an unplanned pregnancy, I would err on the side of caution and use condoms until we know exactly what's going on with your body."

"Yes, that makes sense." Elijah wasn't going to like it, but he'd do what was best for me. Then it dawned on me I'd need to confess about my doctor visit, and he would be upset I kept my fears a secret from him. That was much worse than a thin layer of latex between us. He'd see my silence as lack of trust and wouldn't appreciate my attempt to save him from worrying needlessly. If the situation were reversed, I'd feel the same way. "I look forward to hearing from you tomorrow."

I can't remember much about the drive back to Blissville besides stopping at a pharmacy two towns over to buy magnum condoms. My fog evaporated when I got back into town because I couldn't al-low myself to get my hopes up and daydream about things that might never happen, especially since Books and Brew was hosting my fa-vorite event of the year.

I arrived in plenty of time to avoid suspicion about my afternoon activities. I put on my favorite friendly witch costume and made sure everything was set up in the three distinct areas for our Halloween celebration.

"Hello," Milo said in his Mrs. Doubtfire voice. I turned around and sure enough, he'd chosen to dress as the lovable movie character for his part in the festivities. "Are we ready, my dear?" Even though he was missing his usual night to perform as Peach, he still got to dress up and have fun.

Our Books, Brew, and Boo Bash kept growing in popularity to the point we needed to think about renting a bigger space in the future. It started out with about five kids, and we were now pushing seventy-five precocious kids ranging in age from two to thirteen. They dressed in costume, and we broke them up into categories by age so we could make sure we provided age-appropriate snacks and games. Each age group was given a Halloween-themed book that Milo or I read to them while they enjoyed their snack. Moms and dads who also attended in costume received a free beverage and a pastry. It was a fun night for everyone.

I looked up as Elijah's boss came through the door with his five kids. At least, I thought it was Gabe under the Captain America costume. I knew damn well Josh picked that out for him because he must call Gabe a dozen or more nicknames, all of them starting with the word captain. "Hey, guys," he said, looking a little frazzled.

"Where's your husband, Gabe?" I asked. "He left you to wrestle five kids into their costumes all by yourself?"

"Of course not," Josh said, entering the store with flare. Josh, continuing with the superhero theme had dressed as The Flash. "There's no way I'd miss Darius, Mateo, and Rochelle's first Halloween party as members of our family." Darius was dressed as T'Challa from Black Panther, Mateo was dressed as Superman, sweet Rochelle was rocking a Wonder Woman costume, and Dylan and Destiny were dressed as the Wonder Twins. It was clear the family didn't have an allegiance to either DC Comics or Marvel, which I found endearing. They liked what they liked. Josh looped his arm around my neck and hugged me. "Thank you so much for altering our reservation from two kids to five. I had no idea we'd be expanding our family this quickly when we decided to adopt again."

"It's my pleasure," I said sincerely. "Besides, no one messes with The Hairfather."

Josh threw his head back and laughed. "I'm going to put that on my business cards."

"Are things going well?" I asked, noting the tired look in his eyes.

"As well as can be expected," he replied. "Three kids basically have been thrust into a home full of strangers. Rochelle doesn't want to be separated from Darius for any reason, so school mornings are interesting to say the least. Then there's the nightmares—" He broke off and swallowed hard. "I hate humanity sometimes, Mae." Darius looked up and smiled at something Gabe said to the five of them. "But then that happens, and I know those kids are exactly where they are wanted and needed."

"Yes, they are."

More kids and their parents were arriving, so we started to divide them into age groups. I glanced up when Elijah walked through the door wearing a thunderous expression while he searched the room for me. Had he somehow found out about my doctor appointment? No, it wasn't possible, so something else must've upset him.

"Um, let me take over here, and you see what's wrong with Elijah," Memphis said.

"Okay." I tilted my head toward the entrance to Curious Things knowing Elijah would follow me to the office. The store was closed, so we'd have all the privacy we needed. I expected him to say something right away, but he just paced from one end of the small room to the other.

He finally stopped and pinned me with dark, hurt eyes. "There has to be an explanation. This is my Freckles for crying out loud."

"I'm sure there is, and if you tell me what's bothering you, I might help you find it."

"I wanted to surprise you with some flowers. I knew how tired you've been lately and thought you might like to see something pretty and festive when you got inside your SUV after your event tonight." He must've seen the bag with the box of condoms inside. Knowing his history with Brandy, his mind must've started jumping to all kinds of terrible conclusions.

"Elijah, there is an explanation," I said reaching for his hands. "It's possibly the best kind of explanation. A miracle really," I said. *So much for not getting my hopes up.* "I didn't buy those condoms to have sex with someone else. I bought them because I'm going to need you to start wearing them until I get some test results back."

"Maegan, this is no way sounds like the best possible situation," he said wryly.

"You're not going to catch anything from having unprotected sex from me," I said, reaching up to tweak his nipple.

"That wasn't what I meant, Freckles. I resent anything coming between us, including a thin layer of latex."

"Okay, but you'll need to explain to my father if you accidentally get me pregnant."

Silence. Blinking. Pulse pounding at his temple.

"What's that now?"

"Elijah, I know you haven't missed how fatigued I've been these past few months. I've seen the worry in your eyes when I wake up after a nap. I moved up my appointment with my oncologist from January to today so she could run some blood tests."

"You did this without telling me?" The dark scowl from earlier returned. "You thought your cancer had returned and kept it from me?"

"Elijah," I said, reaching for him. He stepped back out of reach and turned his back on me to face my office door. "I didn't think my cancer had necessarily come back, but I knew something was going on with me. Dr. Lovett runs extremely thorough blood panels, and I knew she'd find any abnormalities. I needed to know what I was dealing with before I told you."

He spun back around, looking crushed and lost. "And?"

"She didn't find any abnormalities, but after talking to her about my symptoms, she said it sounded like I was ovulating." I began shaking all over just thinking about the possibility. "She's running additional tests to see if estrogen is present in my blood. If so, she's referred me to my gyn—" The rest of my words died because Elijah squeezed me in the tightest hug. I patted his shoulders frantically, so he'd loosen his grip.

"How, Freckles? I thought the doctors said you would never have your own babies."

I repeated the conversation I had with Dr. Lovett word for word. "Please don't get your hopes up, Elijah. Dr. Lovett explained there are many places I could land on the spectrum between infertile and fertile. I can only tell you for certain I am not pregnant right now."

"Freckles, I'm afraid to be happy about the possibility. I don't want you to think I've been lying to you all along about my desire to adopt children with you, nor do I want you to think I'll be upset if your original diagnosis is confirmed. I want you just as you are, and the kids will just be a bonus, regardless if we created them or adopted them. Do you believe me?"

There was a light knock on the door then Milo poked his head around. He narrowed his eyes when he saw my tears, so I flashed him a happy smile. "I'll be right there, Milo."

"Okay," he said hesitantly and shut the door.

"Can we talk about this more when we get home? I have a bunch of kids waiting for me."

"Absolutely," Elijah said. "Not until after you have a relaxing bath." He looked at his feet for a second and the solemn expression in his eyes when they returned to mine gutted me. "I'm so sorry I even thought for a second you would—" I cut him off by kissing his lips.

"You wouldn't have jumped to those conclusions if I'd been honest with you and told you about my appointment. I want you to know I deeply regretted my decision while I was waiting for Dr. Lovett to come in. I realized wanting you there to hold my hand doesn't make me weak, it makes me strong because I can admit when I need some-one to help shoulder life's worries. We'll both chalk this up to a lesson learned and not speak of it again."

Elijah nodded then kissed me like he hadn't seen me in years instead of hours. "How long does this little party last?"

"Two hours. Why don't you hang around with Gabe and get a glimpse of what your future will look like?"

"Sounds like a good idea. Do I get a free beverage and snack?"

"Did you wear a costume?"

"I dressed as a police detective who's packing a big gun."

"Maegan," Milo yelled through the door. "We're minutes away from total anarchy."

"I'll see you and your big gun later," I said, planting a quick kiss on him and darting out the door. I was grateful to have the conversation started but wished it had come about under better circumstances.

"Are you okay?" Milo asked when I caught up to him.

"Better than I've ever been in my life," I said, throwing my arms around his neck and hugging him tight. "I can't take you seriously when you look like Mrs. Doubtfire though, so we'll talk later."

We walked into the bookstore together, and the kids started clapping excitedly. No matter how many times I told myself not to get my hopes up, I would cling to the bud of hope blossoming in my heart until I no longer had a reason to believe.

Chapter Twenty-Two

Elijah

"**G**OOD MORNING, PARTNER," ADRIAN SAID WHEN I arrived at work. "It's a rare occurrence that I arrive before you do."

"I overslept," I said sheepishly.

Adrian cocked a brow. "You never oversleep."

"I'm not late, Chicken Whisperer," I said, earning an eye roll. "I'm just not as early as usual." Maegan felt even friskier than normal that morning, and I would've been a horrible person had I not taken care of my woman before sending her off to work. Of course, I wasn't telling him that part. It was my own damn fault for thinking I could just rest my eyes for a few minutes before getting in the shower. I woke up thirty minutes later.

"Captain is looking for you."

"Already?"

"He doesn't look happy either."

"Why does this feel like I'm getting called into the principal's office?" I joked while racking my brain for the reasons I could be in trouble.

"Markham," Gabe called out firmly. I jerked my head toward the captain's office and found him standing in the doorway with his arms crossed over his chest and wearing the surliest expression I'd ever seen on him. "My office, please." He turned and went back inside his office.

"Fuck," I whispered. "You weren't kidding, Adrian."

"What'd you do, partner? Did you forget to update us about the psychopathic biker gang leader with a vendetta, or is there a new asshole coming out of the woodwork?"

"No. I have no idea what this about, Adrian," I said, shaking my head. I looked up to see Gabe had returned to the doorway, and his expression was even more thunderous. "Shit. I got to go." The captain walked back in his office when he saw I was finally doing what he'd asked—demanded—the first time. "My apologies, sir," I said once I walked into his office. I saw the faintest tilt at the corner of his mouth.

"I know all about Adrian's penchant for ribbing his partners and gossiping." He nodded to the door behind me. "Close it, please."

"Uh, sure." I closed the door and took a seat across from him. "What's going on, Captain? You sound...pissed."

"I'm fucking furious, Detective. I can't recall the last time I was this angry."

"At me?" I asked. "I can't think of anything I've done to cause you to be so angry."

"Damn it. I'm fucking this up all to hell." The captain took a few calming breaths then started over. "I'm furious on your behalf, Elijah. I am not furious at you."

"On my behalf?" I asked, sounding as confused as I felt.

"How well do you know and like your former police captain?"

"Well, it was a much bigger department than the one we have here, so we weren't as friendly. The captain didn't attempt to know any of us outside our jobs, and we returned his attitude."

"Did you think he was a competent leader?" I opened my mouth to respond, but Gabe cut me off with a wave of his hand. "I think he's a fucking idiot who doesn't value the lives of the men and women working under him—past or present."

Uh oh. That didn't sound so good for me. "What's happened?"

"So, the man didn't call and speak to you directly?"

"No, sir."

"Good," Gabe replied, nodding his head sharply. "I asked him to allow me the courtesy to have this discussion with you first."

"He honored your request, sir."

"Captain Barker called my cell phone last night while I was attending the Books, Brew, and Boo Bash with my husband and children. I wasn't going to answer it because I fear Josh more than anything, but I worried your life was in imminent danger."

I relaxed a little in my seat. "Can I assume by the delayed conversation the phone call wasn't to warn you Axel was spotted heading south down I-71?"

"Do I detect a tone, Detective?"

"Not intentionally, sir."

"Good, because I get enough of it at home from my husband." Gabe scrubbed his hand over his face. "Listen, I didn't tell you about the conversation I had with Barker last night because I was too angry, and I wanted to be calm when we discussed his proposal."

"Proposal?" My tension returned tenfold.

"Quite honestly, I wanted to tell him to go fuck himself, but I can't make the decision on your behalf. Well, I could in this case, but I respect you too damn much."

"You're making me nervous," I admitted.

"I'm just going to repeat the conversation I had with him, and let you make the best decision for yourself." I nodded. "Barker told me the missing witness, Sonya Wilson, and her family were found."

"Dead?" I asked. Anger, frustration, and disgust washed over me when Gabe nodded. "Sonya was a young, confused woman who wanted so desperately to be loved. She'd had enough of his abuse and wanted a fresh start for herself and her family. They promised her witness protection for herself and her family if she testified. Gabe, they were kept in police custody to ensure their safety."

"The safe house was compromised."

"Or the officers on duty were," I added. "I knew she didn't flee into the night with her parents and younger siblings."

"There was the slim possibility Axel paid her off so she could start over someplace new," Gabe said. I shook my head. "Yeah, I didn't think so either, but I hoped it was the case."

"Can their deaths be tied to Axel?"

Gabe shook his head. "It was a very clean snatch and grab with no evidence left behind at the safe house or at the crime scene. This was done by someone with more skill, precision, and patience than Axel possesses."

"He hired someone to do it for him," I said to myself.

"It would seem because he's still living the clean life. The surveillance hasn't even turned up a single night of drunken behavior. He only goes to his legitimate job, church, and his mother's house for dinner every Sunday night."

"Bullshit," I said. "There must be secret tunnels beneath those places. A guy like Axel Washington doesn't just stop running drugs and guns. He didn't kill off Sonya and her family to start a new life working for pennies compared to his previous weekly haul of cash, and he didn't suddenly find religion. He fucking hates his mother. Did anyone check to see if she's even alive? Has she been seen in public? If not, he's killed her, buried her in the basement, and is using her house as his front."

"Your captain said you'd feel this way."

"About that," I said. "What the fuck does any of this have to do with me? I did my part. I got them the evidence they needed to put the bastard away."

"I was hoping this would be your reaction."

"What other reaction would I have? What's going on? What did Barker say that has you so angry?"

"He called and asked me to loan you out to his department so you could resume your undercover role and lure Axel back into his old life too."

"Barker didn't think to ask me first if this was something I'd be willing to do?"

"His exact words were 'Elijah was made for this job. He understands the sacrifices it takes to bring criminals like Axel Washington to justice.' Basically, he implied you would jump at the chance to return to undercover work, and I was the only one standing in your way. It's why he called me first to see if I would be willing to spare you."

"What did you say?" I asked.

"I told the arrogant fucker I don't presume to know your wishes, nor should he. I also reminded him of his duty to look out for the people serving beneath him. Taking advantage of their willingness to make those sacrifices is the same as signing a death warrant. Make no mistake about it, you'd be walking into a trap for which there would be no escape, Elijah."

I sat there stunned for a minute or so. I had made *many* sacrifices, both as a soldier and a police officer. I didn't regret my choices, but undercover work wasn't the life I wanted for myself anymore. Besides, my feelings weren't the only ones to consider. It had been easy to risk my life in undercover work when I didn't have someone waiting for me at home. Some might say I had a death wish because I'd thrown myself into the underground world with gusto. Captain Barker had based his assumptions on my actions while working for him, but that Elijah Markham no longer existed, and I wasn't a lone wolf anymore. Maegan was my home, my heart, and my future. There was no fucking way I would commit to doing something which could jeopardize our relationship without discussing it with her first. Also, I had my family back. There was no way I was putting my parents through that kind of stress because Captain Barker couldn't control the corruption within his police force. After weighing it out, was there anything to consider or discuss?

"What are you thinking, Elijah?" Gabe asked, breaking into my thoughts.

"I want Axel Washington to pay for the crimes I know he committed. He needs to be held accountable for the things I saw him do, and the things he hired others to do. It makes me fucking sick to know he's walking the streets."

"I understand," Gabe said, sounding resigned as he broke eye contact to look at his hands.

"But, I don't see how my death will bring Axel to justice." Gabe's head jerked up, and his eyes locked on mine once more. "Even if I captured him killing me on video or audio, the evidence would just turn up missing again. What good would it do? Captain Barker need to come up with a plan that doesn't include me."

"Those were my thoughts exactly, but I didn't want to influence your decision. Had you wanted to go, I would've permitted it."

"That means a lot to me, Captain."

"Now, which one of us calls Barker and tells him to go fuck himself?"

I snorted. "It needs to come from me." I pulled my cell phone out of my pocket and dialed his number. I pressed the button to turn on my speakerphone and relaxed in my seat while waiting for him to answer.

"Elijah, thanks for getting back to me so soon, although to be honest, I expected to hear from you last night after your captain discussed my proposal with you. How soon can you be here? I need to—"

"I'm not coming," I said firmly, interrupting him.

"What? How many detectives does a small town need?" Captain Barker snorted like he'd said the funniest thing in the world. "Is cow tipping still a big thing?" I hoped like hell he never found out about the chicken snatching that went on over the summer. "Come on, Elijah. You know you miss playing with the big boys." I nearly laughed out loud when Gabe silently flipped Barker off.

"It's not the size of the police force that matters, Captain; it's how you use it." I glanced up and saw Gabe smirk.

"I'm not sure I follow, Elijah."

"Let me explain in a way you will understand. I am grateful you acknowledged the sacrifices I made while working under your command. I am also humbled you think I could single-handedly bring down Axel Washington for a second time *and* live to tell about it. My survival did factor into your schemes, right?"

"Of course," he scoffed. "I had no intention of sending you to your death."

"That's just what you'd be doing. You told me Axel blames my undercover persona for the reason he got caught, and his hatred grows for me every day he goes without making a drug or gun deal. Not to mention how cranky he is without his daily massages at one of his illegal parlors. It's a recipe for my death, and I have no desire to engage in a suicide mission."

Captain released a short, frustrated huff. "Well, I won't pretend I'm not disappointed in your answer."

"And I won't pretend I'm not disappointed my life has so little meaning to you."

"I'm sorry you feel that way."

"Likewise, Captain. I think I've said all I care to about this matter. In the future, I would prefer you call me directly instead of going through Captain Roman-Wyatt."

"You won't hear from me again, Elijah. Take care of yourself and watch your back. You never know when demons from your past might rear their ugly heads and destroy your happy new life," he ominously said before disconnecting the call.

I stared at my phone for several seconds before I looked at Gabe. "Did he just threaten me?"

"I took it as a threat."

"So did I."

"Elijah, you let me worry about the situation with Axel

Washington from now on. I have connections, and I promise you we won't be kept in the dark."

"Thank you, but I can't—"

"I'm not asking you to turn this over to me; I'm ordering you to do so as your commanding officer. Do you trust me?"

"With my life." *And Maegan's.* My decision to keep the situation from her hadn't changed, and my reasoning remained the same even if a small voice called me a hypocrite and reminded me how it felt when Maegan went to see the oncologist without telling me first.

"Then it's settled. Get back to work. I'm sure somewhere in our town a devious mind is plotting to steal Halloween decorations. You need to be ready."

"You can count on me, Captain." I gave him a jaunty salute which he returned.

"This I know, Detective."

Adrian was waiting anxiously for me in my chair. "Well?"

"Not here." I grabbed my jacket and headed toward the door, knowing he would follow me. "Adrian, we have a serious problem."

"What is it, man?" he asked once we stepped outside the station.

"Colonel Sanders was spotted strolling down Main Street. Better guard your chickens."

"Fuck you, asshole," he said then burst into laughter. "Seriously, partner, what's going on?"

My phone rang, and I saw it was Maegan calling. My heart sped up knowing she most likely had the results from the blood tests from the previous day. "Hey, Freckles. Miss me already?" I tried for a casual tone, but the odd look on Adrian's face said I'd missed the mark.

"Always," she said excitedly. "I have some news. Do you want it over the phone or would you like to hear it in person?"

"I'll be there in five minutes." I hung up without saying goodbye and headed for my beat-up truck instead of Adrian's car. "To be continued, Adrian," I shouted over my shoulder.

Maegan was waiting for me in her office at Curious Things. She tried so hard to keep her face neutral but couldn't pull it off. My Freckles burst into delirious giggles and leapt into my arms. "I have great news, Elijah. Dr. Lovett called and said the estradiol levels in my body are in the normal range. You're going to need to keep using those condoms until I can get in to see my gynecologist. I don't know if birth control is something I should be taking, and I don't want to do anything to ruin our chances of getting pregnant after we get married."

"Freckles, I'm so happy." I held her tight and rested my chin on top of her head.

Maegan pulled back and looked into my eyes. "It's important we don't get our hopes up too high. Just because I'm producing estrogen doesn't mean I have viable eggs. There are still many factors to consider, and I might need assistance conceiving."

"Freckles, I'm up for the challenge all day, any day."

"Oh, I know how willing you are to do your part, but it could involve a sterile cup."

"It doesn't sound as sexy as pinning you down to our mattress and fucking you until you scream in pleasure as I pump your pussy full of—" She covered my mouth with her hand to cut me off. "Too much?" I asked behind her hand.

Maegan nodded. "Having you show up and get me horny wasn't part of my plan when I called you." I loved knowing my dirty talk fired her up, but I respected it wasn't the time or place to act on it. "Are you going to be good now?" I nodded.

By good, I hope she meant a long, toe-curling kiss because it was what the situation called for and what I gave her. When I pulled back, she blinked up at me looking dazed and more desirable than ever before, but I somehow resisted the urge to slide my hand up her skirt.

"I will do whatever it takes to make your dreams come true," I whispered in her ear. "They'll just need to know I won't be entering the little sterile room by myself to jerk off in a cup. I don't want some tacky porn magazine filled with fake tits and tans when I could be looking at you."

"I'll even hold the cup for you." Maegan stood on her tiptoes. "Between my tits as I kneel at your feet."

I groaned pitifully. "Is that the kind of thing you tell a man after you said we can't get up to any naughty business in your office?"

"I'm sorry," Maegan said, but her crafty smile said otherwise. "I do like knowing you'll be thinking about me all day long."

"I think we need to practice the cup holding stunt just in case I am called to action. I'll need to make sure I have excellent aim."

"There's no better time than tonight to start practicing."

I loved the way my Freckles thought. "How soon can you get in to see your doctor?" I asked, trying to steer us back to a safer subject.

"They're booked solid until January, but they've put me on the list to call if there are any cancellations. In the meantime, we…"

"Bag it up," I finished for her.

She patted my chest. "You got it."

It was a very small sacrifice to make when the reward was the joyful gleam in her eyes and hopeful smile on her face.

"I hate to interrupt whatever is going on in there," Jackie Miracle said on the other side of the door, but I had an urgent-sounding message from my daughter. "Is everything okay?"

"This is my cue to leave," I said before I opened the door for Jackie to enter. "Everything is great, Jackie." I kissed her cheek then gave my Freckles a quick peck on the lips. "See you tonight."

I'd almost made it to the door when I heard Jackie's delighted squeal coming from the office followed by her promptly bursting into happy tears. I imagined they were both hugging and crying over the opportunity they never thought they'd have. I looked up to the sky when I walked onto the sidewalk. *If it's not too much to ask, I want a little girl with green eyes, curly blonde hair, and a ton of freckles,* I said to whoever might be listening.

Chapter Twenty-Three

Maegan

I DEBATED HOW MUCH WE WOULD TELL OUR FRIENDS AND FAMILY about the potential changes to my circumstances. On one hand, I didn't want to get everyone's hopes up too high only to find out later I still wouldn't be able to conceive a child. On the other hand, if it did happen, wouldn't it be better if we were surrounded by people to support and love us through our disappointment? Once the decision was made, I had to decide how and when to tell everyone. There had to be a proper pecking order.

My mom was first because she was my mom. Milo heard all the jubilant squealing and sobbing and came rushing in. He joined our celebration because he understood how much the opportunity meant to me. Later that night, I insisted we call Brenda and Jack to tell them the news. I didn't want his parents to feel excluded from our happiness, and they were also overcome with joy for us. Brenda was certain to point out she would love any child Elijah and I raised, but she knew how happy the news made me.

"We should make an announcement at the Halloween party this weekend," Elijah said as we reclined in the bathtub later that evening. I was pleasantly surprised to discover he loved the holiday as much as

I did. "I know we already have costumes, but maybe we change them up a bit."

"Instead of a pirate, you'll be what?" I asked.

"A sperm." I nearly choked on my sip of wine. "Should you be drinking alcohol, Freckles?"

"Elijah, I'm not pregnant, and I'm not trying to get pregnant right now. Drinking alcohol is okay." I leaned and turned my head to look up at him. "Just how the hell would you dress as a sperm?" I had this horrific vision of him wearing a giant sperm costume with his grinning face sticking out of the rounded head.

"I was thinking of drawing a sperm, or twenty, on a T-shirt with the words 'looking for love' beneath my swimmers."

"Instead of a tavern wench, what would I be?"

"An egg, of course," Elijah said in his best *duh* voice. "We can draw some eggs on your T-shirt and then write 'in all the right places' beneath your baby hatchers."

"'Baby hatchers'?"

"You don't think it's catchy?" I shook my head then returned to a comfy position against his chest. "What about the costumes?" he asked.

"Maybe we can find a more discreet way to tell the few people we want to share our news with rather than announce it in a way that's sure to make it to the gossip section of the Blissville Daily News."

"Freckles," Elijah said softly, snaking his arms around to hold me firmly against his chest. "As excited as I am about the possibility of having a baby with you, it's a little like putting the cart before the horse."

"Which one of us are you calling the horse, and is this your way of tempering my excitement?"

Elijah chuckled warmly. "I only meant I want to start planning our wedding. I know you, and there's no way my boys are going to tango with your girls until we're properly wed."

"True," I said. "What do you have in mind?"

"We're going to San Francisco next month to do the final film-ing for *The Paranormal Whisperer*. You know what state is next to California?"

"Oregon? Arizona?"

"Nevada."

"You want us to get married in Vegas?" I asked. "How upset do you think our mothers would be if we did that?"

"They wouldn't be upset; they'd be furious with us, Freckles."

"That's no way to start out a marriage," I chided. "Besides, I need more than a month. How about spring?"

"There are three months we typically associate with spring, Freckles. Which one are you thinking about? Please tell me it's March?"

I shook my head. "Still too chilly and unpredictable."

"April?"

"Too rainy?"

"May?"

"Middle of May sounds like our best option. It's only seven months away."

Elijah grumbled. "Fine. Are we having a church wedding or one here at our home?"

"I prefer here if it's okay with you. I think our back yard would be an amazing place for a wedding. If it rains, we can shuffle furniture around and get married inside. Does that sound okay with you?"

"Sounds perfect," Elijah said, lifting his hands to caress my breasts. "Still tender?"

"Yes, but they don't hurt," I said, wriggling my ass against his hard-on. "Don't stop."

"Never," he whispered huskily in my ear. Then he slid one hand underwater to tease and circle my clit. "Tell me about the kind of wedding you see us having?"

It was harder than hell to concentrate on things like arbors and menus while he played my body like a finely tuned instrument, but I still managed to do it in between gasps, moans, and pleas for more.

"Do you want to hear about the wedding night I envision?" he asked hoarsely. By this time, I was beyond speech. All I could do was undulate my hips and rub against his tormenting finger. "I will strip off your wedding dress and kiss every precious inch of my wife. There won't be anything between us when I finally slide my dick inside your greedy pussy. I will fuck you hard and fast then make love to you soft and slow until you cry out my name. Then I'm going to come deep inside you."

Fireworks burst behind my eyelids as Elijah brought me to a climax with his touch and the vivid picture he painted with his words. Instead of collapsing against him like a limp noodle, I got to my knees and turned around to face him. He was too far gone to get out of the bath, towel off, and suit up for action. I push my wet breasts together and he read exactly what was on my mind.

"Are you sure you're not too sore?"

"I promise."

Elijah stood up so fast the water sloshed over the sides of the tub and splashed onto the floor. He cupped my face, running his thumb over my lips and took turns teasing my nipples as he fucked my tits. It didn't take many thrusts before he painted my chest and chin with his cum. Of course, his inner caveman insisted he rub his dick through his release, massaging it into my skin and marking me as his own. People saw the ring I wore and knew I belonged to him, but in our private moments, he marked me in more personal ways. I loved his possessive nature and all the ways he showed I belonged only to him.

Once we were dried off and in bed, Elijah said, "About those Halloween costumes…"

Two days later, I was in the bathroom putting on makeup for my new costume when I felt a slight trickling between my legs. Even though I hadn't felt it in thirteen years, I recognized it right away. I rushed over to the toilet to confirm my suspicions then called Vanessa.

"What's up, gorgeous?" Vanessa said when she answered.

"Van, I need a big favor."

"What's up?"

"I need a pad. Do you think you could bring one over? I really don't want to send Elijah to the store for them."

"Pad of paper?" she asked.

"Van, I got my period just now."

"What? How's that possible?"

"I planned to tell all of you tonight, but it turned out my menopause wasn't permanent, and my ovaries sparked back to life."

Vanessa hooted and hollered. I could tell she was jumping around. "You're not playing a joke on me, right?"

"I'd never joke about something this serious. Can you please bring me a few pads to tide me over until I can get to the store tomorrow?"

"I'll be there in a jiff. I'll just finish getting ready there if it's okay with you."

"Perfect! It'll be like old times."

Vanessa arrived ten minutes later with a variety of options to choose from. "Wasn't sure if you were talking light flow, heavy flow, liners with wings, or maybe you wanted a little more freedom, so I brought you a few different sizes of tampons."

"Things have changed a lot since the last time I had a period," I said, feeling a bit overwhelmed.

"Speaking of changes," Vanessa said as she looked at the Halloween makeup I'd started to put on. "What happened to your tavern girl outfit? Is she now a zombie tavern girl? I swear, I hope the zombie craze passes sometime soon. Zombie cheerleader, zombie bride, and now you got sucked up in to it too."

"It's not zombie related," I assured her. "Elijah and I decided to wear special costumes for an announcement we plan to make tonight."

"Oh my God. Are you dressing up as an egg and a sperm? You won't be offering any kind of fertilization demonstration, will you?"

"I love the way you think, Van," Elijah said, startling me. "I did, in fact, suggest we dress up as a sperm and an egg, but Maegan doesn't have the same sense of humor as we do."

"I didn't hear you come home," I said, rising up on my tiptoes to kiss him.

Elijah acted like he was sketchy about kissing me with my make-up on, but he couldn't resist temptation. "I guess it doesn't matter if you get any of the goop on me since you'll be painting my face next." Vanessa snorted and I knew her mind had headed straight to the gutter.

"Did you have trouble finding what I needed from the state liquor store in Goodville?"

"That was an extensive list of liquor," Elijah said, eyeing the feminine hygiene products on the vanity. "Um, has something happened?"

"The best thing ever," I said, clapping my hands. "I'm having a period."

"I'll just head to the other bathroom to start getting ready so you guys can talk."

Elijah blinked a few times before he said, "This is a good thing? We're happy?"

"Deliriously so," I assured him. "This means I am truly ovulating. My egg wasn't fertilized so I had a period. This is normal and healthy and good." Elijah held me tight and rocked me back and forth. "Don't worry, Pooh Bear, there's nothing wrong with my hand or mouth."

Elijah snorted. "Maegan, I may be on you like a bee on honey, but it doesn't mean I can't get by for a few days while your body does its thing. I'm not really a savage beast; I just growl and thump my chest like one."

"Fuck like one too," I reminded him.

"So, you called Van to bring you some girlie items, huh? You could've called me, and I would've stopped at the drug store and picked up what you needed. I probably would've needed you to send me a picture of what I was supposed to get."

"You would do that for me?"

"Freckles, I'm not one of those idiots who thinks his dick will shrivel up and fall off if he touches a box of tampons. I'm very comfortable in my masculinity. Expecting you to leave the house to pick things up when I'm already out is a dick move. Rule number one: Love your dick without being a dick."

I snorted. "I don't think I've heard you say that before, but it's very catchy."

"Thank you, Freckles." He kissed the tip of my nose even though I had white costume makeup spread over it. "Ready to continue our transformations?"

Elijah and I decided to change our costumes to Frankenstein and the Bride of Frankenstein and created cute "save the date" cards to hand to our guests letting them know we were getting married on May 18th. We'd send formal invitations later, but this was a fun way to announce our wedding date.

I was thrilled when Elijah's family arrived, and we could officially introduce our families. Jack and Brenda were dressed as the Scarecrow and Dorothy from *Wizard of Oz*. Jack Jr. and Daphne were dressed as Fred and Daphne from *Scooby Doo*. I'd hoped they would bring Isaac and Will but understood they needed a night out without the kids. My parents were dressed as Sandy and Danny from the closing scene in *Grease*. Elijah's dad took one look at Milo and Andy dressed up as Elly May Clampett and Jethro Bodine from *The Beverly Hillbillies* and about lost it.

"We've decided on a wedding date," Elijah said once we had our families in front of us. "I tried to get Maegan to marry me next month when we fly west to film the final segment for *The Paranormal Whisperer*, but she wouldn't agree to it. Something to do with our mothers killing us."

"She's a very wise woman," Brenda said to her son.

Elijah reached into his pocket and pulled out the stack of Save the Date business cards we printed. "The eighteenth of May and not a day later."

Milo and Andy looked at each other and burst into laughter.

"What?" I asked even though I already knew. "There's no way you picked the same weekend."

"March was too cold and unpredictable," Andy said.

"April has too much rain," Milo added.

"May is just right," Elijah said, sounding like Goldilocks. "We had a very similar conversation."

"Well, we can move our date," Milo said gallantly. "It seems like I do everything before Maegan does, so I should let her have this one thing."

"Milo," I growled.

"What? It's true. I was born first, hit puberty first, lost my…um *library* card first, and got engaged first."

"You have such a swelled head it's a wonder you fit through the door," I teased.

"Hey, my swelled head stretched out Mom's baby chute so you could have an easier delivery. My head is misshapen from being stuck in the birth canal while yours is perfectly round. You're welcome."

"Milo!" Mom admonished. "We've only known the Markhams for ten minutes. Maybe you wait a good thirty minutes before you bring up your glorious delivery."

"On Halloween night, no less," Milo told the Markhams. "I'll let you figure out which one of us is the trick and which one is the treat." He blew air kisses then tugged Andy along with him to circulate.

Halloween was my favorite time of the year, and not just because it was also my birthday. People cast off all the reasons they shouldn't do something and lived a little. They wore costumes people wouldn't expect them to wear, and they let themselves feel like a kid again when passing out candy on beggar's night.

"I wasn't sure he was going to make it," Elijah whispered in my ear an hour into the party. I looked at the front door and saw Theo had arrived wearing a pirate costume similar to the one Elijah was originally going to wear. "It's a good thing you painted me green and glued bolts to my neck. I'd hate for Theo to feel bad because I wore the pirate costume better."

"Undoubtedly," I said. "We should go say hello to him."

"I don't think he knows anyone at this party besides Vanessa," Elijah said.

I followed Theo's line of sight, and sure enough, Van stood there still as a statue in her sexy, lady pirate costume as she returned his bold gaze with a raised brow. It was like she dared him to make a move in her direction. Not one to back away from a challenge, Theo headed directly for her. Vanessa pivoted and headed toward the library in the back of the house. I suspected she had a lot to say and didn't want witnesses.

I looked over and saw April and Violet, dressed as Tweedledee and Tweedledum, were whispering to each other in the corner. "I bet they make an announcement of their own soon."

"It looks that way," Elijah said. "Where's Candace?"

"She's in Europe on business. She's bummed she missed the party this year. Candy Apple takes her costumes to the extreme." Then again, Candace was hardcore about everything she did.

"There's always next year. Then again," Elijah said, placing his hand on my flat stomach, "you might not feel like having a big party."

"I'll let Milo throw the party next year."

"Speak of the devil," Elijah said, pointing to my brother heading our way.

"You win, Maegan," he said dramatically.

"What are you—" I reached over and gave him a hard pinch. "You peeked!"

"How could I resist the temptation?" Milo smiled warmly and pulled me into a hug. "Your nursery is as beautiful as you are, and I can't wait until my little niece or nephew is sleeping safely there."

"What kind of theme did you pick?" I asked, fighting the urge to drive over to the house they were moving into the following week.

"Atlantica," Milo said with a smile. "You know how much I've always wanted to be a merman."

"It sounds amazing. I can't wait to see it."

"It is amazing, but the treehouse is unbeatable." Milo hooked his arm around my neck. "Andy and I decided we'll get married in June."

"Am I invited?" I asked jokingly.

"Are you kidding? You're going to be my best girl."

"And you can be my man of honor."

Up above, a door slammed loudly, pulling our attention upward. "Sounds to me like Anthony's had enough partying for one night."

"So it seems," I replied, trying to keep the sadness from my voice.

Anthony's shenanigans caught everyone's attention, but it didn't frighten them into leaving, and the party lasted another few hours before our guests started trickling out.

After everyone left, I sat in the stillness of the living room while Elijah slept soundly upstairs. I should've been exhausted, but I couldn't seem to turn off my brain and came downstairs for a cup of herbal tea. I smelled Anthony's pipe tobacco after my first sip of tea and was glad he'd decided to join me. I knew taking Anthony's ashes to San Francisco to reunite him with Wallace was the right thing to do, but I was going to miss him so much.

"I'll never forget you, Anthony," I vowed, noting the scent got stronger as if he was sitting right beside me on the couch.

Two weeks later, Lyric, his crew, Memphis, the hotel concierge, Anh Yang, and I all went up to the penthouse floors of The Golden Gate Bridge Inn to film the moment when the two spirits were reunited. I don't know what I expected, but there was no obvious paranormal activity to record. There were no moans, dramatic winds, or slamming doors. There was just a peacefulness that washed over the room, letting you know the two men were once again together. An actual shift in the air that made the hair on my arms stand up.

When it was over, I returned to the room I shared with Elijah. "How'd it go?"

"It was peaceful and beautiful," I said in a voice thick with emotion. "Anthony is where he always belonged."

"Come here," Elijah said, opening his arms wide for me.

"It's going to be so quiet around our house now."

"Not for long, Freckles."

Epilogue

Elijah

THE DAY AFTER WE GOT BACK FROM SAN FRANCISCO, Maegan's gynecologist called to say they had a cancellation and asked if Maegan wanted the appointment. They advised her to drink a lot of water because they'd be performing an ultrasound to check out her ovaries. Of course, I wanted to be with her in case they told her less than exciting news. I'd seen plenty of ultrasounds on television shows, so I was prepared for them to squirt the lube on her belly and move the device around. Easy peasy. Then the technician rolled a condom on this wand-like probe and squirted lube on it.

"This might be a little uncomfortable with having a full bladder. Are you ready, Ms. Miracle?"

"As I'll ever be," she said.

Instead of rubbing the wand over her stomach, the ultrasound tech raised the paper blanket draped over Maegan's legs and… *Whoa, Nelly!*

"That's it?" I asked out loud. "The wand isn't going to introduce himself first or at least take her to dinner?"

Maegan and the technician started giggling. Then Maegan let

out a tiny yelp. "No more funny-guy routine. I have to go to the bathroom so bad."

"Not much longer," the tech said. "I'm sorry for the discomfort."

I was sitting up by Maegan's head and couldn't really see the action down below, but I could see the tech moving her left arm around while typing things onto her equipment with her right. Maegan squeezed my hand, letting me know she wasn't having a good time. I felt violated for her.

"A few more pictures and I will let you go to the bathroom," she said and offered a sweet smile to Maegan. "You're doing great."

I dropped an encouraging kiss on her forehead which seemed to help relax her. Once the technician was done, Maegan was allowed to use the restroom.

"When will she have the results?" I asked.

"As soon as Dr. Stephens finishes with her current patient and can look at them. She shouldn't be too long."

"Oh, that's great news."

When Maegan returned, she got dressed and sat on the exam table, staring off like she was a thousand miles away.

"I learned quite a bit from the pamphlets of information they have out in reception. Did you know in some IVF processes they pick out the best eggs and sperm and guide the sperm into the egg? They don't let him choose his own egg."

"He'd probably choose based on looks alone," Mae said. "We don't need the prettiest egg; we need the one most likely to become a baby."

"My swimmers are outraged you think so little of them and are shocked at the self-hate directed at the eggs you're producing. You couldn't produce a bad egg if you tried."

"Hopefully, Dr. Stephens will tell us everything looks good and IVF isn't something we have to worry about right now. It's an amazing process, but so damn expensive."

"I read that too. We'd find a way to make it happen. I'll dip into my retirement account if it's what it takes."

Maegan sucked in a shaky breath. "You'd do that for me?"

"I'd do it for us," I told her.

"I love you, Pooh Bear."

"I love you too, Freckles."

"I think I have a better solution should the need arise," Maegan said. "The deed and mortgage for Bliss House are only in my name. I want to refinance the mortgage once we get married so we both own Bliss House. I know there's a lot of equity in the house, and we could borrow against it for a procedure if we need it."

There was a swift knock on the door then an African American woman with a warm smile entered the room. "Hello, Maegan. How are you?"

"I'm doing good. This is my fiancé, Elijah Markham."

Dr. Stephens shook my hand then looked at Maegan once more. "It looks to me like you're doing excellent," she said then sat in the chair. "I have the blood test results your oncologist sent over and reviewed the ultrasound images. The good news is the timing worked out perfectly to have an ultrasound because you haven't started ovulating for the next cycle, which gives us a better idea what's going on in your body. There's no sign of endometrial issues in your uterus or fallopian tubes, nor do I see any cysts on your ovaries. What I do see are eighteen follicles between the two ovaries, which indicates you have great ovarian reserve." It was like she was speaking a foreign language, but her happy smile said she delivered good news to us.

"What should the count be?" Maegan asked.

"We hope to see between ten to twenty between the two ovaries, so you're right there at the high mark."

"So, you think I'll be able to conceive naturally?"

"Based on your test results and exam, yes. We can either collect a sperm sample from Mr. Markham now, or we can wait and do it if you have trouble conceiving."

I wanted to strut around and boast there was no way I had

poor-performing swimmers, but how the hell would I really know that?

"I think we'll play it by ear," Maegan said. "Would it be safe for me to take birth control, or does it reduce my chances of getting pregnant later?"

"Birth control is often the first step in the IVF process. It's absolutely fine, and I'll write you a prescription if you wish."

"If it's safe, then I would prefer to take the pill rather than use condoms."

I admit I tuned in and out after finding out I was going to be tossing out the condoms soon. I caught the last bit where Maegan told the doctor we were getting married in the spring and didn't want to have unplanned pregnancies. I smiled inside because I had a month to try to convince her to marry me when we headed west again.

"What's going through that brain of yours?" Maegan asked when the doctor left the room.

"You'll find out in good time."

To be continued in *The Lady Took My Name*

Want to be the first to know about my book releases and have access to extra content? You can sign up for my newsletter here: eepurl.com/dlhPYj

My favorite place to hang out and chat with my readers is my Facebook group. Would you like to be a member of Aimee's Dye Hards? We'd love to have you! Go here: www.facebook.com/groups/AimeesDyeHards

Other Books by
AIMEE NICOLE WALKER

Only You

The Fated Hearts Series
Chasing Mr. Wright, Book 1
Rhythm of Us, Book 2
Surrender Your Heart, Book 3
Perfect Fit, Book 4
Return to Me, Book 5
Always You, Book 6
Any Means Necessary, Book 7

Curl Up and Dye Mysteries
Dyeing to be Loved
Something to Dye For
Dyed and Gone to Heaven
I Do, or Dye Trying
A Dye Hard Holiday
Ride or Dye

Road to Blissville Series
Unscripted Love
Someone to Call My Own
Nobody's Prince Charming
This Time Around
Smoke in the Mirror

The Lady is Mine Series
The Lady is a Thief

Coauthored with Nicholas Bella
Undisputed
Circle of Darkness (Genesis Circle, Book 1)
Circle of Trust (Genesis Circle, Book 2)

Standalone Novels
Second Wind

Acknowledgments

First, I need to thank my husband and children for their constant support and encouragement. It's not easy living with a writer who often disappears into a fictional world for long periods of time. They do so many things to help me out so that I can realize my dream. I love you guys more than words can ever express.

To my creative dream team, thanks seem hardly enough for all that you do. Miranda Vescio of V8 Editing and Proofreading, thank you for your tireless work, feedback, and many laughs while editing. Jay Aheer of Simply Defined art is an incredible artist, and I love how she brings my words to life. Stacey Blake of Champagne Formats is also an amazing artist who does incredible interior formatting, illustrating, and designing for e-books and paperbacks. Let's not forget Judy Zweifel of Judy's' Proofreading. She does an amazing job of finding the tiniest details that make a book shine.

To my lovely PA, Michelle Slagan. I'm not sure how I ever did this without you. I love you to the moon and back!

Lastly, I am so grateful for my beta readers and the honest feedback they provide me. Thank you for all that you do, Racheal, Kim, and Laurel.

About
AIMEE NICOLE WALKER

Ever since she was a little girl, Aimee Nicole Walker entertained herself with stories that popped into her head. Now she gets paid to tell those stories to other people. She wears many titles—wife, mom, and animal lover are just a few of them. Her absolute favorite title is champion of the happily ever after. Love inspires everything she does, music keeps her sane, and coffee is the magic elixir that fuels her day.

I'd love to hear from you.

You can reach me at:

Twitter—twitter.com/AimeeNWalker

Facebook—/www.facebook.com/aimeenicole.walker

Blog—AimeeNicoleWalker.blogspot.com